PALS
4.52

D1304885

The Captors

The

Captors

by

JOHN FARRIS

TRIDENT PRESS · NEW YORK

SBN: 671–27038–9
LIBRARY OF CONGRESS CATALOG CARD NUMBER: 79–80981
PUBLISHED SIMULTANEOUSLY IN THE UNITED STATES AND CANADA BY
TRIDENT PRESS, A DIVISION OF SIMON & SCHUSTER, INC.,
630 FIFTH AVENUE, NEW YORK, N.Y. 10020
PRINTED IN THE UNITED STATES OF AMERICA

The Captors

Chapter One

AFTER THEY WERE OUT OF SIGHT OF THE HOUSE CAROL
Watterson stopped her car in front of the gates to her grand-
father's place and shifted to neutral. She smiled at her brother.
"All yours."

"You mean it?"

"Why not? You can handle it. Pittsford Lane is a lot wider
than our driveway, and there's no traffic on Sunday."

"What happens when I get to the Parkway?"

"Cross with the light. You won't have any problems."

"OK," Kevin said, pleased and apprehensive. Carol got out of
the Corvette and waited with the door open for Kevin to come
around. As usual she felt a little awed at having to look up at her
brother. He was one month past his thirteenth birthday, and already he was nudging six feet. A few days ago he had weighed in
at one hundred sixty pounds for the first time; Carol had rewarded him with a trip to Shea Stadium for a twi-night double-
header. She'd endured five hours and forty-six minutes of a game
which she found baffling and boring, and her seat was still a trifle
tender from the experience. But they'd left the stadium close
friends again after having seen very little of each other during
her college years.

"Anything you need to know?" she asked as Kevin carefully
adjusted the deep seat for his legs.

"No."

"Let's go, I'm hungry."

She belted herself into the opposite seat and unconcernedly

lit a cigarette. Kevin let the emergency brake off, looked hard behind him at the sun-streaked blacktop, then pulled out into the road. His shift to second was very rough; the Sting Ray, basically a racing machine which thrived on an expert touch, bucked and nearly stalled. But Kevin eased in the clutch and downshifted to third immediately, gave the gas pedal just enough pressure for a steady getaway. The engine labored nervously, recovered. Carol settled back, glanced at the speed—just under thirty-five miles an hour—smiled, appraised Kevin's reactions. He was concentrating but not tense.

"You're a natural," she said affectionately.

"Trouble is I can't get my junior permit for another three years."

"But then you'll be able to have your own car."

Kevin stopped at an unmarked intersection: the cross road was clay and gravel. Two girls about Kevin's age cantered by on sweating horses and one of them called to Kevin; the other girl turned in her saddle to look and wave.

"Hey, I didn't know about those two."

Kevin muttered, "I just met them the other night. They're from the city. Staying over at Ted Fortner's."

"I wouldn't be surprised if they came riding up to our front door in the morning." Kevin shrugged to indicate his indifference. "Remind them, please, that you're taking your sister sailing." The angle of the late-afternoon sun had changed and Carol put on glasses with rhomboid amber lenses to cut the glare. She admired her brother as he drove on, absorbed in his handling of the low quick-charging car: it wasn't much more than a thin bright skin over a power source as mysterious to her as the core of the earth.

Like Carol, Kevin was still dressed in tennis togs, somewhat grimy now from several highly competitive sets on the family court. He was growing fast but he looked strong, not spindly and out of proportion: he had big hands and feet, but his head was large too and not impossibly shaggy, in the fashion of the day. There were tantalizing glimpses of the man to be in Kevin's face. Beneath a fair, faintly cherubic skin he had his father's solid bones. His eyes were gray as gunpowder, cat-steady. It made Carol feel odd and at times bereaved to be so close to this still-unfinished version of their father, whom she usually found hard to remember.

"Do you think it'll go a hundred and sixty?" Kevin asked as he drove cautiously on. They had the road to themselves except for a black delivery van well back and following slowly.

"Well—" After breaking the Sting Ray in properly she'd hit one hundred and twenty-five miles an hour one full-moon night on the wide Taconic, perhaps a celebration of a sort, or a rite: the car was a graduation gift from Sam and Felice, and the special terror and exhilaration of being twenty-one and all but free were symbolized for Carol in those seconds of charmed recklessness. "I suppose it could," she said, not wanting to elaborate. The Corvette had given her all the speed she wanted, without a tremor. And, remembering, she felt a sharp melancholy underlying her pride in the car: it would be the last thing she would receive from both of them. Once they were divorced there would be separate dutiful presents on the appropriate occasions. She would feel cheated, somehow. It was unfair of her, even childish; but she knew she would feel cheated, and not very well-loved any more.

The Saw Mill River Parkway above Fox Village was clogged with Sunday cars, particularly in the southbound lanes: metallic glitter through a light-blue haze. Kevin turned before he reached the Parkway, drove half a mile south to the traffic light, crossed to the single tree-bordered business street of the town.

The village was quiet, all but deserted. Only a clangorous Esso station beside the Saw Mill and two eating places, within a block of each other at the south end of the small business district, were open. They had already decided on Jake's for Steak, which had an air-conditioned dining room; the other place was a drive-in, and the late-June sun fell brutally on the open spaces of Fox Village.

Kevin parked behind the building, beneath an overhang of the cantilevered roof to keep the open car out of the sun. He handed over the keys with a wide grin and a sigh.

They had a short wait for a table. The temperature inside felt close to freezing, and Carol began wishing she had worn more than the sleeveless one-piece tennis outfit. She stared unresponsively at the assembled family groups. Some were bickering and some looked stifled by the clatter and the Muzak; but a few others seemed content and at peace with themselves on a Sunday afternoon.

She wondered why it had to come now, the breakup, when Sam had been confident the marriage was going to survive a bad year. Her mother's point of view was especially difficult for Carol to understand: Felice was not ordinarily obstinate about anything. But Carol had to admit that, whatever Sam's intentions were, he had made some awful blunders. His disappearing act just before Christmas had frightened and angered Felice, even though she knew how exhausted he'd been. Maybe his trip had been impromptu, for recuperative purposes as he said. Maybe he'd taken a woman with him to Mexico. Carol didn't know but she thought it was unlikely. What Felice thought was another matter.

Kevin was greatly troubled, even if he didn't let it show. He and Sam Holland had always been close. But Kevin also had the emotional resiliency, a hardheaded positiveness, that would enable him to live through a divorce without bitterness.

I wonder how much Kevin knows? she thought. In his unobtrusive way Kevin missed virtually nothing of what went on around him. He might have overheard something pertinent. Carol wasn't sure he'd talk; but if she could convince her brother there was a possibility of patching things up between Sam and Felice—

Carol had not been aware of staring at the Latin young man in the phone booth by the door. Probably he was paying no attention to her. He had the receiver propped between one shoulder and his ear and he chewed at a fingernail on his left hand as he talked. His eyes weren't visible behind aviator sunglasses. Yet Carol had the odd blurry sensation that she was being closely observed; furthermore he looked surprisingly familiar. She was about to smile, not sure why, when the hostess appeared at her elbow. *We're ready for you now.*

Carol turned obediently and the two of them followed the hostess to a corner booth.

After a lengthy search of the menu it occurred to her that she had lost most of her appetite. She settled for a bacon, lettuce and tomato sandwich and iced tea, ordered, then excused herself and went to the ladies' room.

Her hair, which she usually wore in a bulky rope twist over one shoulder or tied back with a long scarf, had become tangled during the drive: she combed it out and looked herself over in the mirror with the rigid scrutiny of a professional model bent on finding fault. She was naturally blond but away from the sun for any length of time her hair tended to brown and curl at the tips like a dying poplar leaf. Now it was too dry, she thought, because she'd baked herself carelessly almost every day during the two weeks at home.

The dark smudges beneath her eyes were plainly visible. They had been something of a plague all her life, appearing whenever she was off her feed or went sleepless. She had the vanity to be grateful for brown eyes, which were somehow enhanced by the darkened skin. She disliked the shape of her eyes, which were large but too round and insufficiently lidded, like a snake's, basically without expression. Still, they were a warm reflectant color, and she had a lazy jesting smile that could happily transform her face. Essentially she was a replica of hundreds of other long-boned and youthful blondes with the bikini shapes and a specific, piquant sex appeal that is for the young alone and heartbreakingly perishable. Carol's saving grace was a certain witty intensity that would endure, and favor her as a woman.

The Mets were playing the Giants in San Francisco and Kevin was sitting with his transistor radio at his right ear, taking it all in. He listened for a minute or two after Carol sat down, then winced at some unfavorable turn in the game and broodingly put the radio aside.

"When do you look for your apartment?" he asked.

"What? Oh—I don't know, Kevin, probably not until after Labor Day. I don't start work until mid-September." While he listened to the game she had been thinking of California, in particular of the wind and harsh sea at Big Sur, and strangely enough—unluckily—she was also thinking of Dev.

"What sort of apartment do you want?"

"I'll take what I can get; everything's so damned overpriced nowadays."

Their sandwiches came and Kevin devoted himself to basting a steakburger with everything in sight: A-1, catsup, mustard, relish. "Since I'm going to be off at school," he said, carefully cementing the top half of the bun in place, "maybe you wouldn't mind staying at home."

"It's a long commute into the city." But Carol knew what he was trying to say; she wondered then if it would be possible for her to do as she had planned. She'd spent very little time in Fox Village during the past four years, her interests had gradually become centered in Berkeley, but with a divorce seeming certain it could make things easier for Felice if she did stick close for a while. Living at home, she couldn't hold down her job and also do postgraduate work at NYU. And it would mean giving up the total independence she was now so eager for. But she wanted them to stay a family, somehow, even with Sam gone. . . .

"Well, maybe I will stay home," she said, conceding that much. "I have some time to think about it." The rest of the summer she planned to be a bum. There would be time to do some plotting and, ultimately, to convince her mother and stepfather that they should stay together. Not that she had any unusual wisdom to offer. She hadn't been so very good at patching things up with Dev. But that was different. Carol still felt forlorn and occasionally desperate over Dev, although it had been the intelligent thing to do: Dev would never settle down if he could avoid it.

But how would it feel to give up on a marriage that had been solid for almost nine years? Was Felice terrified behind her

12

façade of good-humored resignation? *We just feel it would be better to remain friends and live apart, Carol. . . .* That was the official line: Felice would say nothing more.

Damn it anyway, if he'd had a girl or two wasn't Felice tough enough to overlook it? Had Sam gone out of his way to humiliate Felice, rub her nose in an affair? No, he would never do that, his sense of style would forbid it—and he wasn't having some silly second childhood.

Carol decided she would have to know more, and Kevin seemed willing to discuss the matter—in a way he'd brought the whole thing up.

"What's the matter with them?" Carol blurted in a fit of exasperation, and Kevin looked up, mildly startled. "What are they rowing about? Do you know?"

Kevin chewed away at a mouthful of steakburger, swallowed, said finally, "Getting divorced isn't Sam's idea."

"Well, I know that, brother. But is it his fault?"

Kevin looked perplexed; then he understood her. "I don't know if he has a girl friend." The thought hurt him, belatedly: Kevin glanced at his radio as if he was thinking of tuning in the game again and tuning everything else out.

Carol covered one of his big hands with both her own. "He doesn't. I don't believe Sam would do that to her."

"It happens all the time," Kevin replied, but he looked less troubled.

"Look, if Sam had someone else—someone he loved, I mean—then he'd be the one to ask for a divorce. Sam wouldn't try to hang on, keep both things going, tell a lot of lies and make everybody miserable."

Kevin picked at his french fries with a fork, put the fork down and shrugged, willing to believe.

"Have they been fighting?"

"They don't yell at each other. But I guess they fight. Sam's gone a lot." He shrugged again. "Mom gets lonely. Sam won't take her with him when he travels."

"Most of the time he can't. Has she complained?"

"Not exactly. But Mom told him a couple of months ago"—Kevin stopped and looked at the table, trying to get the right words: he had a flair for total recall—"told him that she was tired of being shut out of his life." Carol frowned, finding that uninformative. Kevin went on, "Then Sam said he didn't realize he was shutting her out of his life, and she said, Oh, he was being very tactful about it, he was still a gracious escort and always attentive, even in private. All his, uh, gestures were in the right place, I think she said. And then she said, 'But why are you trying to fool me? I know when there's no feeling, all feeling's gone, no feeling for me, it's the same as if I'm paying you so much for your time and attention. I get full value for my dollar, but everything we used to have, that made the marriage worthwhile, is gone.' I think that's how she put it."

"Hmmm," Carol said, fascinated. "And what did Sam tell her?"

"He said she was, uh, imagining things. He said maybe she could have claimed to be paying for him at one time, but not any more."

"Uh-huh!"

"Mom said, 'Is this my punishment? Why did you put it off? Fight fair, Sam. That's all I ask.' Kevin stopped and looked hard at his sister, perplexed again.

And Carol said again, "Uh-huh!" Her eyes filled with a gleam of comprehension. "That was a dandy fight, for those two."

"What were they talking about?"

"*Epilogue*," Carol said.

"Sam's magazine?"

"Right."

"What about it?"

"Felice put some money into it three or four years ago. Quite a lot of money, almost all she had except for the trust. *Epilogue* was always in trouble. Finally there just wasn't any more money—"

Kevin nodded. "The General wouldn't give him a loan, I remember that."

"So *Epilogue* folded. Sam took that hard. And maybe he felt guilty about pouring Felice's money into the magazine. That could explain his crack about being paid for." Carol left her sandwich untouched and settled back in the booth. *Epilogue*, like other politically oriented magazines with limited circulations and little advertising, had been well-written, admired by many—and it also had been doomed to an uncertain life span and an abrupt end. Sam Holland, during the years of his magazine, had crystallized his politics, progressing—or regressing, according to his critics—from Liberal to Left Conservative. He had written a book called *The New Aims of Anarchy*, which was especially popular on college campuses. He appeared often on television with the eminent political philosophers of the time.

Now Sam turned out a weekly polemic for another magazine; he could take on as many speaking engagements as he liked. But losing the magazine had inevitably meant a loss of prestige. Carol was sure Sam's pride had taken a beating. Perhaps the marriage was now suffering, laggardly, because of this unreconciled failure.

Obviously none of the usual factors could be blamed for the divorce: Sam hadn't taken to booze, or beating up his wife, or indiscriminate adultery. As far as Carol knew, nothing unforgivable had been said, or done. Now that she was somewhat better informed she had the confidence that they could be helped, with patience and tact. She beamed at her brother.

"Thanks, Kevin."

He looked at her uncomprehendingly.

"You gave me a good idea of where the trouble is."

"I did?"

"Neither of them wants a divorce. I should be able to make them see it."

Kevin shook his head doubtfully. "What can you do?"

"Well—I'm not sure. I want to have a hard-nose talk with Sam when he gets home. Maybe if he and Felice—"

"Miss?"

Carol looked up, distracted. A man of about thirty was standing at her elbow. He was tall, bushy-haired, well-dressed—in the heat of summer he was wearing a vest. He was also wearing wraparound sunglasses with bulbous lenses. His face was long and lugubrious; there was a slight pout to his thick lips. He seemed embarrassed about something.

"Yes?"

His voice was annoyingly soft; it was difficult for her to understand him. "I don't like to interrupt you, but—that's your blue Sting Ray parked outside?"

"Behind the building? Yes."

"There was a fire under the hood; some wiring, I think."

"Oh, my God!" Carol said.

"It wasn't serious, though," he continued, placatingly. "I noticed the smoke when I drove up and thought I'd better lift the hood. Which I did. I had a foam extinguisher handy—carry it in my truck. Foam is the best thing for electrical fires. So the fire's out, and probably there's not much damage if you want to have a look—"

Carol was already out of her seat. Kevin hadn't overheard everything, but he knew something was wrong with the Corvette. "Want me to come?" he asked quickly.

"No. I'll be right back. Stay and finish your sandwich." The man had already walked away. Carol waited for a glue-footed waitress to unblock the aisle, then caught up with the man outside.

"What could have happened?" Carol moaned. "I've only had my car three weeks."

"Well, as I said, it doesn't look bad. Insurance will take care of what damage there is." He had a slow-paced drawl which was familiar to Carol: he was from the Southwest, she decided. Arizona or New Mexico.

"I'm grateful that you noticed something was wrong."

"Couldn't help admiring your fine automobile."

"How did you know the Corvette belonged to me?" Carol

16

asked. "We've been in the restaurant for—" She bolted ahead of the man. The hood of the cornflower-blue Sting Ray was raised. Carol stepped under the restaurant roof, looked down at the carburetor housing and engine block of her beloved car, dreading a blackened and foam-splattered mess.

There was an all-but-invisible film of road dust, but otherwise everything looked new and undamaged.

Carol lifted her head indignantly, saw the bushy-haired man standing to her right, his face expressionless but sweaty. Immediately behind them, parked between the Sting Ray and the service door of the steak house, was a black Volkswagen van. Carol had a glimpse of the dark-skinned youth behind the wheel, his face turned toward them, something anxious and predatory in that face, eyes lost behind aviator sunglasses. But she knew him: Carol was sure of it, and she was struck by the oddity of seeing him here, of all the unlikely— She started to speak, but an instinctive surge of panic closed her throat.

The other man was holding something; it looked like a white can of shaving cream, the nozzle pointed toward her.

"What—" Carol said, her voice breaking, an instant before the bushy-haired man pressed the button on the can and sprayed her in the face with something that felt very much like liquid fire.

"Would you like something else?"

Kevin glanced at the waitress. In the top of the fourth the Mets had tied the score at three all and were threatening again, with runners on second and third and one out. His eyes shifted to the uneaten sandwich on Carol's plate, then to the small lobby of the steak house, where a lot of people were waiting for tables. He didn't see Carol. She'd been gone for more than ten minutes. He smiled at the waitress, who looked tired. "May I have another glass of milk?" he said.

"You certainly may." Like women of all ages, she was instantly susceptible to his smile, when he felt like really turning it on.

The next batter struck out, to Kevin's disgust. Hodges sent up a pinch hitter, who went for a bad first pitch and fouled out to the third baseman, ending the rally. Kevin wished Carol would come on. He put the radio down beside his plate, leaving it so they wouldn't think he was trying to run out on the check, and went outside.

It was a little past five but still very hot. A two-car Penn Central train was pulling away from the unabashedly quaint red frame station near Jake's. Kevin expected to find Carol by the Sting Ray; the hood had been raised. But she wasn't there. Neither was the bushy-haired man with whom she had left the restaurant.

From where he was standing Kevin could see the Esso station; she wasn't over there, either. Kevin looked carefully around the parking lot, separated from the railroad tracks by a six-foot stockade fence. Carol wasn't sitting in any of the other cars. He watched as the train receded in the distance, bound for the city. He didn't know what to think, but he was beginning to get mad at his sister. He didn't buy the idea of Carol going off with the bushy-haired man, but she had undoubtedly gone someplace—without bothering to tell him.

She must have had a good reason. Probably there was something wrong with the car which couldn't be fixed at the Esso, especially if there wasn't a mechanic on duty. It was a safe bet that on Sunday there wasn't. So the bushy-haired man had driven her to a garage he knew about. There was no more to it than that, Kevin decided.

He approached the Sting Ray to see for himself what the trouble was. Nothing looked wrong to his inexperienced eye. But there was a white envelope wedged behind the fan belt, where it would have to be seen by anyone attempting to lower the hood.

Kevin freed the envelope, stared at it. There was a strip of tape from a label maker pasted across the front, raised white letters on red tape. It wasn't addressed to anyone in particular.

It simply said, whimsically, OPEN ME.

Chapter Two

INSTEAD OF DRIVING ON TO THE CARRIAGE-HOUSE garage Sam Holland left his Mercedes in the drive directly in front of the three-story Colonial house. He grabbed his two-suiter from the right side of the seat and went quickly up the steps to the long front porch, almost jogging, and let himself into the house. The center hall was brightly lighted, but only a single lamp burned in the living room to his left, and no one was there.

"Felice!" Sam called.

A man came promptly from the kitchen at the rear of the house, walked down the hall toward him. He was of middle height and wore a faded, wrinkled wash-and-wear jacket, a badly knotted tie. His hair was going and his complexion was bumpy and mottled. But he had dark lustrous inquisitive eyes and the stride of a fencing master, or a gymnast.

"Mr. Holland?"

"Who are you?" Sam asked, but he had seen enough of the breed to know.

"Fox Village Police," the man replied perfunctorily, showing him identification in a shabby leather folder. He was a detective lieutenant. "My name is Peter Demilia."

Sam put his suitcase against one wall. "Are you in charge?"

"More or less. Chief Demkus called in the FBI. Special agent Gaffney is supervising. Why don't you talk to him?"

"Has there been any word?"

"I'm afraid not," Demilia said. "Your wife is in the kitchen, Mr. Holland—" But Felice Holland had appeared in the doorway at the opposite end of the hall.

"Sam," she said, sounding weak and glad. They met halfway, wordlessly. Sam held her very tightly, absorbing a tremor which she had probably suppressed for most of the evening.

"What's being done?" Sam asked quietly.

"I don't know—not very much. I don't think there's much anyone can do. It's been nine hours, Sam!"

"I'd better see this Gaffney."

He kept an arm around his wife as they went into the kitchen; Demilia followed. Two men were standing by the massive round captain's table at one end of the thirty-foot-long kitchen. One of the men was on the short side, in his late forties perhaps, squint-eyed and astute, with a stippled pugnaciously handsome face, deeply lined around the mouth, a face that looked as if it had been chiseled out of sandstone. His hair was grizzle gray at the ears, flame red on top. It was a hot night; he had taken off his coat and rolled up his shirt sleeves and was drinking iced coffee. Sam was impressed by the width of the man's wrists, the leather-hard look of his sun-reddened forearms.

The other man was Felice's father, General Henry Phelan Morse, U.S.A. Ret., a slouched crippled giant of sixty-eight whose face had become mostly creases and pouches, with slitted hangdog eyes and a nose engorged by time and love of Southern Comfort whiskey. He wore a youthful-looking hairpiece most of the time and, strangely enough, what might have made him seem ridiculous worked for him instead. In spite of his years and only a leg and a half to stand on the General retained a surprising amount of the virility and steel-clad authority that had characterized his life and career; beside him special agent Gaffney, who evidently was quite a man in his own right, seemed diminished to the status of a subaltern.

The FBI man put down his glass of coffee at Sam's approach and introduced himself. "Robert Gaffney, Mr. Holland." Sam shook hands with him and then with the General, who as usual gripped his hand as if he was trying to pull a stump out of the ground.

"Sorry to drag you away from your speechmaking, Sam." To Sam the implication was that nobody really needed him, so why should he have come at all?

"I think you should have let me know sooner," Sam replied curtly, barely glancing at the General. "It's difficult to get a flight from Pittsburgh on Sunday night." To Gaffney he said, "How many of you are working on the investigation?"

"There are eight of my men. Claude Demkus has assigned most of his detectives." Demkus was chief of the Fox Village police, a highly mobile and efficient force in a rich semirural community.

"All of you parading in and out of this house? If the kidnappers are watching, Carol may be dead by now." Sam saw the look of sick terror in Felice's eyes and wished he hadn't said that, but he'd had a long agonizing trip back and he had obeyed a rash desire to assert himself in some way.

"If anyone was watching the house, Mr. Holland, we'd know about it. But as a matter of routine Lieutenant Demilia and I came in by way of the General's house next door. We'll take the same precaution when either of us leaves. The investigation is being coordinated from Chief Demkus' office."

"I'm sorry," Sam said. "I shouldn't have assumed— Could you tell me about it now? The agent in Pittsburgh didn't have much to say."

"Sam, hot coffee?" Felice asked.

"Yes, please. Why don't we all sit down?" Demilia had quietly left the kitchen. The General, of course, preferred to remain standing, although he was far from comfortable that way. He stood with his back against a brick wall, glass in hand. Drinking it straight, one chunk of ice. *How about you?* Sam thought, with an unquenchable flash of resentment. *Are you scared, General?* But instead of frightened he looked stimulated, enlivened by events, perhaps a shade regretful that he wasn't running the show.

Felice brought coffee and slipped into the chair beside Sam. She glanced at him apologetically. "Sam, would you mind? A cigarette?" Sam looked blankly at her, then remembering she had given up smoking a few days ago, for what seemed like the fiftieth time since they had been married: all those Cancer Society commercials on television had prompted her most recent attempt.

Sam lit filtertips for both of them, handed one to Felice. She took it gratefully and dragged deeply once, then closed her eyes like a child too starved to eat. "The kids played tennis most of the afternoon," she said, as if it steadied her to do the talking. "They went down to the Village about four-thirty for hamburgers. Asked if I wanted to go along, but I had my hair to wash." Felice opened her eyes and stared unfocusedly at the cigarette in her hand. The other hand was clenched. Above Sam's head ice rattled in the General's glass as he sipped his whiskey.

"Where did they go? To Jake's?"

"Yes. They had to wait a little while for a table, and then they ordered, but Carol apparently wasn't hungry, she didn't touch her sandwich when it came. They talked quite a bit, Kevin said. About us."

"About us?" Sam repeated, and Gaffney, catching something in his tone, flicked his eyes across Sam's face.

"And then a man came in and told Carol something had happened to her car. He talked in a low voice and Kevin couldn't overhear all he said. It was something about an electrical fire under the hood of the Corvette, Kevin thinks. Carol went outside with the man—followed him outside. And after ten minutes or so, when she didn't come back, Kevin went to look for her. Carol was gone, and so was the man. The Corvette hadn't been damaged in any way. Kevin found a note under the raised hood."

"A ransom note?" Sam said, and Gaffney reached into an inside pocket of his coat, which was folded over the chair next to him. He handed Sam a sheet of paper.

"This is a typed facsimile," the agent explained. "We'll put the original through our lab to see if anything useful turns up. The original message was printed by a common type of label maker, raised white letters on strips of quarter-inch red tape. These were gummed to a sheet of heavy white typing paper."

Sam read the brief message twice.

> WE HAVE CAROL WATTERSON
> NO POLICE NO FBI
> SHE WILL BE KILLED IF YOU
> DONT DO AS WE SAY
> GET 225 G USED BILLS
> FIFTIES TWENTIES
> YOU WILL HEAR FROM US

He let the paper fall to the table, his face taut with apprehension. "It's been a while since I've heard of a kidnapping for ransom."

Gaffney nodded. "Kidnapping goes through cycles of popularity. There are certain types of crimes which publicity seems to breed: kidnapping, mass shootings, political assassination. Quite often such crimes are the work of nonprofessionals, individuals whose previous criminal records, if any, are of minor offenses."

"Then the threat to kill her—"

"I don't want to mislead you. At this point we can't accept that as a bluff."

"Please, *please*," Felice murmured, her head bowed.

Sam said, "The note refers to *we*. Does that mean more than one man is involved?"

"It seems likely. But we don't know if Carol was taken by force."

"How else could she have been taken?" Felice asked, exasperated. Sam looked at his wife: he could all but see the bones of her face showing through her skin. She'd already endured nine hours of this. He knew it was useless to try to get her to bed, so he held one of her hands tightly, giving what comfort he could. He was beginning to find that concentration came hard.

He drank some of the steaming coffee, forcing it down, wincing. But coffee helped.

"Was Kevin able to give a good description of the man who came into the restaurant?"

"He remembered the man as tall, thin, bushy-haired. A reddish cast to his hair. Kevin couldn't say how old he was; the man wore dark glasses which covered a third of his face."

"What else do you have to go on?"

"Frankly, Mr. Holland, we have very little. We're hoping that someone who was in the vicinity of the steak house around five o'clock saw the two of them get into a car. The restaurant was full at that hour, and a gas station across the way was open. But, as of this moment—" Gaffney didn't quite shrug, which would have been unprofessional of him. Instead he reached for his glass of iced coffee. "We can draw some tentative conclusions about the kidnapping from what we already know, and there are certain areas of speculation which might prove to be fruitful."

A bumping and scratching at the screen of the back door froze them all.

Even as Gaffney glanced toward the door he dropped his hand to the butt of the revolver he wore in a belt holster. Sam turned his head and saw Riggs, Kevin's setter pup, with his nose pressed against the screen, a paw raised to scratch again.

"Oh, Lord!" Felice said. "We forgot to feed him. Poor Riggs." She got up immediately and opened a pantry door, took out a package of Gaines-burgers and went to the back porch. "Good boy, Riggs," she said soothingly, breaking open the package. "We're sorry—here's your supper."

Sam said to the FBI man, "What conclusions?"

"The amount of money specified in the note is two hundred twenty-five thousand. Your wife has already told me that you would have trouble raising that kind of money, particularly on short notice."

Sam nodded. "We'd have to mortgage the house to make it, or sell a dozen paintings in a hurry."

"So the kidnappers obviously were aiming at me," General Morse said harshly. "It has to be someone who knows I can pick up a telephone and order five times that amount, in cash, no questions asked."

"Someone in your organization?" Gaffney asked politely.

"I have employees and agents all over the world, of course; but they're clerks and purchasing agents and salesmen, that's all. Most of them wouldn't know me if they saw me."

"What about Metts?" Sam said, looking around at him. "He knows as much about your business as you do."

The General knocked back another half ounce of whiskey, staring at Sam, his eyes unfriendly. "Vernon Metts has been with me for twenty-six years; I've trusted him with my life more than once. Kidnap my granddaughter? He's a rich man in his own right." He laughed, studying the FBI agent. "It could be a dissatisfied customer, wanting to get his money back. But I don't have dissatisfied customers."

"Still, it's worth looking into," Gaffney said, refusing to be baited.

"I've sold dozens of lots in the past year," the General replied. "All transactions are a matter of record. The CIA might help you with your paper work, but I won't." He grinned, relishing his jibe; Gaffney allowed himself a trace of a smile.

Sam said wrathfully, "Let's keep our minds on Carol!"

"When they call the money will be ready," the General said, somewhat subdued by Sam's tone. He mopped his steamy face with a handkerchief.

"When they call." Sam turned to the FBI man, trying unsuccessfully not to look dismayed. "How long do you think that will be?"

"Assuming the kidnappers have planned this thoroughly, I doubt if they'll try to get in touch before noon tomorrow. They would want to—soften you up, and they'd know that General Morse's bank would need time to fill an order for a two-hundred-thousand-dollar package of used fifties and twenties."

"They must have been planning this for weeks."

25

"That would be a safe bet."

"Carol's only been home for two weeks."

"So I understand. Unless one of the kidnappers knows your family well, chances are that when they began to plan it Kevin was the intended victim."

"Kevin?" Sam said, shocked again.

"But when your stepdaughter came home from college they might have changed their plans. Kevin is a good-size boy, and looks even bigger than he actually is. The kidnappers couldn't be certain how much trouble he'd give them. A girl is usually much easier to handle."

Sam felt that he needed air; he went to the windows which looked out on the spacious west lawn. In the moonlight the white trunks of birches were sharply, gracefully drawn against the night sky. He took off his glasses and began to wipe moisture from the lenses. There was no wind, which accounted for the unusual humidity. The warm air smelled faintly of honeysuckle. He heard the sounds of the hungry setter wolfing its meal, and he heard Felice crooning in an undertone to the dog.

"How about a drink, Sam?" the General suggested. "It'll be a long wait."

"Not now, thanks."

"Mr. Holland, your wife said you could give us the name of the village in Ireland where Joseph and Mattie Dowd are visiting."

Sam said automatically, "It's a little place in County Wexford; I wrote the name down and put it in my—" He turned slowly away from the windows, staring at the agent, his lips pressed irritably together. "What do you want with the Dowds? You can't think they know anything about this!"

"They may, without realizing it. Something they might have observed during the past few weeks, seemingly harmless in itself, could be useful to us now."

"That's farfetched. I don't see why you have to bother them. They've been with Felice eighteen years, and this trip to Ireland

26

is the first real vacation they've had. Once they know about Carol it'll be ruined for them."

"I'm sorry, Mr. Holland. I can't afford to overlook any possibilities."

Sam reluctantly took out his wallet and found the right slip of paper after a search. "Village of Saint Clare."

Gaffney asked him to spell it, then rose and left the kitchen. The dog was making a peculiar unnerving sound. Sam and the General looked at each other, and both realized at the same time that it wasn't Riggs at all.

Sam found his wife on her knees on the dark porch, arms folded tightly across her breasts, weeping.

"I don't know, Sam," Felice sobbed as he helped her up. "I don't know; I'm trying to keep my mind off it. But what if they—what if C-Carol—"

"All they want is money; she'll be all right. They'll let her go."

"Oh, Sam, oh, God, I want to believe that!"

"Better take her up to bed, Sam," the General muttered.

"I intend to."

Felice broke away from him. "Oh, no, Sam," she protested, her voice strained, "I have to stay *up*, they're going to call and—"

"According to Gaffney they probably won't call before noon tomorrow. He knows about these things."

Felice looked at him in disappointment and frustration, her tan a gray-yellow shade in the underlighted brick kitchen. She shook her head slowly, tears streaming. "Not until n-noon? Oh, I can't—I don't think I—"

She began to shake with sobs. Sam put both arms around her; this time Felice didn't resist. He guided her up the crooked low-ceilinged back stairs to the second floor, then along the hall to her bedroom. Once she had wept she barely could keep her eyes open. In the bathroom they shared Sam ran water into a glass, found the prescription Seconals they both took occasionally and gave one to Felice, to ensure that she slept. Then he helped her undress. When he pulled the sheet over her bare breasts Felice gripped one of his wrists with a strength that surprised him, looked mutely out at him as if from a tunnel, eyes sore but dry.

"Stay with me, Sam."

"I'll be right back," he promised. "Before you fall asleep." He kissed her lips, which were swollen from biting.

"I wish—after this—I wish the two of us could just get away, to some place we've never been. I'd be—so happy to meet you again, Sam Holland."

He smiled at her passion for their own lives, eyes stinging, and he was still smiling when her eyelids closed and she drifted away, her breathing becoming deep. After a couple of minutes Felice's fingers loosened on his wrist, and Sam placed her hand at her side.

He closed the bath door three-quarters of the way but left the light on within, thinking there was a chance she might wake up—or be awakened by one of the nightmares which she had taken with her to bed.

After turning the window air-conditioner on low Sam went out. He paused a minute to look in on Kevin, who was sleeping restless and brawny in his shorts, which were unbuttoned and revealed a tentative light smudge of pubic hair. The bedclothes were in a tangle and half on the floor. Sam couldn't help staring at the shadowed length of Kevin; for him it was like seeing a stranger in a well-loved little boy's bed. He thought of kidnappers trailing Kevin, sizing him up. What if they had tried to take him and had been clumsy, or careless? Kevin would have fought tenaciously, Sam was sure of that. He had taught his stepson a few useful things about self-defense. Kevin would have fought until he was unconscious, or dead.

There was an obstruction in his throat which Sam couldn't force away. He went slowly downstairs to the kitchen, feeling prematurely bereaved, helpless. The kitchen was empty now. On the back porch Riggs barked sharply once, then grumbled and settled back to sleep. The General's smeared glass was empty

28

too, sitting in the brassy gleam of light from the fixture above the captain's table.

Lieutenant Demilia made a sound in his throat as he came up behind Sam.

"Is everything all right?"

"Yes, my wife's asleep. I gave her a Seconal. Where's the General?"

"He went home after an argument with Gaffney."

"What were they arguing about?"

There was amusement in Demilia's soft eyes. "Procedure, I believe. The General has threatened to conduct his own investigation."

Sam said grimly, "I think I'd better have a talk with General Morse before morning."

"I wouldn't worry; it's his way of expressing anxiety. He wants to be doing something. We'll think of a way to keep him occupied."

"Do you know anything about Gaffney?"

"We've worked with him on a couple of other matters. He's good. At your wife's suggestion we've set our equipment in the library, Mr. Holland. You may have some questions."

Sam led the way to the library, which adjoined the living room in the one-hundred-and-fifty-year-old house. Sam did most of his writing in this paneled and oak-beamed room. The furnishings were antiques, mostly English, and there were good paintings on the walls: a Rouault, a Soutine, a Pollock, two bold works by the Spaniard known as Hipólito.

The investigators were using a folding game table in one corner; as Sam walked in Gaffney finished testing one of their two tape recorders, which were built into standard attaché cases.

"The recorders are voice-activated," Gaffney explained. "As soon as you or your wife answers the telephone—it can be any phone in the house, by the way, not just this one—everything said will go down on tape. This gadget is an ordinary voice amplifier, which will enable our people in the room to hear both ends of the conversation. And they needn't pick up the receiver of the telephone in order to hear." He smiled. "Wonders of the electronic age."

Demilia said, "It's possible these days to be in Washington and listen to conversations in, say, San Francisco, just by dialing a telephone number. The telephone in San Francisco doesn't ring, which isn't much of a trick when you know how to do it. But every word spoken in that room is subsequently transmitted, over telephone lines, back to Washington."

"That's one of the things about the police—and the FBI—that really frightens me," Sam remarked, an edge to his voice. He went to the bar, installed in a sideboard, to make himself a badly needed drink.

"We have the technical means of doing this, Mr. Holland," Gaffney said, and Sam could imagine the look he gave Demilia—*Remember who you're talking to.* "But we don't do it."

"Of course not," Sam said, glumly and almost inaudibly; he didn't want a public-relations job done on him at this particular moment. Nor did he want the investigators to feel they had to be careful of every word said in his presence, because he was a journalist who had been critical in the past of certain FBI practices.

He turned his head and smiled, willing to be friends. "I suppose you can't have hard liquor on the job, but there's cold beer if you want it."

Demilia looked parched and susceptible, but both men shook their heads. "I'll go ahead then," Sam said, selecting a bottle of Beefeater gin and taking ice cubes from the compact refrigerator fitted into the sideboard. "How will the recordings help you?" he asked Gaffney.

"They may be useful in providing, by means of a voice print, positive identification of one of the kidnappers. Also, if the call should be placed from a pay phone, we may pick up background noises—sounds of construction, for instance, or a train—that could give us a fix on the location of the telephone."

"I see. What happens when they call? Can you trace it?"

"Possibly. But they should know enough to limit their call to sixty seconds. There's no way the telephone-company technicians can make even a partial trace in that length of time."

"We'll have to keep our man talking, then."

"That's a must, if it can be done without arousing suspicion."

"They'll be suspicious of everything," Sam said, feeling hot and miserable. The window air-conditioner in the library didn't seem to be functioning properly. He turned it up as high as it would go. "I suppose the kidnappers will arrange for a drop. Isn't that what you call it? Will you try to pick up the man who comes for the money?"

"No," Gaffney said. "It wouldn't be worth the risk to Carol. There's no point in trying to tell you now just what we'll do. That depends on the situation from moment to moment." He was testing the other tape recorder. Two, in case one failed at a critical time, Sam thought. Although he partially resented Gaffney's evasion about their plans, he was aware that the agent had complete confidence in himself and in his routine. Sam wished he could share in that confidence.

When Gaffney completed his test of the tape recorder he lifted the receiver of a telephone on the other side of the card table. "Direct line to Chief Demkus' office," he explained to Sam. Then, as someone came on the line, "This is Gaffney. We've finished setting up here. What did the phone company have to say about—Good. Anything of interest from the girl's car? I didn't think there would be. Yes? As well as could be expected. I'll be sure to tell him, Chief. Good-bye."

Gaffney hung up. "The Chief wanted you to know that everything conceivable is being done, and he personally guarantees you'll have Carol back soon." Sam smiled wryly. "He'll stop by in the morning to see you and Mrs. Holland. Oh, and Carol's car is at the State Police building just south of Hawthorne Circle. General Morse drove it well out of the area for us, just in case somebody was watching to see what happened to it. Might be a good idea if you brought it home yourself tomorrow." Gaffney suppressed a yawn. "I wouldn't mind having another glass of that cold buttermilk your wife served earlier," he said.

"Right. Lieutenant Demilia?"

"I'm a city boy myself. But I'd appreciate a Coke."

Gaffney accompanied Sam to the kitchen. As their long shadows fell across the porch Riggs, uneasy in his sleep, growled. "I understand the General gave you a hard time," Sam said, opening one of the doors of the restaurant-size refrigerator.

"Not really. He asked sharp questions; there was some give-and-take. He wanted to be convinced I knew my job. Just as you want to be convinced, Mr. Holland."

Sam gave the agent a glass of buttermilk, then poured a Coke over ice. Gaffney leaned against the captain's table and admired the handmade cabinetry, a wealth of old glass displayed in a glass-front cabinet, the gleam of copper on antique brick and the spacious hearth where log fires on cold winter mornings were a ritual.

"Fine old house. Well-preserved. Have you lived here long?"

"We bought it five years ago, when it became available. Before that it was in one family for over a hundred years. Felice had been lusting after this house since she was a girl. Felice and her mother summered next door while the General was off fighting his wars."

"Do you find it difficult living so close to your father-in-law?" the FBI man asked, wiping at a childlike moustache of buttermilk with his handkerchief.

Sam was well aware of what was coming but he said, sardonically, "It might be less difficult if the six acres between us were an impenetrable swamp. But there's no swamp, so when he's not halfway around the world on business he's here, keeping things running smoothly for us. That's what he thinks. As you've become aware, he's a dominating old bastard. If Joe and Mattie Dowd weren't the most patient people on earth—I guess they feel sorry for him. He's alone over there, except when Vernon Metts flies in from Europe; the General is too suspicious to have live-in help on his place. And he despises restaurant food. If Mattie didn't feed him from our cupboard, like a stray dog, I suppose he'd have starved to death long ago."

Gaffney grinned. "So the two of you don't get along."

"We keep up a pretense; it's easier on everybody's nerves."

"You differ politically, I take it."

Sam said, "We're fundamentally different, like apes and alligators. The General has been out of the Service for nearly twenty-five years, but he's still very much the professional soldier—mercenary is a better word. He has no morals. He's made a fortune promoting competition between backward nations eager for the latest in small arms. Battles have been fought and people have died because of the General's activities. The Bureau must have a dossier on him half a foot thick."

Gaffney said without hesitation, "We have several dossiers that thick."

"So you watch him closely."

"General Morse is a legitimate businessman who operates, with Washington's consent, in a sensitive area. Justice always keeps an eye on him; his business is on a cash basis so of course the Tax boys have him in perpetual audit. He's scrupulous about permits and documentation. He doesn't deal in stolen weapons or military explosives. It isn't the dramatic, hazardous business he hints at: clandestine meetings, running guns into a deserted beach before dawn, all that. The truth is he's succeeded because he's aggressive, shrewd, a pitchman; and he can figure profit margins like a CPA."

Sam said, "I'm convinced that what anyone sees of his business is what he wants them to see. But we won't get into that: I tend to be a fanatic on the subject of arms dealers." He hesitated, his expression crushingly remote. Then he smiled sadly. "I'm curious: what sort of file does the FBI have on me?"

Gaffney chuckled. "I know you've been arrested a couple of times during peace demonstrations. I don't think that's worth much space in our files."

"The General wouldn't agree. As far as he's concerned I'm a

33

damned nihilist." Sam looked dourly amused. "That's what he calls me, five minutes after we set out to have a serious discussion on any topic. In public the most the General will allow, with a very thin smile, is that I have 'strange politics.'" Sam shook his head in accustomed bemusement. "Would you believe that ten years ago I was a perfectly ordinary Liberal Democrat?"

"I can't imagine. What got into you?"

"Well, I think it was exposure to the General and his views, as well as the trend of the times, that changed this benign boy into the contentious radical he is today. Now, when the General is really in his cups and annoyed with me, he comes out with his ultimate epithet: I'm a 'spaghetti-brained Marxist.' You don't know how vile that can sound until you hear it from Henry Phelan Morse himself."

Gaffney smiled and said, "I would expect that your wife hates politics."

"We find other things to quarrel about. Bridge. French cooking. Vladimir Nabokov. Carol is going to be the politician in the family—" Sam's voice trailed and he glanced at his watch. It was now past three in the morning.

"The General told me you and your wife are considering a divorce," Gaffney said, completing the change of mood.

Sam said with undisguised annoyance, "There won't be any divorce, although of course the General would be delighted. Felice hardly saw him while she was growing up, but lately he's rediscovered his 'little girl.' I guess he's going through some crisis of identity I don't know anything about. Or else he's just getting sentimental and possessive in his old age." Sam shrugged. "I don't know why I let the old boy irritate me. Apes and alligators. The last couple of years I've spent more and more time away from home. Too many speaking engagements, too many causes I couldn't turn down. Felice couldn't go everywhere I went; she would have been bored if she had. So we lost touch emotionally, as married people often do. Felice is not a woman to settle for a figurehead husband. I've told her that my marriage means a great deal to me. I think I've begun to prove it, by cutting my schedule drastically. I'd say we just need time to—bum around together. Mend our ties."

"What do you think of your stepchildren, Mr. Holland?"

"Why the personal questions?" Sam asked, cleaning his glasses again.

"I've met Kevin, but I've only seen photographs of Carol. I'd like to know something about her."

"I wouldn't claim to be an expert on Carol; girls her age change personalities with almost every breath they take. Because I travel so much I saw her quite often at Berkeley. She's enthusiastic, impetuous—engaged three times already, if I recall—"

The FBI man said quickly, "Engaged now? Or recently?"

"No. She broke up with a boy named Dev Kaufman about five months ago. I think they were planning to be married. They were living together. Her mother doesn't know this, by the way."

"I understand. But this Kaufman is out of the picture now?"

"And out of the country. Traveling around Europe. He wants to be a painter."

"Sorry to have interrupted you."

"It must have been important," Sam said, looking closely at Gaffney. "If Carol were simply missing, I could suspect Dev. He's impetuous too, and he was crazy about her. He might conceivably lock her up someplace until she agreed to marry him. But he doesn't need the money. His father is in the movie business: producing, distributing. Are you trying to say someone Carol knows may have grabbed her? What about the ransom note?"

"Ransom notes don't always mean what they say. Sometimes they don't mean anything. Kidnappers are frequently complex and devious people."

"And unbalanced?"

Gaffney lit a cigarette. "There's no need to overstimulate our imaginations. I have no reason to believe that this is anything but

35

a snatch for ransom, well planned and so far well executed. Why don't you go on about the kids? Apparently you get along with them very well."

"I'd say so, considering I'm not their father. Carol confides in me; I think she has a high regard for my opinions. She's appalled by some of the things that are happening in our increasingly closed society; four years at Berkeley have made a political activist of her. We enjoy bouncing ideas off each other. Kevin is more reticent, scholarly. At the moment he's fascinated with marine biology. I taught him skin-diving and fishing, and his grandfather taught him to shoot and handle hawks. I'm happy to say Kevin prefers the water. The General tried to give him a two-thousand-dollar shotgun for his birthday recently. I had a long talk with Kevin, and he agreed not to accept it. That didn't improve the old man's attitude toward me, but it was the right thing to do."

"I suppose Carol and Kevin know about your present marital difficulties?"

"They know enough; neither of us has really talked it out with them."

Gaffney took his glass to the sink and rinsed it. "This is a rough time for you and you've been more than patient with me, Mr. Holland."

Sam said, "I want an answer to one question. No hedging, no qualifications. Carol's in danger, isn't she?"

"Yes."

Sam took a deep breath. "I appreciate that."

"You'll have to decide for yourself how much your wife should know. You might try getting some sleep now, if you can. Pete Demilia and one of my agents will be here through the night. I'll be along bright and early in the morning."

"If I take some work upstairs with me I might get drowsy." Sam added, with a humorless grin, "And that quart of Beefeater I just opened might help too."

They walked together to the library and Sam gave Demilia his Coke. "By the way, the telephone on my desk is a business phone. After three rings an answering service cuts in."

"We noted the difference in numbers," Demilia said. "Thanks, Mr. Holland."

Gaffney asked, "Is that K-a-u-f-m-a-n? Where's he from?"

"Los Angeles, I think," Sam said absently. "No, Beverly Hills. You aren't going to bother Dev, are you?"

"That shouldn't be necessary," Gaffney assured him. Sam put the bottle of gin under one arm, stacked several folders and a tall glass filled with ice on his clipboard and left the library.

As soon as he was gone Demilia picked up the receiver of the direct-line telephone, looked inquiringly at the agent.

"Dev Kaufman," Gaffney told him. "He and Carol Watterson were living together while she was at Berkeley. I assume he was a student there too. We ought to know where he is now, what he's doing, what he has to say about Carol Watterson."

"Maybe," Demilia said, with a hint of eagerness, "he's with Miss Watterson now."

"That would be damned unfortunate for him."

It started after he opened the bathroom door, when the light from the bath angled across the canopied Victorian bed, across the naked unevenly browned back of his wife. Apparently she had resisted sleep long enough to unpin her hair, which was a streaky ash blond. Carol's hair was pale, uncoarsened, feather-light, but they were of the same build, mother and daughter, their bones were the same.

That was enough to start Sam thinking of Carol; it was enough to bring on an unpleasant spasming of muscles in his chest and upper arms, the pincer-like squeezing of his heart, renewed sweat after his cold soak in the tub. He took off his glasses and the room slipped out of focus, high shadows and indefinite light, like pale morning sunlight glistening on frozen snow. Felice became remote, inert, undetailed in her slumber.

"Stay with me, Sam," she had pleaded, and he felt an eagerness to be in bed with Felice, to sleep with his hands on her firm and smoothly muscled body.

But as he approached her he became myopically aware of the white eagle, guardian eagle, emerging from shadows by the foot of the bed, wings frozen in beginning flight, and he drew back with a snort of distaste. Felice thought it was kicky and she had paid the antique dealer too much for it, in Sam's opinion. He despised the bird, and tonight, because of the kidnapping, he seemed to see a special menace in the off-white out-thrust head, porcelain claws. It was foolish, but if he stayed, slept with Felice as she wanted, he was certain he would dream of birds more evil than this one cast in porcelain: birds in motion, swirling darkly at him, smothering him with heavy wings. . . .

Sam turned away shakily and closed the bathroom door. *You're tired, boy,* he thought derisively. It was a fair reminder that he was not getting off the merry-go-round any too soon; he couldn't afford to get that tired again.

He sat on the edge of his own bed. The muscle spasms continued, making it difficult for him to pour the shot of gin over ice. His first swallow tasted as bitter as hemlock; he was afraid he would heave it up. But he drank a little more, and the taste was smoother, appealing, benumbing. He drank still more and sighed, losing apprehension, escaping panic. When he'd finished the first shot he poured another and at last, drinking sparingly for the better part of an hour, Sam felt dead calm.

He had no heart or mind for work tonight. He turned off the bedside lamp and lay back in his dressing gown, eyes on the raked moonlit ceiling. He was nerveless, but a million miles from sleep. Morning would be dreadful; morning would be an impossibility. But somehow they would all have to endure it.

Chapter Three

THE SUNRISE WAS LOVELY.

From the white bed Carol watched the sky change very gradually, star-flecked gray to a tea-rose shade to a few minutes of clear glistening amber before the normal early-morning blue began to assert itself.

It was quiet, had been quiet, except for the flushing of a toilet earlier. Now a woman was singing, in some distant part of the house—if that's what it was—singing in a sweet soprano voice about Suzanne by the river. She also heard a rattle of pans.

The double sash windows through which she had observed the dawn were closed, but the room was cool enough, even a little chilly. There was a blanket across her bed. She could feel the rough texture of it against her bare arms. She had slept comfortably, Carol supposed. Hadn't moved a muscle. She had no desire to move even now, although she had been awake for some time. There was a growing pressure in her bladder, though; she would have to do something about that before long.

At some time during the night they had removed the wet medicinal bandage from her eyes: though they were still inflamed and somewhat swollen, her eyes felt much better. From time to time her vision was blurry, but blinking cleared that up.

The girl soprano down there—down? It was hard to tell; Carol couldn't say for certain if she herself was "up" or "down" —the girl was really very good, and the song was poetic, wistful, melancholy. Carol knew some of the words, but not many. She felt like humming along, but her throat was a little sore. Also

39

that thing was around her neck. It wasn't uncomfortably tight, but she did become aware of it when she swallowed hard, or coughed in an attempt to clear her throat.

Some water would be a big help, Carol thought.

She turned her head on the pillow, to the left. Beside the white bed was a white iron pedestal table with a round white marble top, and on the table there was a milk-glass plate with an old china pitcher on it. White, of course. So much white, Carol thought, displeased. Like a hospital. But she was confident she wasn't in a hospital: this room was large and had odd angles, a ceiling that sloped in different directions, interesting furniture. And in the strengthening light it was apparent that total "whiteness" consisted of a blend of different shades of white, from rich ivory to a stark eggshell.

Intent on the pitcher, Carol sat up and instantly felt giddy; her stomach flexed like a rubbery hand. She heard the slipping rattle of a lightweight chain.

When she could she turned her head curiously and saw the close-linked chain snaking brightly over her right shoulder, across the spacious bed, falling out of sight into the last of the shadows in the room. She traced the chain with the fingers of one hand to the place where it joined the band around her neck, a band made of heavy padded leather—like a dog collar.

A dog collar. Her fingers appraised it. There was the buckle. She raised her other hand and tried, experimentally, to undo the buckle. But it was fixed in some way so that she couldn't.

Oh, well, she was thirsty. Carol forgot about the chain and collar and reached for the pitcher, which to her delight was filled with cold water. She sipped it gratefully. As delicious as spring water, she thought. Her giddiness had passed and it was no effort for her to sit up, cross-legged. She noticed that she was wearing a man's white shirt, the sleeves rolled past her elbows, and faded denim shorts, the color of the sky outside, that came down to just above her knees.

But hadn't she been wearing—

Carol sat very still. She had come to dread those moments of blankness, of bleakness, when something unpleasant, even frightening, seemed to be trying to squirm loose in her mind. But if she didn't move, just fixed her attention on some neutral thing— the sky, the colorless water in the heavy old pitcher—the moments would come to an end, and she would feel like herself again. Her neutral, undemanding, uncaring self.

Now then. That was much better. What difference did clothes make, as long as she was clean and comfortable?

Carol put the pitcher down carefully on the antique plate. Her mother had collected milk glass, Carol recalled, she'd had tons of it at one time: there were still a few good pieces in the display cabinet in the kitchen at home. She wondered how her mother was this morning. She hoped Felice had slept well. She had certainly slept well herself, would've been feeling just fine except for her eyes, which watered and blurred occasionally; and the sore throat was a nuisance. Undoubtedly she had caught a cold somewhere. Well, you couldn't have everything, Carol sternly reminded herself—and it was a pretty day. Carol looked around the room, now that she could see it well. There were cheerful patterns of sun on two walls. She approved of what she saw.

The headboard of the bed was elaborately made from heavy wrought iron and there were two faces in the center of the design, or rather masks: Janus masks, comedy and tragedy. The bed itself, and the pretty little white table, sat on a platform which raised them about six inches from the floor. Directly above the bed, at least eight feet from where she was sitting, was a small recessed window, like a dormer window. The other windows, through which she had watched the sunrise, were diagonally to her left, and approximately fifteen feet away. The wall in front of her contained an unscreened fireplace with a mantel. There were birch logs for ornament in the fireplace.

To her right Carol saw a tall narrow door—she decided the bathroom must be behind it—and, diagonal to that, where two walls met obliquely (it was certainly a strangely shaped room) there was a stairway, descending. *So I'm up*, Carol thought,

41

pleased with this discovery. From her position on the bed she could see only the top step of this stairway. The ceiling, she noted, continuing her inventory, was about fifteen feet at its highest point. From this point hung the single light fixture in the room, a severe white globe with a large glass lens in the bottom of it. The floor was completely carpeted, in white, of course. Over by the windows there were two sling chairs in white stitched cowhide, shiny, looking like Kevin's baseballs before he used them. Separating the chairs was a huge polar-bear rug, its fur thick and tufted like whorls of whipped cream. The yellow eyes and fangs and pink tongue were the only spots of color to be found. A big white double-doored chifforobe was angled between two walls to her left—and that was it. No other furniture. It was a room for sleeping.

Carol swung her legs to the opposite side of the bed and stood up beside it. The chain slithered down one arm. There was a lot of chain, and it seemed to be fastened to the frame of the bed. She gave it a yank. Fastened firmly. She frowned. It seemed absurd to her, unnecessary. *I'm not going to run away*, she thought.

And instantly the blankness, the sensation of something uncoiling, threateningly, in the cool sunless back regions of her mind. She put both hands to her face to steady herself. Carol shuddered, but it was a small shudder, as isolated and meaningless as a lone bubble rising to the surface of a still pond. As soon as it was gone she was calm again, no longer annoyed.

There was some perfectly good explanation for the collar and chain, otherwise she would be worried about it. And she wasn't. That was the truth. She was not *worried* about anything—except, perhaps, the possibility that she might flood the nice carpet unless she reached the bathroom quickly.

So she ignored the chain and collar, which chafed her neck slightly, and walked to the door nearby. Sure enough, the john. She undid the snap of the denim shorts and made another discovery—no pants. Also no bra. Whoops! Oh, well. She shifted the chain, which was tauter now, no longer slumped over one shoulder, from left to right and sat down. Urinating was unexpectedly painful, it burned her at first. Carol concentrated on the makeup of the old-fashioned bathroom. White, all white. That was beginning to be tedious. The tub was an obvious antique. There was no window. But there was something to look at, on the wall facing the toilet, an unframed oil painting, possibly very old: the surface was crazy-cracked. It was a painting of a hunchbacked dwarf having sexual intercourse with a buxom coarse-featured peasant woman.

Carol stared at it, both fascinated and repelled by the gross sensibilities of the artist. There was also a little dog in the picture. Carol hadn't noticed him right away. It was an ugly picture, not so much pornographic as downright ugly, but she couldn't help grinning. Because in the picture the little dog was about to—he was going to—

She gasped and chuckled and began to laugh aloud, partially smothering the laughter with her hands. And, without warning, the laughter turned to formidable sobs, and she cursed the man warped enough to hang a thing like that in his bathroom.

Tears still falling, her breast heaving with hiccups, Carol stood and pulled up her shorts, groped for the toilet chain above her head and yanked it, went stumbling back into the bedroom, the chain she wore sagging to her feet, almost tripping her up. She sank down on the edge of the bed, used a corner of the sheet to dry her wet and burning eyes. She held her breath to get rid of the hiccups, but that didn't do any good, and neither did a long drink of water. She began to prowl the room, jerking the chain free whenever it hung momentarily on something.

She discovered that she could approach within three feet of the high windows, close enough to glimpse an empty stretch of pasture below, between green woodlots. There were hills, blue with haze, in the distance. On tiptoe and with her arms outstretched, her neck pulled against the collar, Carol could barely press her fingertips against the glass. A bird flew near, and quickly out of view. The sunlight streaming in was all but blinding: she covered her sensitive eyes and retreated, gulping air, and kneeled on the bearskin feeling thwarted, cross and despondent.

When she looked up a young man was standing at the top of the stairway. His hair was black and curled thickly over his shirt collar. He wore dark glasses. He was also wearing Levi's with a tooled leather belt and a bell-sleeved fancy white shirt, front unbuttoned to the middle of his tanned hairless chest. He looked very dark-skinned and tribal against the white background. He was carrying a tray.

"I want to go outside," Carol complained.

He came on into the bedroom. He was barefoot, like Carol. He put the tray on the bed. She watched him closely. Her hiccups had gone.

"What's that?" she asked.

He looked at Carol for only a moment, inscrutably; the dark glasses bothered her, as if they concealed something terrible— a bad scar, a broken mind. She lowered her eyes momentarily. He turned to go.

"*Wait* a minute," Carol said anxiously, jumping up. He stopped. He was wide-shouldered, lithe, slightly bowlegged, and he waited with an athlete's calm containment, an ease that was reassuring. She felt less intimidated by him. She approached slowly.

"What would you like?" he asked.

Carol pushed a sheaf of blond hair away from her face. "Just —stay."

He gestured toward the bed. "Your breakfast is ready."

She looked at the tray, at the plastic dishes, the shirred eggs on strips of broiled ham, fresh orange juice in a plastic tumbler, corn muffins with butter melting on them, a pot of tea.

"Aren't you hungry?"

"I don't know," Carol said vaguely. But she sat down and began to eat. She found the food delicious. There was only a plastic spoon to eat with, which was inconvenient, but she managed. "Don't go away," she asked him, between mouthfuls.

She heard singing again. Both of them looked up. Carol smiled, but the young man didn't look pleased.

"I don't remember your name," she said earnestly, "but your face is familiar."

"Is there anything else I can bring you?"

Carol thought about it. "I'd like some flowers." She chewed solemnly on a piece of cornbread, then giggled.

"Flowers," he repeated, nodding.

"Peonies," Carol specified. "But not white peonies: it's too white in here already. Make them red."

"Red peonies," he said, and then, formally: "Are you comfortable?"

"Sure," Carol said, pouring herself some tea.

"Very good." His voice sounded forlorn to her; she glanced inquiringly at him. He did look sad about something. "Say!" Carol said suddenly, remembering. "Hadn't you better hurry? You'll be late to old what's-his-name's lecture." His expression didn't change; he continued to look broodingly down at her. And Carol (although she knew very well she wasn't supposed to *worry* about anything) was afraid she'd offended. But then he took off the sunglasses, folded them and put them in his shirt pocket, smiled. His teeth were far whiter than anything else in the monochromatic bedroom.

"I'm never on time anyway."

"That's right, you're never on time." So it was all right to tease him; she hadn't been sure how he'd take it. He was very touchy, she knew that much. Proud and touchy. But terribly nice.

"Don't you want to drink your tea?" he asked.

Carol shrugged. She'd eaten every scrap of food, and it had filled a void which she hadn't been aware of. "How about a cigarette?" she ventured.

"Of course." He produced a pack from his shirt pocket, lit one for her, then, after a slight hesitation, lit another for himself. Carol put one hand behind her and leaned back on the bed, luxuriously exhaling a cloud of smoke.

45

"That was awfully good," she said, indicating the breakfast tray.

"Your tea's going to get cold."

Carol was about to tell him she didn't care for any, but he'd been so helpful and kind she didn't have the heart. She sat up again when he handed her the cup and saucer. "How about yourself?"

"I've had breakfast," he said.

She sipped the tea so as not to hurt his feelings. It was luke-warm, excessively sweetened. Even so there was a bitter after-taste on the back of her tongue. But he seemed so eager for her to drink it all that she went ahead and drained the cup.

"You could tell me your name," she said.

"Yes," he said, with a sparing smile; but he didn't. Carol decided it was to be a game. She sincerely liked him, although he wasn't the best company: he seemed ill at ease. Well, she was the hostess, up to her to make him feel right at home. She patted the bed beside her. "Why don't you sit down?"

He declined, with a quick shake of his head.

"You know—I probably shouldn't tell you this—but there's the strangest painting in the bathroom. By the way, this isn't *your* room, is it? Good. I wouldn't want to criticize if it was. Whoever lives here owns only one painting, and *it* is a dilly." Carol giggled, thinking about it. She had begun to feel slightly tired, well relaxed, a trifle on the warm side. Her vision was blurring again. That was really crazy, to own only one painting, with so much white wall space in the bedroom. But maybe he hadn't wanted Carol to see all his other paintings, so he had taken them down and hidden them from her. Oh, well. "Any-way, this painting—you just have to see it for yourself. Why don't you go have a peek? I don't think I could begin to describe it to you."

He shook his head again, with so much sadness in his pitchy eyes it all but broke Carol's heart. "I have to be leaving," he said, and bent to pick up the tray with the breakfast things.

Carol felt genuinely contrite; she knew she was at fault

46

because he obviously was not enjoying himself. Impulsively she leaned over and kissed him full on the lips. It was to have been a soul kiss, warmest regards, but he jerked away after a second's contact, looking startled and curiously violated.

"It's all right," Carol said, watching him mistily. "I always did want to kiss you, I think. You were so—aloof and serious. Let's be friends." She reached up and opened the front of her shirt for him. He bowed his handsome head slightly. His lips had parted; he seemed to be in pain. "If you want to—if it would make you feel better," Carol said, "you can make love to me." She cupped her breasts with her hands. "I think they're pretty nice, don't you?" His pain deepened; muscle bulged in his wide jaws. "I know all of you boys want to make love to blond women," Carol said conversationally, trying to put him at his ease.

He almost ran for the steps, the breakfast things bouncing and chattering on the tray. Carol was mortified. She knew she wasn't supposed to *worry*, but he had looked so angry and upset with her that she couldn't help it.

"Wait!" she said. "I'm sorry."

He paused at the top of the steps.

"I'm really *very* sorry," Carol said tearfully.

"It's—" he began, stammering, "it's all r-right, you—" He shook his head hopelessly, his lustrous black modishly long hair all uncombed now.

"Will you come back to see me?"

"Button up your shirt," he said, his voice guttural, unfriendly in command. She complied, meekly.

"Soon," she said.

"All right." His promise was barely audible. Then his head swung toward Carol; there was a glitter in his flat eyes that fascinated her. "Listen, *chica:* I want you to promise. Don't do that again. Don't unbutton your shirt. Not in front of me, or *any*body."

"I won't," Carol said, chastened.

He went down the stairs quickly. Carol looked after him for

several seconds. Then she yawned, her interest waning. She really liked him, though. She certainly hoped he would come back soon. It was lonesome by herself. There was nothing to do. She lay back on the bed, her bare feet propped on the wrought-iron headboard. The little dormer window was filled with blue sky. Carol regarded it patiently.

I could get up there, she thought. *The chain is long enough.*

She kicked aimlessly at the iron, rocking the bed, eyes on the bright blue pane above. *I could get up there and—*

No one was singing now. It was very quiet. The room had become warmer. Carol brushed sweat from her forehead with her fingertips. The chain made a noise. She hummed drowsily to herself.

I could get out, she thought.

After a while—she had no idea of how much time had passed —a different man came up the stairs to see her. She was still watching the changeless blue in the dormer window, waiting for a cloud, or a bird.

"Hello, dear," he said, standing at the foot of the bed.

"Hello." Carol wasn't sufficiently interested to look around at him.

"Is everything all right?"

"Sure."

"You're not worried about anything, are you?"

"No, I'm not *worried,*" Carol said obediently, and resumed humming to herself. He didn't ask her anything else. She supposed he had gone away. She didn't look to see.

I could get up there, she thought judiciously, *if I really wanted to.*

But I don't. Do I?

Chapter Four

AT FIRST LIGHT FELICE CAME FULLY AWAKE IN HER bed, sitting up convulsively, staring at the dawn-luminous tilted mirror of the vanity opposite. Her throat was dry and closed; she felt light-headed and oppressed. Her first thought was of Carol.

"Sam," she said, despairingly, and looked for him, but he hadn't slept beside her.

A glass of water had staled on the commode by the bed; she drank part of it anyway, then fumbled for her pillbox and two tranquilizer tablets. When they were down she lit a morning cigarette: Sam had been thoughtful enough to leave half a pack for her.

The room was cool and damp. Felice got up. The sheets seemed to be wet enough to wring; she wondered how she could have sweated that much in a single night without awakening. She put on a robe and went into the bathroom. The door to Sam's bedroom was closed. She opened it an inch and looked in. He had fallen asleep on his back, arms outflung. He was snoring lightly and still wearing his glasses.

Felice went in quietly and took off the glasses; Sam didn't stir. She looked at his face for half a minute, avid, absorbed as always. He had a young lean handsome face with high cheekbones, deep eye sockets, a wide mouth with a small white scar at one corner of his upper lip. His face was lined just enough to nullify any impression of boyishness. He was getting a little bald at the back

49

of his head. She thought of these things and was comforted by what was familiar and predictable.

Still she had to remind herself that she had seldom seen even an inch below the surface of Sam Holland. Felice could not decide if she was at fault for wanting the impossible. Her husband was neither cold nor selfish, an emotional enigma; he had humor, he could love and talk openly of loving. But Felice had the heart of a big raggedy spaniel, happily plunging into relationships. She had good intuitions and trusted them. Sam was forced to approach new people by degrees, always guarded, although there was nothing oppressive about his reserve. A touch of melancholy, perhaps, of irony, as if he lived in enchanted blind alleys. Blame the austere upbringing, the lack of parents, the long groping search for a sense of personal worth. He was the only man who had ever puzzled her, challenged her, kept her subtly off balance. She had adjusted to his ways and his drive without conscious thought; she had loved him—still loved him—but often with a sense of defeat that was all but unshakable.

Felice had a warm soapy shower. The tranquilizers worked, changing grinding fear into a low-key, bearable apprehension. She was able to plan. Breakfast first, for all of them. Then cancel the luncheon date. She would need a few things from the A&P; Kevin could go with her, later in the afternoon. With Mattie Dowd gone for a month she was having to learn to shop all over again. There was that tentative thing with the Colvins for evening: drinks, a few rubbers of bridge, with the old mother talking their ears off. Cancel, gladly. Pretext? Sam too tired, although used that one a couple of weeks ago . . .

As soon as Felice turned the shower off she heard Sam cry out. She dried off hastily, then wrapped the big towel around herself and went into his bedroom. He was sitting up, rubbing his forehead, wincing, showing the tooth rimmed in gold. His off-color hazel eyes had that deep tarnish that appeared when he had worked long and hard, drunk too much, slept poorly.

She noticed the bottle of gin, half empty, on the carpet beside the bed.

"Sorry," he said. "I didn't mean to sound like a wounded bull. Gin headache, and a stiff neck along with it."

"I'll run a hot bath."

"That would be the best thing." He cracked a smile for her. "How are you?"

"I just keep flapping my wings, hoping I'll take off. Waking up must have hurt you. It was almost like a scream."

"I was having a choice nightmare. Do you ever dream about funerals?"

"Oh, God! Don't tell me about it."

"Supposedly it was the funeral of my mother. I hadn't set eyes on her since I was three days old, so I was curious to see the old girl. It was a nice dim chapel. No flowers at the bier; that bothered me. But someone was playing the organ beautifully, and there were mourners. I don't think I knew any of them."

"Sam, I really don't want to hear."

"I approached the coffin—as one must—and looked inside. But it wasn't my mother. It was me. I could see where they had plugged the bullet hole in my forehead with mortician's wax. Then, just like that, I was inside the coffin looking out, and the lid started down—"

"All right," Felice said, furious. She went into the bathroom and turned on the taps for his bath, then continued to her room, where she put on a shift and pinned her hair up and applied a light coat of pale-pink lipstick.

"Felice," she heard him say, and reluctantly she returned to his bedroom. He hadn't moved. His hands were clasped in his lap. He smoothed the carpet with one narrow foot.

"I forgot, for a minute. I forgot about—"

"No big thing. Your bath's almost ready." She hesitated, then said, "I still don't understand why you didn't go to the police about it. You had a bullet hole in your windshield."

"One bullet hole, no bullet. They would have been polite and regretful, and maybe there would have been three paragraphs in the Lubbock papers. I'm sure one of the wire services would have picked up the story. I suppose I didn't want anyone else getting ideas. Brethren of the Radical Right, it's open season on Sam Holland, who has bad-mouthed us once too often. Not the biggest trophy head around, but he travels light and alone, and you all bear in mind that little Communists get to be big Communists."

"But you *saw* the one who took the shot at you."

"I saw a face on a dark street. It was only a glimpse. I don't know what he looked like." Sam passed a hand over a bristly jaw. "He might have been serious enough to try again, so after I bashed in the broken place with a brick I wasn't inclined to hang around town. If there *had* been a bullet in the car somewhere, then I might have brought in the cops. Naturally it could never be proved, but I've thought that it would be a nice irony if the gunman had been using a rifle from the arsenal of Henry Phelan Morse. He's furnished plenty of material aid and comfort to those Minuteman types."

"Shut up, Sam," she warned him, in a voice he seldom heard. He nodded once, wearily, accepting the reprimand, and went to his bath, shedding his pajamas on the way.

"Give me twenty minutes," he said.

As soon as Felice reached the first floor a man came out of the library and introduced himself as special agent Crockett. It was still a shock for her to realize these men were in the house, and what they were there for. Like Sam, this agent was in his mid-forties, trim, bespectacled.

"Is there any news?" she asked him.

"I haven't heard anything. Mr. Gaffney will be here soon, though, and he'll bring you up to date."

Felice offered the two agents breakfast and went back to the kitchen.

Early as it was—ruckus of birds, grass beaded from the dew, trees still dark and motionless against a sky hinting of opal—

her father was already there. He was drinking buttermilk on the porch, watching Riggs course for an unwary rabbit or woodchuck. The ten-acre pond at the rear of the two properties was misted over, showing a core of gold from the just-risen sun.

"Good morning," she said, brushing a kiss against his frail cheek. "Did you sleep?"

"Not a wink," he grumbled. "Who's up?"

"Sam, so far."

He grunted something, turned his head to look for the dog. Felice asked how many eggs he wanted and retreated to the kitchen, concentrating on the breakfast menu. She thought she was functioning smartly, well coordinated, with all emotions sorted, graded, compartmentalized. *Eight eggs, no, make it nine* . . . There was a slippage, a little blank space. And then she became aware of the General standing behind her, saying in his half-throttled whiskied voice:

"You've been holding that damned door open for almost three minutes; can't you find what you need?"

Felice turned and looked up at him, her mind in its peculiar terrible stall; her legs felt overused, unbearably wobbly.

"What—what are they going to do to Carol?" she whispered.

The General's unstable blue eyes opened a little wider. "Not a damned thing. They're taking good care of her."

Felice shook her head, bewildered, annoyed. "I don't believe it. That's what everyone wants to believe, but I *can't* any more. It's all the same to the kidnappers, isn't it? Whether she lives or dies?"

"She'll be back in this house tonight, Felice."

"What makes you think so?" she asked calmly, eyes on his face, daring him to be right.

"Because they're good. They took Carol in broad daylight, without a fuss. Maybe Gaffney's crew will turn up some kind of eyewitness, somebody saw something that looked a little funny, but that's a long shot. I sat all night trying to figure from what we already know how the rest of it's going to happen, and this is the way it looks to me. There's three of them, all young—"

53

"Three? How—"

"They asked for two hundred twenty-five thousand. That's seventy-five thousand a man, and even in fifties and twenties it wouldn't be hard to carry that kind of money around. The whole amount could be packed solid in a thin-line attaché case. If these boys were stupid and greedy they might have gone for the whole hog instead of just taking a good-size bite. Say, three-quarters of a million. I can afford it, but that kind of money creates problems. My bank has to get the bills from the Reserve, which takes time, and also it would take a good-size suitcase to hold it all. These boys want to collect fast and inconspicuously. Now, when the call comes they'll likely specify one of those tan attaché cases, probably ten million of them in the whole country, and they'll instruct Sam to put that case with the money in his car and drive down to La Guardia airport, timing it so he arrives about six P.M. That's the peak traffic hour, and La Guardia is always jammed then. He'll be told to report to one of the luggage-claim areas, American or TWA, and put the case down with some incoming luggage and get the hell out of there. You know what a mob scene that is, people lined up six deep trying to get their bags. A dozen cops couldn't keep their eyes on that one little case. But I don't think the pickup man would just walk away with it. No, he'd have a larger case, with a trick bottom, like shoplifters use, and he'd just slip his own case down over the one Sam left and ten minutes later he'd be on a plane for Chicago or someplace to join up with the others."

"And Carol?"

"One quick phone call after his plane touches down, and the police will have Carol home in no time."

"You make them sound—very businesslike, and not frightening."

"They're taking damned good care of her," the General said again, kneading her shoulder with a hand well scarred by the beaks of the hunting birds he had trained. "They may have other schemes in mind for transferring that cash, but otherwise I know

I've got them pegged. Now be a good girl and get some breakfast cooked. If you could use a tranquilizer I've got a few on me."

"No, thanks, I've taken two already. They're too seductive. I want to stand in one place all day braiding my hair."

She made coffee first so the General would have a cup, then put a frozen breakfast Danish in the oven to heat. She carried coffee to the FBI men in the library. When she returned the General was sitting at the table staring out at the first blaze of day on lawns and beds, on masses of peonies and rambling rose and late-blooming azaleas.

"Felice," he said abruptly, "you shouldn't let what's happened confuse your thinking about Sam."

"What do you mean, General?"

"You were all set to have Sam move out, let old Johnny Chesler draw up the papers."

Felice poured coffee for herself. She said, careful about her wording, "I had reached the point where—I didn't know what else I could do."

"You still hold out hope there might be a change in Sam?"

She was a long time in answering. "I believe we've been totally honest with each other. I believe he sincerely wants this marriage." The General sat hunched over his coffee. He looked at her, slow, sidewise, unblinking. He said nothing more. He had taken no pains of late to disguise his hatred of Sam. He had never understood how she could marry two men as fundamentally different as Sam and Doug Watterson. The General had loved Doug like a brother and still mourned him. *Have you forgiven me, General, because I no longer mourn for Doug? He was the most exciting thing that ever happened to me, all that slapdash Texas charm, I was cockeyed in love with him. I lost him, and the world changed. I adapted and met Sam, whom I loved—do love, but in an altogether different way. Everyone adapts but you, General. You solidify.*

And yet she had a measurable amount of affection for the old man; she put up with his obtuseness and maddening interference

55

in her personal life. Her mother had been a happy flagellant, so Felice supposed that much of her mother, at least, lingered in her. . . .

If Sam stayed, if they tried seriously to work out their differences, then inevitably there would be open warfare between Sam and the General. And, inevitably, she would side with her husband. The General would be badly hurt. But he alone was to blame.

Sam and Kevin came down to breakfast together. Unexpectedly the General was cordial, talkative. He explained his theories about the kidnappers while Felice served them. Sam just nodded, preoccupied, but the General's conviction was good for Kevin, bringing him out of his depression. He asked astute questions. The General knew him very well, she thought, watching the two of them with a trace of envy. Kevin's moods could be shattering. Last night he had blamed himself for what had happened to Carol. During questioning he had shouted at Gaffney, pounded up the stairs to his room in tears. Luckily he was growing up with men around the house. She loved Kevin too much, and understood him too little. Felice knew she never could have raised him by herself.

Before they finished eating the telephone rang. Their reactions were predictable. Felice shut her eyes, not panicky, just dead certain she had forgotten how to breathe. Then without looking at anyone she walked the five steps to the wall telephone and answered. It was a buddy of Kevin's, about the cruise. Kevin made it as brief as he could, returned to the table unfocused and depressed again.

Sam said, "That's going to happen. People call. We can't be jumping five feet every time."

"I'd better let them know I can't go on the cruise," Kevin said. He had been counting on it for almost a year. Twelve boys from the yacht club in Rye were flying with chaperons to the Virgin Islands; the plan was to island-hop from Charlotte Amalie aboard a blue water sailer. The boys were divided into teams, and each team had chosen a navigational or scientific project to complete during the cruise.

"You're not going until next week," Sam pointed out. "Carol will be back long before then."

"She'll be back in this house tonight," the General vowed, for the tenth time. Kevin looked from one to the other and said nothing more; but there was trust in his eyes, and that made Felice uneasy. They were promising Kevin—promising themselves—far too much.

Gaffney came. He managed to be encouraging without having any hard news. Again the General expounded on his ideas, speculation having become God's truth to him by this time, and Gaffney listened intently, nodding, saying when the General had finished, "You've certainly given us some angles to think about, sir."

"The way I see it, you bug that case, sew a little transponder into the lining, and track him every step of the way. After they've released Carol, then you grab him."

Gaffney told Sam and Felice what they must do when the kidnappers called. "Demand to talk to Carol. Probably they won't let you, it wastes too much time, but demand anyway. Make the caller go slow on instructions; tell him you're writing everything down. Break down and cry a little if you think you can be convincing. Use up time."

He had brought with him an artist from the Bureau in Washington. After the table was cleared Kevin sat down with the artist and they went through a volume of transparencies called an Identi-kit, putting together combinations of facial features until a reasonable likeness of the man Kevin had seen in Jake's emerged. It took a long time. The General stayed through a second cup of coffee and then went home to spend the morning on the telephone, placing and receiving calls from all over the world. Sam moved his papers and typewriter upstairs.

Felice washed dishes, collected laundry. A girl came on Tuesdays and Fridays to do the washing and cleaning. Felice thought of a plausible excuse to keep her away that week, telephoned. Then she made brief calls canceling personal obligations through the week, exasperating old and dear friends by refusing to chat. By ten o'clock she could no longer think of ways to keep herself busy.

The FBI artist had finished his charcoal portrait. Studying the elongated, partially masked face gave Felice some bad moments: she wished she hadn't asked to see the drawing. She had begun to believe the kidnapping could be understood as a business venture after all, conducted by men who were ruthless and coldly precise in their methods, but not necessarily evil. They would look upon Carol as merchandise to be exchanged in good condition for X number of dollars. An honorable transaction. But there was brutality in this man's face. If Carol caused the least bit of trouble, if she annoyed him, he could hurt her without hesitation or remorse.

"I'll try him without the shades and the fright wig," the artist said, turning to a fresh page. "Thanks, Kevin; you don't need to stick around."

Kevin got up from the table, eyes slightly squinched as if he had a headache. He went outside without a word, screen door banging behind him.

Fifteen minutes later Felice saw him from an upstairs window, standing motionless beside the pond, Riggs lying in the grass at his feet. On impulse she went downstairs and outside, past the two-room guest cottage where the Dowds lived, past the enclosed green-surfaced tennis court. She could feel the heat of the sun on her bare shoulders, heat rising moistly from the stubble of the cut field beyond the hedged lawn. There were cooling trees on the shore of the green pond, twin elms that had somehow escaped the blight. Ducks coasted in the domino of shade alongside the small boat dock. Riggs got up at her approach and stretched himself and tried to snatch a yellow butterfly with his teeth; Kevin merely looked around and then back again at the sweltering pond.

"It's like when I was ten," Kevin said, "and Tim Beckley

walked out in front of that ready-mix truck. And we waited almost all night in the hospital in Mount Kisco, just waited."

"I remember. Then it turned out not to be as bad for Timmy as we thought." She stood beside him for a while, hands in the pockets of her shift. "None of this is going to be as bad as we think it is. Because we're plain scared now, and it's easy to let our fears run over us."

"When do you think they'll call?"

"Soon," Felice said. "It has to be soon."

Chapter Five

BY THE TIME SHE HEARD BIG JIM'S FOOTSTEPS ON THE stairs Carol had put together nearly half of the elaborate jigsaw puzzle, which was a reproduction of one of Degas's studies of dancing girls.

"Lights out, Carol," Big Jim said.

Carol held a small butterfly-shaped section of the puzzle in the air, not taking her eyes from the chop-board on which she was working. She sat cross-legged on the floor, the metal chain three-quarters taut, like a high-tension line connecting her to the white bed. "Just this one piece," she begged.

"All right, dear. I'll wait." Big Jim sat in one of the white sling chairs and crossed his legs. He was smoking, and he'd brought an ashtray, which he held in the palm of his right hand. Carol asked automatically for a cigarette. Big Jim balanced the glass ashtray on one bony knee and lit a cigarette for her, leaned over. Carol turned her head and he placed the cigarette between her lips. It was a menthol; she didn't care for those. She liked Handsome Dan's brand the best. Thinking of Handsome Dan activated the pinched lonesome feeling in her heart. He hadn't come to see her today.

She scowled at the puzzle, pretending to be in all kinds of difficulty. Actually she had seen where the piece would fit, but she wasn't ready for lights-out, and so she stalled.

Big Jim wore dark-gray Hush Puppies that were becoming shapeless from age. They were dusted all over with white, as if he had spilled talcum. But Carol knew what the white really was: marble dust. She'd listened to the chink-chink of chisel against stone most of the rainy afternoon.

"When can I see the bust?" she asked.

"Oh, it won't be ready for a long time, Carol."

"But you promised to show it to me first."

"I will," he said good-humoredly. He leaned forward again and gently plucked the piece of puzzle from her fingers. He notched it into the proper place on the board and sat back, looking down at her with a hint of amusement. He never really smiled, but most of the time he was in a relaxed easygoing mood. He was nice-looking, except for a lack of hair and the unfortunate thickness and grape-stain color of his lips. His eyes were dark and attractive and his nose had a good noble height of bridge. There was always a pale spot above his nose where he shaved a break between his eyebrows.

"Can I finish my cigarette?" she asked, getting up. The chain made a noise sliding against the metal of the bed. Usually the chain didn't bother her; she seldom thought about it any more. But for the last hour or so she had become increasingly aware of the chain as an impediment and a discrimination. No one else wore chains. It wasn't fair. If she didn't have the chain on she wouldn't have to stay Up all the time. She could go Down if she wanted to. Even Out. That was what she wanted more than anything. To be Out. If she were Out, then she could—

"What are you doing?" Big Jim asked, and Carol looked guiltily around at him. She flushed; there was disapproval in his eyes. Without realizing it she had been tugging with one hand at the chain, hard enough to displace the bed a couple of inches. She stared at the marks on her fingers where she had gripped the chain so tightly.

Carol lowered her head as much as she could, still feeling guilty. "Nothing."

"Aren't you comfortable?"

"Yes, I'm comfortable," Carol said in a subdued voice, glancing at him, wishing he would forget about it. *See, I'm not doing anything now.* The ashtray was a heavy one. If she had it, she

61

thought, she could knock him in the head, knock his brains out—

The emotion rather than the image confused and upset Carol: she was not accustomed to overpowering emotions. Why would she want to do something like that to Big Jim?

"You look nervous tonight," Big Jim said, studying her through a haze of cigarette smoke, his eyes narrowed down. "Does working on the puzzle make you nervous?"

"No, I like working on the puzzle," Carol said. She felt desperate to change the subject. The ash on her cigarette was nearly an inch long; she reached out and Big Jim held the ashtray for her. "Somebody came today—somebody else, I mean. It wasn't Handsome Dan."

"You have very good ears," he said, looking benign again. "No, it wasn't Handsome Dan."

"Was it somebody I know?"

Big Jim shook his head. "One more drag on that cigarette, and then into bed."

"I didn't hear Gorgeous Gertie singing today."

"I'm afraid Gorgeous Gertie has come down with a cold."

"Oh, that must have been her coughing."

"Right you are." Big Jim snubbed his own cigarette and came up out of the chair. He was eight inches taller than Carol. When he looked down at her she could see the light reflecting on the big bald spot toward the back of his skull. Deftly he pinched the cigarette from between her fingers and deposited it in the ashtray. Then he put his hand at the back of her blond head, cupping it. He had hard warty hands, nails mangled. She didn't like for Big Jim to stand this close, to touch her—it reminded her, dimly, of something shocking that had happened on a hot blue day, it reminded her of Big Jim transformed by a crispy mass of red hair and evil-looking sunglasses, his lips pursed in concentration as he—

Knock his brains out, and—of course, of course—RUN!

Run, she thought, licking her lips, staring helplessly at Big Jim. But that was foolish, where would she go? She liked it here.

"I like it here," she said, appeasingly, as if he'd questioned her.

62

"That's fine, dear. But you are edgy tonight. Naow, ah suspect it's on account of because you din drink yore tea at suppertime."

Usually it tickled Carol when he faked a drawl that way, she couldn't help giggling at his silliness, but this time she didn't respond at all, because in kidding tones he was accusing her of something quite serious. It was important for her to drink her tea at every meal, drink every drop. It was one thing they all insisted upon.

But she just hadn't wanted it, that's all. She was bored with tea. So she had poured the whole cupful into the toilet.

Somehow Big Jim seemed to know what she had done, and, obediently, she was about to tell him, so he would quit watching her with those dark, fitfully amused eyes and pursed sausage lips, tell him so he would turn out the light and leave her. But something unexpected occurred: a coldness crept into her heart, a cold resolve to lie. It was very very difficult to tell Big Jim any sort of lie. By concentrating on this coldness and an exhilarating sense of purpose, however, she was able to say it.

"Yes, I drank my tea."

"Hmm," he said, still watching closely. And then he believed her, and she felt a tiny jolt of triumph. "I guess Ba—I mean, Gorgeous Gertie slipped up. No harm done." He reached into his shirt pocket and withdrew a plastic bottle half filled with red-and-white capsules. He shook two out. "Be a good girl and take these for me before you go to bed."

"All right," she said, because she was supposed to say it; but it was another lie.

But Big Jim wasn't going to leave it up to her. He went into the bathroom and filled the plastic tumbler with water and brought it to Carol. He stood beside her while she swallowed both capsules.

Carol put the tumbler on the table beside her bed and curled up on the bed, nestling her face against the pillow. "Good night, Big Jim."

"Good night, Carol. Gorgeous Gertie tells me we'll have pancakes in the morning."

"I want mine with maple syrup."

"You shall certainly have it." He turned out the light and Carol watched over one shoulder as he went down the steep stairs and through the curtain that shut out the light from below. For a few moments it seemed totally dark in the room. The pillow was cool against her cheek. Carol yawned. Most nights all she had to do was lie down and pow, just like that it was morning, and the breakfast tray was on the way up. She never remembered sleeping at all. . . .

The alarm was a subtle one, no more than a skipped heartbeat and a shifting in the currents of her blood. She sat up, the bed creaking, the chain rattling against one hollow post. She did not want to take the capsules. She did not want to sleep, because there were things to think about, things that troubled her.

A long time ago there had been a dog, a tawny shepherd named— Carol tried hard to think of his name, but it eluded her. She yawned again and lay back. Her mind was fogging slightly.

. . . And the shepherd had roamed happily and confidently all over the neighborhood. But sometimes he made a nuisance of himself or accidentally frightened children, so it became necessary to chain him to a post in the back yard. The chain had made him miserable. He howled and leaped and tried to slip his collar, but, although he fought and bit at the chain until he lay exhausted with froth on his lips and mad yellow lights in his eyes, he could not be free.

Then one night he dug at the foundations of the post, dug deep around the concrete and with implausible strength and determination simply pulled the iron post over. She had watched from her bedroom window as he dug silently and tenaciously through the moonlit hours. She watched him run free with mingled feelings of loss and relief: it had not been right. He had run and run, and they never saw him again. It was not right to chain dogs, or people. It was wrong for her to be chained.

Carol sat up on the bed, which squeaked a little. Her throat was dry. There were funny lights before her eyes, sparkling, slowly exploding, receding trickily, confusing her, distorting perspective. She walked awkwardly, one hand paying out chain to keep it from rattling. She felt as if she were inching along a tilted surface, and her knees bumped together. Her heart fluttered and her head was filled with lemony air. She missed the bathroom doorspace and bumped the jamb hard, hurting her nose.

There was a bathroom light, but she didn't turn it on. Her breath stirred in her chest like dried leaves. She groped and found the john, lifted the lid. With a foot she pushed the door behind her until it was wedged against the length of chain. Then she braced herself with one hand and leaned over the john and stuck two fingers of the other hand down her throat.

Carol gagged but didn't retch. The gag reflex set off the alarm in her bloodstream, restored the coldness of rebellion to her unsteady heart. She prodded again and vomited, then went to her knees on the tile floor, too dizzy and sick to stand.

Again, she thought, feverishly, and pulled herself up. She turned on the cold-water tap and leaned backward over the tub, letting the water gush down her throat until she was bloated and choking. Then, tears streaming down her cheeks, soaked to the waist, she rolled stomach-down with her head hanging and made herself vomit again, this time into the tub.

The abuse almost caused her to faint, and Carol slipped senselessly to the floor. But after a few moments she blindly dragged a towel from the rack. She wet it, then soaked her face until it no longer felt waxen. She had the hiccups. She felt as if she was going to fly into hysterics. She was certain they had heard her and had come upstairs. They would make her drink a pint of their oversweet tea, and she would go to sleep and never wake up.

When it became possible Carol rocked to her knees, like an old mama buffalo wallowing up out of a rice paddy, grasping the lip of the tub for support. Her head was clearer now, and she didn't feel as if she might nod off at any moment. She sank blunt teeth into her lower lip and stood erect. The whipsawing of the chain had forced the door open partway. She opened it more and looked out. She heard nothing except the cold rapping of rain against the double windows. A run of lightning turned the white bedroom to a scintillate blue. She walked back to the bed, the floor level now. Nevertheless she put one foot in front of the other with extraordinary care. Her heartbeat was nearly normal. Her hands tingled, but there was strength in them.

She would not sleep until she was ready. She would remember what she needed to remember. It was a victory. It established her as a person again, not a cowed unthinking chain-wearing thing.

Dull shaking of thunder, like—

Like combers slamming phosphorescent against the Big Sur coast, slamming down there in the dark and dwindling away to salty foam as the next big one tucked and lunged, and oh God how safe there with Dev in the A-frame on the high spit of sand. There beside the huge stone fireplace with just enough scattered fire left to cozy up the dark and reflect from his eyes, from the hanging glossy lock, the naked chest and tanned straining thighs as he—

There was a clear arc of lightning outside the gleaming windows; involuntarily she threw up her hands.

Oh God oh God what am I doing here?

That's your blue Sting Ray parked outside?

Carol fell face down on the bed, covering her damp head with the pillow. The dog collar felt like iron at her throat. As the rain fell heavily on the roof she was swept into a drowning panic.

Please get me out of here, Dev!

But that was over. Dev was gone. She couldn't hope that he would help her.

Because of the collar she had to sit up after a while to catch her breath. She held the weight of the chain in her hands, too depressed to curse it. Above her head the square window glowed from a pulse of lightning, darkened again. The rain fell ceaselessly, and Carol shuddered. The shudder turned into a comfortable yawn. She was beginning to feel the least bit drowsy after all the punishment her body had accepted: drowsy and reconciled. But the alarm ran through her blood again, plunged like a steel needle into the heart.

She stood up on the bed, careful not to shake it, not wanting to make noise. But she sensed that the rain had effectively sound-proofed the room.

She could easily reach the deep sill of the window with her hands. By climbing—bare feet gripping the Janus masks worked into the iron headboard—she found that she could raise herself high enough to see through the pane.

Not that there was anything to see. Rain, darkness.

The sill seemed deep enough and wide enough to sit in. If she could look down, then she would know just how high she was.

The bed trembled as Carol thrust herself upward; she supported herself on elbows and forearms, clawed for a handhold and found a lever of some sort, then twisted and wormed higher until she had one hip seated on the recessed sill. The space was small. She discovered that she could sit in reasonable comfort with her head and shoulders bent, one leg tucked under her, the other hanging down. There was still about seven feet of chain left.

For the first time during her captivity she was able to see in all directions from the white bedroom. Carol stared through the rain and murk, unable to read the land. Then below, off to her left, almost out of her line of vision, she saw the light of a tall window slanted across the muddy well-trampled ground. Beyond it she could make out a shed of some sort, or a garage. Lightning flickered a few miles away, and she received an impression of distant hills. She closed her eyes tightly and counted slowly to sixty and looked out again. Now she thought she could see pin-points of light, moving, vanishing, reappearing. Far off. She had no sense of distance. They seemed to be the headlights of automobiles. Her discovery excited her.

The window was of the casement type, opening outward. It could be locked by means of the curved lever which she had grasped to pull herself up to the perch she now occupied. Carol played with the handle. In the up position the window was un-locked. When she pushed against it she felt the window give slightly, but it seemed stuck in the frame. Probably it had been painted over numerous times since it was last opened. Just outside, the roof dropped steeply to a metal gutter, now brimming over with rainwater.

Twenty feet, no, twenty-five to the ground, Carol judged. She looked out again. Thunder, rain, the weaving, shifting pinpoints of light. They seemed no closer. She yawned. It had been fun getting up there. But it was now time to go down, go to sleep.

The thought set off a fit of trembling. *No.*

No, that was what Big Jim and the others wanted. They wanted her to go to sleep and never wake up.

In the automobiles, out there, were people who could help her. If they could see her, then they would come to help. The tawny shepherd had dug himself free and had run, *run,* but she needed help; she could not break the chain that made her a prisoner.

Prisoner, Carol thought, shuddering violently. Oh, Dev, oh, dear Dev, Jesus, help—

If she could just open the window, climb out onto the roof, then someone would notice her there. Someone who could make Big Jim let her go.

Carol pushed against the stuck window, but she was not in a position to get her maximum strength into the effort. She stopped to catch her breath, then turned awkwardly, getting both knees under her. Her shoulders were wedged against the raked ceiling of the window space. She locked her hands and this time shoved with her forearms, straining forward, gasping with effort.

The window swung wide on a broken hinge and Carol pitched out into the rain, tumbling headfirst down the slippery roof slant; she sprawled across the gutter, which tore partly away from the roof on impact.

The flailing weight of her legs carried her over the edge. She started to plummet straight down. But the chain snapped taut and the dog collar dug cruelly into the soft flesh beneath her jaw and she came to a jarring stop in the air, her back arched, hands upflung.

In the bedroom the iron bed was jerked back a foot and a half until it crashed against the wall, inclined at an angle.

The bright links of the chain dug a quarter inch into the wood of the windowsill.

Comedy smiled blindly in the dark and Tragedy grimaced, as if in the throes of a frozen scream.

And Carol Watterson was suspended by the neck in the rain, hands brushing against her thighs, turning slowly, palely, with each pendulous motion of her body.

Chapter Six

WHEN THE TYPEWRITER STOPPED AND SHE HEARD SAM
moving around in his room Felice shut the heavy loose-leaf book
and shoved it under her pillow. Sam came in after a while, a glass
with a generous portion of gin in one hand. She turned her head
on the pillow. From the puffiness of his eyes and the way his
mouth was stitched into a half grimace she could tell he had
been doing an unusual amount of drinking, fueling his attack on
the typewriter. But he wasn't drunk. It would be better for him
if he could get good and drunk, she thought, and she smiled half
sleepily, pleased to see him.

"Not sleeping?"

"Just lying here," Felice said.

"I'm sorry—the typewriter—"

"No, it doesn't bother me."

"Let me get you a drink."

"No. Just sit with me, Sam."

The rain had let up; she hadn't really been aware of the rain
for the past half hour or so. It was now after midnight. And it
was Saturday, she realized. But she didn't want to think about
that. It was not credible. Not Saturday already. She hoped it
wouldn't rain much longer. Most of the week they'd been
blessed with hot sun. She and Kevin had literally worn each
other out—with tennis, swimming, horses—while poor Sam had
stuck close to the telephone. If she'd had to stay in the house
she'd be a lunatic by now, Felice thought. Sam had known that.

He'd insisted she get out, and the games and the sun had relaxed, even stunned her, as thoroughly as medication.

Felice moved over to make room for him on the side of her bed. "How's the article coming?"

"I can't tell; I haven't had the heart to stop and read through it." He leaned over and kissed her forehead. He was unshaven, his chin a stubbly gray, and his face had begun to look emaciated. "You're dark as a squaw," he said approvingly. She touched the side of his neck and felt all the stiffness and tension that was in him. It worried her.

"Your turn tomorrow," she said. "Why don't you and Kevin go sailing? You've only been once, and June is almost gone." Sam shook his head automatically. "You *need* a break," she said insistently. "I'm fine now. I can handle it if they call." Sam sat back and rubbed his eyes, fought a yawn. Felice dropped her hand. "Besides, I don't think anyone's going to call. It's been too long."

Sam looked unbelievingly at her. She smiled back at him, calmly. "I think it's obvious now. This is like *The Collector*. It's some poor demented boy who has the nerve to kidnap her. But he wouldn't hurt her; he's not violent. He's lonely, and he wants companionship. He saw Carol and fell for her and let his fantasies get out of hand. That's what it's about, Sam." There was a shading of urgency in her voice. "So I'm not worried about her—"

"There was a ransom note. We can't ignore that."

"It was just a—ploy, meant to mislead us."

"But why write a note at all?"

"Sam," she said, trying to be patient, "there's no other explanation. He never *intended* to call. But Carol is perfectly all right. She's safe. Eventually she'll talk him into letting her go. Or—"

"I think you're letting your own fantasies get out of hand," he said, too sharply.

Felice said, "—or the FBI will catch up to him."

"I wouldn't put too much faith in them."

Felice sat up. "But look how much they've found out already. And Gaffney always knows more than he's willing to tell us!"

"I—I don't want you to be upset, Felice. They just don't have that much to go on. And they're already looking in a four-state area."

Felice studied him for a long time, and her face hardened and her eyes lost their light of assurance. She said in a low bitter tone, "What do you want me to believe, Sam? That Carol is dead?"

It was viciously unfair and she knew that immediately. He was shocked; his lips moved but he couldn't speak. She made a small lunge and wrapped her arms around him and said painfully, "Sam, Sam, I don't know why!" He soothed her forgivingly; he kissed a bare shoulder and then a pale breast, the dark bolt of nipple driven through the center of it. Her skin was still very warm from the sun, and he was stimulated by the heat and desperate flavor of her. She bent like a bow as his blunt fingers dug into the flesh of her back. Her eyes were wide and alert to the demonstration of need. "Sam?" she said, breath a sharp explosion in his ear.

They were both rigid and expectant for a few seconds, then the strength went out of him. He got up. "I don't think I would do you any good," he said hopelessly.

Felice felt a clear rush of anger; she was ashamed of her reaction, and brought it under control. She sat cross-legged, uncovered, turning her head to watch him as he walked to the windows overlooking the drive. "My pleasure, then," she said, waiting patiently for her heavy heartbeat to slow, her fingers curled lightly on sensitive thighs.

"Maybe tomorrow I'll be—" His lips were white. He lit a cigarette for himself, his hands awkward; he scorched a finger-nail on a quick-burning match. "I *would* like to get out," he said, peering nervously at the rain. "Provided this clears up. Just to get away from the damned telephone, you know?"

"I know."

"I didn't mean to be so blunt with you. You could have the right idea after all. Gaffney's thought from the beginning that there was something odd about this—snatch, as he calls it. I think he suspects Dev Kaufman could be behind it."

"Good Lord! Dev?" She gave Dev some thought. "The time I met him—what? two years ago?—he seemed intense and excitable, and—very much in love with Carol. But I can't conceive of him doing something like this to her. Besides, Dev is in Europe."

"He's supposed to be. Everyone thinks that's where he is. But he left Madrid more than three weeks ago. There hasn't been a trace of him since then."

"It would be easy to find out if he'd come back to the States."

"I think so." Sam yawned, rubbing his swollen eyes. "I'm starting to go numb," he complained. "It's the damnedest sensation. My head wants to swing around and around as if it was on a pivot."

"Go to bed," she said kindly.

"No, I thought I'd keep you company a little—"

"Sam, go to bed. You're out on your feet."

He shrugged and grinned sheepishly at her. "If you're sure you—"

"I'm fine. And you can't go sailing tomorrow without at least eight hours' sleep. You'd fall out of the boat and drown."

He mumbled, "Bob Kennedy used to say that nobody drowns in Long Island Sound any more, they decay first."

"*Bed*," she told him, and got up swiftly to accompany him into his own room. There was a litter of balled-up yellow papers on the bed and floor. She moved the ink-stained typewriter and cleaned up. She made Sam take off his frayed twill work trousers and nearly buttonless shirt—his favorite costume for writing—and switched on the fan of the air-conditioner to replace the cigarette-polluted air in the room. When she looked around Sam was fast asleep on his side, hollow-cheeked, his fists lightly clenched. She covered him with a sheet and a spread, turned off the lamp.

73

The book was Carol's. She had taken it from Carol's room. Felice experienced a residual sense of wrongness whenever she opened it, but she couldn't stop herself: these poems and essays and pages of sometimes harsh self-examination were the best link she had with her daughter now; she had become dependent upon them.

She was surprised by Carol's ability, by the rough-edged unsentimental poems. When she came upon revelations meant for no one else's eyes Felice was often shaken, then touched by her daughter's humanness, her candor and judgment. And she would have a great deal to think about during the sleepless hours with the book weighing heavy in her lap. Carol was quick-changing before her eyes, like an actress on a runaway strip of film. It was difficult to keep up, to put aside the cherished misconceptions of who her daughter was, and why. Presumptions and prejudices had to be rolled away like heavy stones, allowing Carol room to grow and be herself, to prove her point. Felice read and reread. Eavesdropping, yes—but perhaps it could be justified, she thought.

Let me explain, Carol. When you were a child and could trust me with every emotion and every thought we had a closeness we'll never have again, and being the usual sort of mother that's what I remember best about us, and return to most often. Because it's not so easy to be sentimental about the growing-up time and the growing apart, the necessary time of becoming equals, with all that means to women. There were quarrels sometimes, with a setting-aside of trust, and I think of opportunities I had to make things smoother for you, and missed, because I didn't always understand what you wanted. All in all we got along well while losing touch; affection was more than a habit with us, thank God, and I suppose you don't think too badly of me now.

Equals. So am I intruding, stealing what is private and untouchable? I hope you wouldn't feel that way, if you knew.

I can hear your heartbeat again, and that's what I care about. We're not so different—and you can't imagine the relief I feel knowing that. We're not such strangers. I could talk to you now, easily, with more confidence than I've had in a good many years. Carol, when you come home—

There she had to stop and close the book and work the cold fish-hook thing out of her heart a little at a time, and after it was gone her hands trembled for several minutes; her breath had a tendency to gather like cotton wadding in her lungs.

Chapter Seven

CAROL'S BOOK

Dec. 4

QUITE A PARTY SUNDAY, ALTHOUGH THAT'S NOT WHAT we had in mind when Dev invited Paul Kobrak and his retinue over to talk about the film they're going to make. We ended up with twenty-five or so in two rooms. I suppose it was the usual thing, half of them just wandered in from somewhere else because it sounded like we had a good thing going. It was a *very* serious evening, with a lot of weighty discussion about The Film (Truffaut's or Resnais' names invoked at proper intervals, greeted by orgiastic sighs and profound nods). Nobody was toking up. Or could it be that overly solemn and self-conscious ritual is on its way out around here?

Anyway, the movie: It'll be called *The Oakland Method,* referring of course to the plans for civil disobedience worked out for the draft protests at Oakland Induction Center last year. Ergo the film will deal with the Politics of Confrontation. Apparently Kobrak has considerable footage from here and there, but no script yet. And there won't be a script. Some overeager disciple (she must be new) brought up the subject and Kobrak gave her a full thirty seconds of his rather empty stare, then grandly raised one hand and tapped his temple with a forefinger. Meaning, I suppose, that his vision was complete, but much too precious and vital to commit to paper. Bullshit. Kobrak is an interesting-looking man, a big-shouldered farm-boy type who reminds me of the immortal Kesey. But I doubt he has any of

Kesey's talent or madness, and certainly not that lovely sense of buffoonery. Take away Mr. Kobrak's major pretense (that he's a genius) and underneath you'll find a rather stupid man. Coming up with a script would mean he'd have to write and spell, and I can't imagine he does either effectively.

Even so Dev sees something in him. Since I've known Dev he's been antimovie (I can drag him out about once every three months to see one, if I'm lucky). He can be a bore about it. I suppose it's due to his family's involvement with the business in Hollywood: there's nothing glamorous or inspiring about making movies when you've grown up hearing shoptalk. But Dev knows a great deal about the mechanics of film making and editing. It's possible he and Kobrak can achieve something worthwhile. At least Dev is intrigued and involved—and much easier to live with.

They spent the better part of an hour debating the central metaphor of somebody else's film. Dev got very fidgety but he stuck it out. I couldn't, so I went into the kitchen to wash glasses, displacing the obligatory pair of lovers. All parties in our neighborhood are depressingly alike. People drifted in and out of the kitchen and I had to tell a couple of frig raiders to keep their hands off our food. They'd walk off with the furniture if you didn't watch.

A man I know vaguely—he's a teaching assistant in the English Dept. and works for the *Berkeley Barb*—established a position with his back to the stove. He must have been talking for twenty minutes before I really noticed. He has this thing for me and is convinced that if he shows enough soul he'll lure me away from Dev. So he was working hard at projecting soul, lots of body English and so forth; but I wasn't paying attention. I had a headache coming on and it looked as if everybody was going to be there until the earlies. After a while he just shut up and looked at me mournfully. Confess I felt a little sorry then. I put another beer in his hand; that brightened him up. "So," he said, "when may I have the pleasure of meeting your delightful sister?" "Believe me," I said, "I would like to introduce you; but I don't have a sister." "No?" he said, and pretended to be nonplussed. Then he smiled and hooked a hand inside my elbow and showed me to the door.

"Standing by the Larry Rivers litho—a very fine litho, by the way." (It was Claes Oldenburg, by the way. Somebody swiped it two nights later.) The girl he was talking about hadn't been there earlier. She didn't look as if she knew anyone. She was smiling rather vaguely, as if she was listening to two conversations at once. I didn't see any family resemblance. She was my height and we were built the same. (Altogether there were four girls in attendance Sunday night who could have stepped from the same mold. Let's face it, I have a very common body.) Her hair was deep red; she wore it long and it looked clean. She had very pale delicate skin. She'd overdrawn her eyes, I couldn't tell much about them.

I stared at her too long and she became aware of us and stared back, curious and friendly, as if she was slightly myopic and couldn't decide who we were. I smiled, caught—what can you do?—and she made her way through the bunch. By then I was tired, headachy, feeling a little silly; so I said, "Hello, Sis; I haven't seen you since we were separated by the Great Blizzard of Fifty-one." That set her back on her heels, but only for a couple of seconds. She blinked and glanced at the Soul Man and seemed to realize this was for his benefit. So she said with a straight face, "I never dreamed when Mummy plunged back into that snowdrift that the two of you would come out alive." "You'll be happy to hear," I said, "that she finally thawed out and is running an authentic Turkish bordello in Fall River, Massachusetts. Do tell me, how's plucky old Dad?" She arched her eyebrows. "Well, I'm only allowed to visit him once a year —rules of the monastery, you know. But in that saffron robe, with his head shaved, he is the sexiest thing you've ever laid eyes on!"

Pretty silly stuff, but not any worse than the general run of conversation at these parties, and it got us started. We hit it off

78

well and somewhere along the way what's-his-name got to feeling excluded and left us. Fortunately.

She had a Danish name, Lone, which is pronounced something like loan-ah (that's as close as I can come to spelling it). Lone Kels. It turned out she knew Kobrak, had acted in an earlier film of his. She wasn't a student. It was difficult to find out anything about her, really, because she was high on something, although far from being stoned. I could believe she was an actress, though. A good one. Basically we had the same equipment, as I said, but she was sexier. (Somehow redheads are always sexier.) It was not a matter of posture or display; Lone wasn't obvious at any time. But she could focus her sexuality and beam it anywhere in the room. She gave me a couple of off-hand demonstrations, from a sense of rivalry, perhaps, or just because she thought I might be interested. I caught Dev giving her some lengthy speculative looks. Next to Miss Kels I felt as if I was still wearing a ponytail.

And, while giving the man of her choice a good zapping, Lone could simultaneously make it plain that she didn't want him wandering over and horning in on us girls. She was not much more than a year older than me. I wondered where she came by her education; maybe some women are just born turned on like that. Fascinating; and all this while on a high.

As the night got a little older it occurred to me she was playing a part, playing it expertly. But I didn't know who she was supposed to be. Or wanted to be. Then she mentioned that she had seen Vivien Leigh the week before, in *Gone with the Wind*. Twice. So that was it. She was fooling around with Vivien Leigh as Scarlett O'Hara, improvising, having a marvelous time, adapting the qualities of actress-in-character to her own specifications and potential. I wondered if she'd had her hair dyed for the occasion.

And still later when the high wore off and she found herself out of character, from fatigue, perhaps, I had a few glimpses of Lone herself: not a very private person but still she has moments of shyness which are appealing. She's been wounded, even brutalized, but not hardened yet. There is something unnaturally wild in her too, held tightly most of the time, guarded with a fanatic's strength.

I don't really know why—nothing's passed between us, at least not on a conscious level. But I received the impression that sexually she's taken on all comers, and if I wanted her I could have her. She has that flavor of utter wantonness that doesn't seem tainted, it's almost like innocence.

We could be friends. But it was up to me to say Come around again, and I didn't. I was noncommittal. She seemed to expect that. When it was time for her to go she left alone. Does she have friends? Or just pursuers? I'm sorry for her. But I'm afraid too.

I don't know what time they all went home. I took myself down to Beth Liska's pad and spent the rest of the night there.

Dec. 9

A dull briny day and Sam was here early by way of Oakland AP. But looking as if he had just come off Death Row at San Quentin. He has that greenish haunted appearance they must get over there. Just when Dev was beginning to show signs of vitality . . . the men in my life. Sam drove on to San Francisco. Stopping at the Mark as usual. He's here for a three-day socio-political conference at SF State. Michael Harrington and Herb Marcuse are on a panel with him; should be interesting if I can get away, but I think tonight is all the time I can spare. Couldn't think about going over if Dev hadn't started his week at the Bevatron. Maybe I can be of some use to Sam. We'll save Enrico's and North Broadway for last and do all the corny tourist things and have a stupendous feed and drink to excess. I can always stay overnight with Sam if he gets the suite he likes. Or even if he doesn't. Now that I'm a Mature Woman and all over the terrible urge to be laid by Samuel Holland I could sleep very peacefully in the same bed with him—as long as it's a big bed. Hard to believe how badly I was hung up on

Sam a few years ago. Growing pains, or something. Lord, the daydreams! I'm sure he's competent in the sack, like a billion other men. Maybe I'll ask him. Poor Sam, the shock would all but kill him. I'm quite confident he's never entertained any improper ideas about me. Despite my arrangement with Dev I would count myself as pretty square, and Sam is even more so. To be cont'd.

Well, it cleared during the afternoon and the show at dusk from the Top of the Mark was sufficiently glorious to give even Sam a huge lift. We had quite an itinerary planned, Fisherman's Wharf, everything, but we just sat there in the lounge drinking and talking and canceling plans right and left. And in three hours' time I got pretty close to the heart of Sam Holland. But even with a batch of double martinis in him he wasn't ripe for exorcism. I'm not sure I was up to it anyhow, or knew the right incantations.

Fact one about Sam: his marriage is going bad and he can't do anything about it.

Fact two: he's very close to a nervous breakdown. He's been driving himself extremely hard for two years and the engine has overheated to the point where he can't turn it off. I would say, although I loathe amateur shrink stuff, that fear is behind his drive. Fear evolving as a ferocious sense of urgency. He's afraid for the future of this country. We all are, of course, but Sam is obsessed by the increasingly deadly cynicism and moral failures of government, by the critical lack of communication between hostile and destructive forces (i.e., the black and white power structures in America), by unsubtle and punitive pressures on those who wish to exercise their right to dissent. And he particularly fears the collective paranoia (as he calls it) of the Far Right crowd.

It took some doing, but I got him to talk about something that happened in Texas a few nights ago: he was shot at on the streets of Lubbock, probably by some idiot who labels people without bothering to find out what they really stand for. Sam was in a rental car. He had just left the Texas Tech campus, where a student political group had invited him to speak.

"Army training," he said. "When I see anything that even *looks* like a gun pointed my way I flatten out. If I had gawked for a second or so he would have nailed me. Square in the face."

He tried to smile about it, but came up with a pretty ghastly smile. No wonder he looks haunted! Several times during the evening he mentioned the incident again. He would stare into space or just shake his head, horrified. "I don't get it. So he disagrees with me. Fine. But *kill* me?" I was having my share of martinis (undoubled), and feeling pretty well insulated. Even so something in his voice chilled me to the bone.

Instead of going to Enrico's we had a late dinner at a little place on Powell Street. I doubt if Sam ate more than a few bites. He apologized frequently for brooding. I could tell he just didn't feel well. But he seemed to want my company. We walked back up to the hotel and he suggested a nightcap in his suite. We talked for another hour at least; I tried my tactful best to get him to open up about his troubles with Felice but he stayed vague on the subject. It got late and I wasn't enthusiastic about making the long trip back to Berkeley that time of the night, so I didn't argue when Sam suggested I stay there. The sofa in the sitting room made a very comfortable bed.

I woke up early, first light almost; Sam wasn't in the suite. He might have slept for a while on top of his bed—the spread was badly rumpled. And the fifth of gin he'd had sent up for our "nightcap" was less than a third full.

I found a note. He said he'd gone out for a walk and probably wouldn't be back before I left. I wrote on the back of his note, thanking him, trying to be cheerful and breezy. But the effort was flat.

Home to Berkeley, and two classes I couldn't afford to cut.

About three this afternoon Sam called. The conference has been canceled, for a number of reasons, leaving him with a five-day gap in his schedule before a flock of speaking engagements in S. California and Arizona. Not really worthwhile to fly back to New York and then out again. He sounded disconsolate, not knowing what to do with himself.

I had an inspiration. One of Dev's uncles owns a place below Carmel, near Pt. Sur. They seldom use it during the winter. It's isolated but not impossible to find. The coast there is rugged and often cold and shrouded in Dec., but you can count on a fair percentage of good days. I thought Sam would enjoy and benefit from a spell of beach walking and thought collecting away from all distractions, including telephones.

He was doubtful when I mentioned it, but I can be persuasive for the right cause. Called Dev at the lab, who called his sister in LA. She's the unofficial keeper of the keys and knows the family's migratory patterns well. She assured Dev it would be all right to loan out the house. (Dev had explained that Sam would be working on a book; his sister has a weakness for authors and things literary.)

Gave Sam directions. He left immediately so he could arrive before dark.

Dec. 14

Four wet days in a row. I'm struggling along trying to ignore the flu. I think it's going to catch up to me, though.

Dec. 18

If I stay in bed another minute I'll go nuts. Dev has been around the house most of the afternoon. We're putting a severe strain on each other's nerves. I can stand a messy house but not Dev in a messy house. It looks as if Dev is losing interest in *The Oakland Method;* he isn't particularly diplomatic, and he's lost his temper a couple of times trying to reconcile Paul Kobrak's visions and lack of craft.

Sent him out to do some shopping while I tried to put a shine on the humble old place. I'm very wobbly, nose dripping, etc., but anything is better than staying in bed. This spell of sickness knocks out a trip home for Christmas: I'll have to spend six hours a day at the library over the holidays trying to catch up. Jolly, jolly holiday.

Felice called around five. She was very concerned and wanted to know did I know where Sam was. To be cont'd.

Dec. 20

Yesterday, thank God, was a sunny, gusty day, almost warm, perfect for a drive. I didn't really have to talk Dev into it. We got to be friends again, sort of, on the way to Big Sur. The sea air scoured out my wheezy lungs and opened up my nose. I would have felt priceless if I hadn't been so worried about Sam, the Wandering Boy.

The beach house was locked up tight. The key was right where it always is, in a little moisture-proof box buried in the sand between two beach pines. The house was stuffy, as if it had been closed for days, and faultlessly neat. It was obvious that Sam was gone. But we prowled around anyway. I don't know what we expected to find—blood in the sink, perhaps. (As a matter of fact there were three drops of blood in the basin in one of the bathrooms. Sam must have cut himself shaving and missed the spots when he was cleaning up.)

Dev prowled around outside and came in looking odd. He hadn't found anything except a dead seagull on the south patio, badly torn up as if an animal had gotten to it. He found a shovel and buried the remains—Dev is very tenderhearted about birds and animals. Then he scrubbed the patio with sand and a stiff brush.

During the drive down I'd half convinced myself that we'd find Sam there, thoroughly under the spell of the Big Sur country, just wandering the beach or sitting in the sun, not even aware of what day it was. Now I didn't know what to think. What most worried Felice—aside from not hearing from him— was the fact that Sam had abruptly canceled all of his West

Coast speaking engagements a few days ago. The lecture bureau didn't know where he was, either. And he'd given no reason for the cancellations.

We drove back to Carmel and had a late lunch. And finally Dev said what we'd both been thinking: it was only sensible to go to the Monterey County Sheriff's substation and report Sam missing. It's wild country down there. Sam can certainly take care of himself, but he might have gone back into one of the canyons and broken a leg or something. Or misjudged the tides and—

I was happy to find the flaw in those arguments. If he'd had an accident, where was his car?

Dev still wanted to report him missing, which would have meant publicity. I couldn't make myself believe anything serious had happened to Sam. Then I thought about the shot that had been fired at him in Texas and wasn't so sure. But I didn't think we should put Sam on the front pages because he'd been out of touch for a few days.

Before dusk we returned to the house and walked the beach until it was too dark to see anything but the cold spill of the surf; we said not a word. But we didn't need to talk. It was our place, we had fallen in love there. Later Dev built a driftwood fire and we drank mulled ale and sat very close, knees and fingertips touching, and passed most of an hour seducing each other with our eyes. First the cold walk and the wind and the surf, then a searing fire and just enough ale and an orgy of anticipation— When we finally made love it was the fastest thing that ever happened to either one of us. Half a minute later I passed out in his arms with a blanket wrapped around me.

When I woke up the wind was banging a loose shutter and the fire had fallen in on itself, a few red vines still clinging to gray walls of ash. Dev was holding me. I could tell he hadn't closed his eyes.

"I'm going to study painting," he said. Just like that. He has less than a year to go to earn a doctorate in particle physics.

I knew he wasn't just talking about a nice hobby for his spare time. When Dev decides he wants to do something, he wants it to the exclusion of everything else. At fifteen he set out to become a chess master; he devoted a year and a half to nothing but chess. He didn't go to school, but then he wasn't required to. He'd already completed a full year of college work.

Eventually two things happened: he found out that he didn't possess that final degree of exquisite fanaticism it took to be the best in the world. Also he discovered girls. So he gave up chess, and he doesn't play now.

At nineteen, after he completed college, Dev took up Group 7 racing cars. He might be the best in the world now—or dead—but a hair-raising accident put him in the hospital for a couple of months, distorted his vision just enough to keep him off the tracks forever.

"Let's not talk about it now," I said. But he hadn't asked my opinion; he hadn't left room for discussion. That was Dev's way.

Dec. 21

I'd been putting off a call to Felice most of the day, trying to think of something to tell her that might sound halfway encouraging.

About four the doorbell rang and there was Sam Holland, smiling calmly at me. He was still pitifully thin but he had a good tan and his eyes were clear. I invited him in and then gave him hell. He was genuinely appalled to learn how much trouble he'd been causing. He hadn't disappeared, he said. Didn't Dev and I get his thank-you? Hadn't Felice received the letter he'd written her? He'd entrusted both letters to the proprietor of a motel in Indio, where he stayed one night during his wanderings. That explained a lot, but not everything. I hauled him into the bedroom, put the telephone in his hands and shut the door.

Twenty minutes later he emerged looking subdued and chastened. "Everything's all right," he said. "I think." We had drinks and Sam told me about the trip he'd taken. After four days of lazing around Big Sur he was much improved but still in no mood to make those half-dozen speeches he'd been booked for. So he begged off and drove over to the San Joaquin Valley to see how things were currently going for the migrant farm workers, do some interviewing for a possible article. Then he continued as far south as Mexico before doubling back and showing up here.

Sam arranged to catch an eight-thirty flight out of Oakland AP and I got cracking in the kitchen to fix supper for everybody. Dev came. As usual he and Sam were up to their ears in profound conversation five seconds after they said hello. They raked over the breakup of the hippie community in Haight-Ashbury (Dev claimed public hostility had a lot to do with it, but he admitted that hippie communities are by nature volatile and unstable, and indiscriminate use of certain drugs intensifies the pressure-cooker atmosphere of violence and self-destruction). That got them onto the possibility of a viable drug sub-culture. Sam brought up LSD. Dev, who used it extensively for several months (before I met him), argued that LSD's value in unlocking human potential is exaggerated. Dev contended that the real hope for humanity lies in Esalen-style encounter-group meetings. (There we're in complete agreement. We've both been to Esalen, but separately. I felt like a big pussycat for weeks after, brimming over with potential and good fellowship, but everyday living gradually turned me into an aspirin-swallowing neurotic again.)

Dec. 28

Christmas was cozy and fun. Dev left yesterday to spend a couple of days with his family. I could have gone along, but only his sister, who is a doll, really accepts me; the usual ethnic thing and we just have to get used to it, I suppose. Anyway I had much work to do on two longish papers, due the end of Jan.

Came back from the library and found this rather dog-eared Santa Claus card tacked to the front door. It said: *Hi, remember me? If you get bored during the break give me a call.* It was

Lone. Well, I almost did call her but decided against it, and felt like a rat. She must be lonely and apparently she digs me, harmlessly. I don't know. I just have too much else to cope with right now.

Jan. 5

Hard to find the time any more to add anything to this misbegotten journal. I haven't written a decent poem for weeks. Everything comes out sour and neurotic. (I'm using that word too much lately.)

Dev and I are on the verge of having a Big One, which is all I need to go with premenstrual tension. He is taking no pains to disguise his dissatisfaction with nearly everything. There is no integrity in science any more. To be free, to hold onto his own integrity in a valueless society, he has to find a way out of his personal prison. He is going to *paint*. Maybe he'll be a lousy painter, he tells me (if I could just get him out of the habit of pacing while he's talking to me I'd be a contented woman), but the important thing is to quickly break with what you find destructive in life and clean out your mind, live truthfully, create hopefully.

"I think we need at least a year," he said. "Maybe it'll take three years, who knows? In Europe, preferably a country where we don't know the language, can't read the papers. We'll live as simply as we know how."

The awful hell of it is, I can't argue with him. Because I know how intensely he is suffering from his disaffection, and how certain he is that he's found the cure-all at last. But I'm saddened because I can't share his—I was going to write *enthusiasm*, but it isn't that. Just a bleak determination to turn everything upside down, empty his life, fill it up again—with *something*. Painting, this time. And this time, unlike the other times, will he fill his life completely?

This is what keeps me awake at night. How are *we* going to be fulfilled, Dev? By living in a place where we don't speak the language—even to each other?

Chapter Eight

GENERAL HENRY PHELAN MORSE CAME IN OUT OF THE wretched night and paused in the lobby of the police building, which was no more than a new wing of the long-standing Colonial village hall. He nodded to the officer who was on duty in a glassed cubicle with the dispatcher opposite him. The General pulled off his hat and let it drain. Then he continued grimly down a wide corridor, listing badly over a black and thorny-looking cane.

Near the end of the hall he opened a door marked *Interrogation* and went in.

Ordinarily the fourteen-feet-square room had only a metal table with a gray top and four wooden chairs in it. But the room had been turned into a crowded command center for the investigation of the kidnapping of Carol Watterson. There were detailed maps on the walls, four telephones, police radio equipment, a teletype, a slide projector and screen, a chalk board and an artist's layout board.

There were two men in the room, both using telephones. Peter Demilia glanced at the General and raised an eyebrow and went on talking. After hanging up the receiver he jotted a couple of notes on a pad.

The General said, "Where's Gaffney?"

Demilia pointed to the phone. "I was just talking to him, General. He's in Kingston."

"Anything in that Volkswagen van?"

"Enough to keep the mobile lab crew working for a couple of days."

"But there's no evidence yet that Carol was taken in that particular van."

Demilia looked sleepily at him. "Whoever drove it last cleaned it up pretty good afterward. But short of steam-cleaning and sandblasting you couldn't possibly remove all evidence of use and occupation. The lab boys have found detergent, soil samples, traces of vomit, hairs, a scrap of human skin, urine. There are fragmentary fingerprints and one good palm print. I suppose altogether they lifted a couple of hundred latents. Maybe one of them will be helpful." He hesitated, then said, "The best clue so far is a few flecks of yellow paint in the treads of three of the four tires on the van. The paint is the type used for warning stripes on the highways in this state, and for marking off restricted and parking areas."

"Fresh paint?"

"Only a few days old, they say. We're still checking state and county maintenance departments here, in Jersey and in Connecticut. Twelve miles of route two-ten west of Stony Point, over in Rockland County, were striped on Monday."

"I assume Gaffney is bringing the owner of the truck rental down to look at the man you picked up this morning."

"No reason, General. Our Mr. Flicker has proved to everyone's satisfaction that he was busy writing bad checks in Louisville until Tuesday of this week. The bus driver who brought him East remembered him only too well. Flicker talked nonstop about inventions he was going to invent and books he was going to write. Outside of the hippie hair there's no great resemblance between Flicker and the man who chose to call himself Homer Sewell of Barstow, Tennessee."

"There's no Homer Sewell?"

"And no Barstow, Tennessee. About a thousand blank State of Tennessee drivers' licenses were stolen eight months ago from their Department of Public Safety. Now we know where one of those licenses ended up." Demilia rubbed the back of his neck. "Still lousy out, General? How about some coffee?"

"Thanks," the General said, and limped across the room to study a map of Orange and Rockland Counties. The teletype woke up, hammered out a message, fell silent. Demilia poured coffee into a plastic-coated cup and added two cubes of sugar: he knew the General's habits well by now.

The General took his coffee without looking away from the map. "Almost six goddam days," he said; Demilia noted undertones of desperation and panic in his voice.

"We've had good breaks so far," the detective said mildly. They had sifted through the credit-card receipts at the Esso station in Fox Village, then called on a couple dozen people in two states. A family of seven in a ranch wagon had stopped about five on Sunday for gas and restrooms. Patient questioning of the five children had resulted in their first break. A twelve-year-old girl had been sulking alone in the back of the wagon, facing Jake's for Steak. She had seen an older girl in a cute tennis outfit stagger and collapse as if fainting. A tall bushy-haired man had helped her into a black delivery van. They were both half concealed behind some kind of sports car with the hood up. The truck had been a Volks, the witness was positive about that, because her Uncle Sherm, who was a florist, had recently bought one like it, only red. The van drove away fast, then turned south on the Saw Mill. The witness hadn't noticed the driver. The whole thing looked funny to her because the man just sort of threw the girl into the back of the van. But she hadn't said a word about what she'd seen because she was so mad at her parents.

Two hours after the APB for a black Volkswagen van two Columbia County sheriff's deputies spotted one on a run-down riverfront street just outside the city limits of Hudson, New York. They checked it out routinely. The keys were in the ignition.

The van was staked out by police and FBI for twenty-four hours. In that time no one went near it. They learned, meanwhile, that it had been rented for two weeks. Homer Sewell of Barstow, Tennessee, had paid a cash deposit.

After a full day it was concluded that the van had been abandoned; it was then taken to a police garage for examination.

The General stared at the map for a long time, letting his coffee grow cold. His shoulders had rounded.

"Two-ten west," he said finally. "That runs straight through Harriman State Park and Sterling Forest. Isolated areas, nothing but hiking trails."

"Yeah," Demilia affirmed, knowing what he was getting at.

"It went wrong," the General said reluctantly. "The only thing I didn't count on. If they'd planned to kill her in the first place they would have called and tried to collect their money. No, it went wrong somehow, and Carol's dead." He was rigid, face flushed here and waxen there, like the work of a bad mortician. Only the eyes were fervently alive. "Bear Mountain, Harriman. That's where you ought to be looking. By God, they killed her—" He broke off, still staring, and now there were tears of outrage in his eyes.

Demilia shook his head slowly. "There's a chance, General."

"By God," the old man groaned, "you find them! You'd better do it goddam fast or I'll be out looking too, and if I get to them first you won't have anything to bring in! I'll cut them up in chunks for my birds."

"Yes, sir." Lieutenant Demilia, despite the fact that he'd been a cop for a good while and had heard all kinds of threats, was rather impressed. This wasn't just a scared old man talking tough. The General, for a man of seventy or so, had plenty of iron left in him. He looked as if he could handle himself well in a scrap, even with one leg off at the knee. . . . "Yes, sir, General," Demilia said again, restively, when it seemed as if the General had locked his bitter tearful gaze onto him for the remainder of the night.

The General shook himself, blinked, and for a few moments he looked dazed and unaware of his surroundings. Then he put on his hat and reached for the formidable cane.

"I want to be notified," he said sternly, "as soon as there are developments. Don't forget that, Lieutenant. Don't let anybody here forget it."

"I won't, sir," Demilia promised, and although he'd been out of the Army for a decade, he was powerfully seized by an urge to salute as the General turned away.

Chapter Nine

ALONG ABOUT TWO IN THE MORNING THERE WAS another squall of rain, with wind and sharp thunder that jolted the solid old Colonial house.

Felice scarcely noticed; she looked up only twice from the last pages of Carol's handwritten journal. These pages were about her increasingly sad and troubled days after the breakup with Dev. And she had written often about Sam.

Feb. 16

Dev has been gone for five days.

It isn't any good remaining here, I know that now. I thought I could tough it out in the apartment until graduation, but I feel like I've overstayed at a funeral. Last night I woke up half a dozen times, and the last time I was sobbing so hard they must have heard me in the street. So I'm going to move. It shouldn't be hard subletting right now. Beth knows a couple who are looking. They can have this place today if they want it. Just give me time to pack.

The problem is finding a place to lay my head for the next three or four months. I could move in with Lone, of course. She has room and I know she'd be delighted. Yesterday when I ran into her at Dwinelle Hall she dropped a couple of hints hard enough to break my toes. But I don't think so. In her brighter moods Lone is good company. But she has more than her share of quirks and fetishes I find hard to condone and impossible to

94

live with. I think she honestly tries, but she can't seem to get along without pills of some kind. Amphetamines, probably; or amyl nitrate. I hope not. She is a strangely endearing, impulsive person, so I suppose it was inevitable we'd become friends. The last couple of weeks she's been especially solicitous and helpful without being too pushy.

Still, I couldn't. I just couldn't share living space with Lone Kels. Like so many women who are basically carnal she's on the slovenly side, and the drug-oriented can't be bothered with mundane housekeeping. She does keep herself clean, but I'm sure I would take on the role of Keeper and Lone's not that domesticated, so, inevitably, we'd be at each other's throats. I'd have to keep my guard up and the whip cracking, particularly when the boyfriends, the tough, scarred, promiscuous cats, came prowling around. And I'm not in a whip-cracking mood. I just want to leave alone, be left alone.

So I'll accept Gary and Beth's offer, that dark little eight-by-eight room. With both of them teaching and working on their doctorates I doubt if they spend more than four hours a day in their pad during the week. And there's not the remotest chance Gary will take a hack at me if we happen to find ourselves alone. His only vices are an occasional lid of Acapulco Gold when the budget allows and the, ugh, *National Enquirer*.

Feb. 25

I've got the deep blue sinks. I don't want to write, talk, eat, sleep, or go out. I just sit here. And I hate myself. And I want to be with Dev, with Dev. Oh, God!

Mar. 14

Sam couldn't have called at a worse time. I had just climbed up out of the blue sinks for about the tenth time, but the latest effort left me exhausted and indifferent. Yesterday Beth went to a great deal of trouble to cook her ragout, which ordinarily I can't get enough of, but it was an ordeal just to eat it and say the proper things. I guess I wasn't convincing in my enthusiasm because I could tell Beth was disappointed and hurt. I could have cut out my tongue for hurting Beth's feelings. I'm no good for anybody these days. I know I shouldn't have moved in with the Liskas. I thought I was a hardy no-nonsense type—broken romance, so what? A few tears, a few bad moments, he's forgotten.

It's torture. It is pure hell. He is not forgotten. I don't think I will ever forget Dev. Or stop hurting in this godawful cancerous way.

I didn't want to put Sam out but he had the whole day on his hands and he insisted on driving over and yanking me out of my fouled little nest. Bless Sam Holland. It turned out to be a marvelous day, more summer than spring, with that breathtaking clarity which we have all too seldom in the Bay Area.

We drove north through the grape-growing, wine-making counties and had a long splendid lunch at a little restaurant I'd heard about, near Santa Rosa.

Sam was chipper and looked fit. He'd even put on a few pounds. He very tactfully didn't remark on my appearance. I hadn't seen him since before Christmas, during his own personal dog days, but he'd been to the Coast frequently during the past three months, and had dutifully called from the airport each time.

We split a bottle of claret with our smorgasbord, which loosened my tongue slightly too much, and I held forth for the better part of a half hour, a syrupy monologue about Dev and how I missed him and how it was for the best after all, and when I started hiccuping in a silly grief-stricken way (hiccups, apparently, are my acne, my buck teeth, my stigmata) I had to beat it to the ladies' room to cry and wash my face. But I have to admit it did me a heck of a lot of good. And Sam didn't seem any the worse for wear when I reappeared.

He was less eager to talk about his difficulties with Felice. He frowned when I prodded, and hemmed and hawed and allowed that they were making progress, but communication was a difficult thing all of a sudden, and, well, they'd just have to see. I let it go at that.

Sam had a surprise for me, which he saved for dessert. During the past week he'd had lunch with his editor to discuss the new book Sam was going to write. Somehow the subject got around to me and my craving to find a niche in the literary world. Two days later the editor called and told Sam that his house would have a place for me, as an editorial assistant, come September. I didn't know what an editorial assistant was, but I pretended I did. Sam's publisher is one of the oldest and most respected in the business and their lists are crammed with famous names, so it should be fascinating.

We drove south toward Marin and the Golden Gate Bridge; then, because it was that kind of day, we decided on the spur of the moment to go up to the summit of Tamalpais.

The view was all it should have been, from the blue Pacific slash beyond Muir Woods to Tiburon and the sun-glazed North Bay. The park wasn't crowded on a weekday so we did some walking. I began to feel a little sorry I wasn't staying in California. But after four years I had begun to miss the tension and gritty competitiveness of New York. A classic case of home-town nostalgia, I suppose.

A funny thing happened. Two big glossy crotchety ravens, each more than two feet long, suddenly swooped down across our path. They began walking around in circles, impeccable as bankers, bobbing their heads and carrying on about something.

You don't often see them that close—they're reclusive birds. They weren't more than forty feet away. Maybe they weren't aware of us because we were standing in the shade. There was something noble and awe-inspiring about these two. Tribes of coastal Indians once considered them to be gods. I've always been something of a bird watcher and I like them all, even the goshawks and peregrine falcons the General keeps for sport—but I prefer falcons from a distance, not eye-to-eye.

Apparently Sam doesn't care to be eye-to-eye with any bird.

I turned to suggest we try to move a little closer to find out what the ravens thought of us and there was Sam, making tracks down the path, going back the way we'd come. But he was walking stiffly, jerkily. He stumbled and I caught up to him. His color had gone bad and his face was squeezed up as if he'd just swallowed something poisonous. I spoke to him; like a sleep-walker he kept going for another twenty yards or so. Then he stopped and hunched his shoulders and mopped his forehead with a handkerchief.

"Sam, what's the matter? Are you sick?"

He tried a smile. We were out of sight of the ravens.

"I didn't know you were afraid of birds," I said.

He shook his head as if he was baffled by his reaction. "I'm not," he said. "I mean, I haven't been for years. I thought I was all over that."

On the way back to the car I got him to explain. It had to do with Sam's uncle, of course, the one who had raised him. Uncle Hat, he was called, because he had no hair and caught colds easily, so he wore something on his head all the time, even in bed. Which makes him sound sort of quaint and folksy, but he was a complex and tortured man. Self-educated, a talented amateur musician, he worked all his life at unskilled jobs. He was de-voted to his wife and daughter, particularly the daughter, who (according to Sam) was an accomplished bitch by the time she was fifteen. Apparently old Hat was sexually hung up on his daughter, and she all but drove him crazy. Occasionally Hat would erupt, outbursts of sadism. Sam was always the victim.

Sam was only eight the year his uncle worked for the zoo. There was nothing to the job; Hat was a night watchman, with a slightly more prestigious title.

The daughter was in the hospital for a minor operation, tonsils or something, and the mother was staying all night with her. Instead of paying a few dollars to a baby-sitter Uncle Hat took Sam with him to the zoo.

Like any boy would, Sam got bored in the office where Hat

98

had stashed him and he wandered out to see the animals. It was a good-size zoo and he managed to get lost. Hat was furious by the time he located Sam.

A whipping was in order, but Hat believed in unusual punishments. He dragged Sam to the birdcage, unlocked a door, shoved him inside.

The birdcage covered half a city block and was four stories high. The climate and lighting were controlled, simulating a tropical jungle. Sam found himself in near-darkness with a thousand exotic birds for company, all of them irritable and screeching at him. He was in a mortal panic to get out of there. As he was blundering around he fell into a shallow pool and was cut by the sharp fronds of some tropical plants. He thought the birds were attacking him. By the time an assistant curator heard him screaming and pulled him out of the bird cage Sam was off his rocker. It took shock therapy to bring him around, a year as an outpatient at a psychiatric clinic to get him back to normal. Hat lost his job, of course, but criminal charges against him were dropped. Unfortunately.

We were tired after Tamalpais and talked very little on the way to Berkeley. When he dropped me off Sam leaned over and kissed me on the forehead. His eyes were terribly sad. I guess he was still thinking about that little boy in the bird cage. Or maybe he was thinking about Dev.

"Things work out for the best," he said tritely, almost sounding maudlin. But the emotion in his voice was genuine. "Remember that you mean a lot to us." He seldom lets his emotions show, and I was touched. This Sam is quite a guy. I hope Felice realizes it in time.

Mar. 20

Broke down today and wrote to Dev's sister; I told her I had some papers of Dev's which he'd overlooked when he was cleaning out his file at the Physics Dept. I just want to know where he is and how he is, and Jean is my only hope there. Probably Dev is just fine. The son of a bitch.

Mar. 27

Lone has a new boyfriend.

I shouldn't say new; I have the impression he's known her for a couple of years, and has wandered in and out of her life. But he seems to have made up his mind that Lone is for him; he's sticking very close to her. It's hard to say if Lone is in love with him. She's remarkably alive, all juices flowing; sexually the relationship must be very good. But there's a puzzling kind of tension between them: Lone is almost too eager for his approval; that's not like her.

His name is Richard Marsland. Lone calls him Rich. My first reactions to him were all negative. He's a perfect stud type, big, rangy, with a square face and small ears and knobbly cheekbones, a surefire grin. His hair is surfer wild, chopped like spinach. He is older than he seems: I'd say early thirties. He's spent a lot of time on the beach because he has the coloring, a raw splotch or two where skin ulcers have started, a permanent sun squint. No eyes visible at all, just shadowy niches under a tawny overhanging of brow. I figured an IQ of possibly one hundred, giving away a few points in a fit of generosity.

The first half hour or so after we met he didn't say anything to reflect on my judgment. He said nothing at all, just sat, nicely self-contained, and grinned from time to time while Lone and I chatted. He wasn't giving me the automatic stud business, so in that respect he wasn't true to type.

I made a couple of attempts to include him in the conversation, including the usual what-do-you-do-with-yourself gambit. I expected he worked a tuna boat or sold skis in season.

He said, with that wide utterly relaxed grin, "I'm an injustice collector."

I decided that I'd fairly let myself in for the put-on, so I asked

100

the right questions to give him a chance to complete his routine and braced myself. Lone looked dead serious, damn her.

When her boy Richard started talking in earnest I jumped his IQ fifty points immediately, and occasionally added a bonus of ten. Liar or not, he was by no means existing on a dab of brains.

He'd learned the brokerage business while taking a PhD in Business at UCLA. Even before finishing his schooling he began a hedge fund with three other young brokers; within four years the thirty percent fee for managing the wildly successful fund had made them all millionaires. Rich Marsland retired at the age of twenty-seven.

For a while he did nothing except travel around, hitchhiking mostly, looking at things, listening to people. He listened to what was wrong with them, and what they thought was wrong with everybody else. He came to some perfectly ordinary conclusions: people are, on the whole, badly served by the institutions they have erected and are forced to support. Their governments make empty gestures and false commitments while chewing up vital resources. Most schools are an insult to native intelligence. And so on. There was one intriguing conclusion: bad institutions are directly responsible for mutations of the human spirit. They breed monsters who ultimately will become powerful enough to destroy humanity, for the sake of this ideal or that inalienable right.

The problem, then, in the name of humanity and common sense, is to do away with institutions altogether, or break them down to the point where they can be operated with complete integrity. A primary function of the institution, however, is to protect itself, at any cost, from dissolution. Violent revolution as a means is not justifiable because of the human suffering involved; and the end result is new institutions, which in time become as intolerable as the old.

Uh-huh, I said, still wondering what he was getting at.

"With a few other people I've spent the past couple of years studying the common characteristics of institutions, seeking ways to ethically destroy them. Of course this has to be done without dislocating the culture and inviting anarchy."

"Is there a way?" I asked.

He shook his head emphatically, showing not a trace of humor. "No."

"Chalk up two years," I said, and laughed, because he'd had me on pretty good, and he smiled then, just a little. Lone didn't smile or say anything right away, but she looked rather urgently at him, as if she was excited by the arcane philosophy he'd been handing out.

"Why don't you tell her about—"

"No," Rich said, thoughtfully. He was staring straight at me. Then Lone, chastened, sneaked a glance, sort of a guilty glance. I felt damned irritated with both of them; for no reason I could define I decided again that I didn't care for Richard Marsland. But he's Lone's problem, not mine.

April 5

A variation on The Dream again: This time the baby wasn't in the nursery when I went to look, and Dev was so nonchalant I knew he'd taken the baby away. I made him tell me. He said it just wouldn't do for us, a baby at this particular time, his family would not approve, therefore he had done the sensible thing and given our baby to a Chinese family living on a junk in San Francisco Bay. He said they needed the baby and we didn't. He made this sound so plausible that I had to agree with him. But I missed the baby terribly—it was a blond little girl, with immense plum eyes—and so I sneaked off and went down to the bay. I knew I could find the Chinese junk without any trouble, and be with my baby for a while. But when I got there the bay was as crowded with junks as Hong Kong harbor, all of them looking exactly alike. . . .

I woke up from that one at dawn with only a mild case of the shakes and I thought I'd forget about it soon enough and go about my business, but it didn't work out that way. I knew what was prompting The Dream. When Dev and I started really having troubles and I realized what might happen to us I thought about tying him down that way, skipping the pills at the critical time. I'm ashamed that I would have considered it for even a second. I was getting desperate, but that doesn't excuse me. To use Dev that way, use a child—Before long I was in a muck of self-loathing.

The day just got worse and worse. I wandered purposelessly around the sunny campus with my hair tangled, wearing a dress that should have been ironed, muttering to myself, maybe, like Ophelia with Hamlet's scorn echoing inside her naïve little head. At last, Ophelia . . .

I was suicidal, for the first time in my life, and that was no surprise at all. The idea of it seemed inescapable if not particularly welcome. It seemed like a justified act of atonement for my essential loathsomeness.

The Berkeley hills were April-green, the campus was spilling over with rhododendron and azalea under a wafer-crisp blue sky and there was a salt breeze along University Way. And it had become too much trouble for me to think, to see, to breathe. I understood them all very well, the leapers and drowners and pill swallowers. It was no great decision, accompanied by waves of self-pity and cymbal clashes. No tragedy, no loss. You just reached a point where you had to turn out the light and accept the dark, and whatever came with it.

I took my new-found wisdom to the Campanile and rode up in the elevator. Once upon a time the self-destructive ones who couldn't waste time getting to the Golden Gate Bridge used the Campanile tower for their dives, so the authorities glassed in the observation room. I had no immediate plans for doing myself in, just knew it must happen soon. At the moment I wanted to get away from the streets, I needed something resembling an ivory tower. The Campanile was noisy but convenient.

I spent a lot of time walking around slowly, looking out over the East Bay, deciding how I was going to do it. Accept the dark.

It gave me quite a start a few minutes later to realize I was no longer thinking of my essential loathsomeness. I was thinking about washing my hair.

Leap and drown, or swallow pills. Or a quick jerk of the razor blade at the wrist, and lean forward over the lip of the bathtub like that friend of Beth's a couple of years ago, poor frenzied kid.

I yawned, and wondered when I had washed my hair last. It was cozy up there in the observation room.

And I caught sight of myself reflected vaguely in the sun-warmed glass, the blue bay in the distance.

Loathsome, I thought. I yearned to go sailing.

The Campanile carillon kicked off on the hour and a couple of kids nearby squealed and grabbed their ears. Standing that close to so many bells has different effects, depending on your mood, I suppose. Today, for me, it was like being slapped, many times, roughly but compassionately, by someone who knows the body needs a careful mauling from time to time. And the music the bells made was strong music, to drive out devils. Soon I was crying and hiccuping and not caring much what anyone might think.

With or without Dev, damn it, I wanted to live! I was going to live.

Chapter Ten

MIKE SILLS AND VIRGIL MUNDAY CLOUTED THE CAR, A '65 Mercury, from the off-alley parking lot of the Shawmore Garden Apartments in Norwalk at six-fifty Friday evening. It was raining then, and it kept on raining while Mike drove up to Bridgeport to see a couple of girls he knew. The girls weren't around so Mike and Virg hunted up a quickie grocery and Virg kept the proprietor looking the wrong way while Mike loaded up with cold beer and walked out with it under his slicker. They drove back to the girls' apartment house and drank most of the beer in the car while they waited. But the girls never showed.

"The hell with it," Virg said. He was fifteen and they'd let him out of the Home a few days ago. "I hate this goddam town. Let's go."

"Go where?" Mike said. "Back to Norwalk?"

"Shit, no, man, what's in Norwalk?"

"Good question. OK, then, Buffalo."

"Buffalo?" Virg said, startled. "You crazy? Why Buffalo?"

"I got a sister in Buffalo."

"Yeah, and I got a sister in Floral Park, but I don't want to go to Floral Park. Let's head south and see what happens. Maybe we'll make Miami. I hate this goddam rain."

"Look, in Buffalo we can get rid of this Merc. My sister'll know somebody give us a price on it."

"How much?"

"It ain't in such bad shape. Four, five hundred."

"Hey."

"Sure."

"Where the hell is Buffalo anyway?"

"We can make it by morning easy," Mike promised. "Sooner."

"Maybe she'll put us up for a while."

"Sure, Gwen digs me."

"Maybe she's got a friend I can screw."

"You can screw Gwen, long as you don't tell her how old you are."

"It ain't how old I am that counts," Virg said, scowling manfully. "But if she looks like you I wouldn't want her anyway."

What with getting lost and avoiding tollways it took them more than two hours to reach the Hudson. A few miles east of the Tappan Zee Bridge Mike pulled off and consulted a map he'd found in the dash compartment. After a hell of an argument he persuaded Virg it was worth fifty cents to use the bridge, it would save them a lot of time. And chances were nobody was looking for the car just yet. By then it was past two in the morning. A new storm was peaking over the Hudson and rain had begun to fall again, making coin-size splashes on the windshield.

A State Police car was parked near the tollbooths but the trooper in it hardly gave them a glance. Yellow warning lights were blinking on the long humpbacked bridge and, halfway across, rain and wind began to buffet them. Mike swore, finding it hard to see and steer. The interior of the car was a steambath, but opening a window even a crack let in a flood. He wondered if Buffalo had been such a great idea after all. At least this time of the night the Thruway was all but deserted.

Mike was going sixty and the rain was really hitting; he could feel how unstable the back end of the Merc was at that speed, with the roadway awash. But it didn't matter, he just wanted to be somewhere, and if the goddam car fish-tailed into an overpass abutment he didn't care about that, either; let it.

The high beams picked up a hitchhiker beside the road maybe a hundred yards away. Mike had to look twice and change his mind about what he was seeing and then he hit the brakes too hard. The Merc fought the road and the water and just didn't skid out of control. By then they were practically on top of her. Virg shouted something irritable at him. He'd been dozing.

"Take a look," Mike said.

She was walking on the shoulder, well in from the edge of the road but still shying from the lights. They saw drenched blond hair and a man's shirt pasted to the body so thoroughly it had no color of its own, and tanned bare legs.

"Well, Jesus," Virg muttered as the girl strolled past, pretending not to notice them. He rolled his window down a couple of inches. "Hey, baby!" he shouted, getting a faceful of rain. She didn't hesitate or turn her head. Momentarily her wet body was bathed in pink from the brake lights, and then she was swallowed up by rain and darkness.

The two boys looked at each other.

Mike said, "I don't know, maybe she was in a wreck."

"Pull off."

Mike drove onto the hard-surfaced shoulder. Virg opened the dash compartment and took out the flashlight he'd noticed earlier. He grabbed his slicker from the back seat, worked his way into it, got out of the car. It wasn't a hell of a good flashlight, weak batteries probably, and he couldn't pick her up with the beam. Too late he remembered he was wearing new shoes. He cursed and slogged in the direction the girl had gone, aiming the flash. After twenty yards or so the back of her slicked blond head became visible.

"Wait!" Virg yelled, and ran.

When he caught up to her he seized her right arm above the elbow and turned her, forcing the light on her face. She pulled her head back. There was something around her neck; it looked like a dog collar.

He lowered the light to get it out of her eyes. Just as he'd thought, she was naked under the shirt. "Where you going?" Virg asked. She tried to run away from him; not a word out of her. She was strong and he had trouble holding onto wet flesh. "Look," he said, bitterly annoyed. "Just trying to help."

She made a protesting sound, shaking her head urgently. Her thickly lashed eyes were wide and shock-blank. That big dog collar around her neck bothered Virg. He didn't like any of this. How, he wondered, was he going to get her back to the car —drag her? And then what? They just might have some kind of nut on their hands.

A big semi was coming toward them, ablaze in the murk. Virg tried to pull the girl away from the light. She froze at the sound of the truck, turning her back to it. Maybe, Virg thought, if the driver noticed them at all it would look as if they were taking a walk—at three in the morning in a goddam rainstorm. But the truck didn't slow down. As soon as it was past the girl pried Virg's hand from her arm, gouging him in a couple of places with her fingernails, and fled.

Virg started after her at a run but he splashed through a puddle, soaking his trousers to the knees, and he gave up. Mike, the son of a bitch, was still sitting in the car. Virg walked back, sodden and fuming. He should have just busted her one. The sight of her naked breasts, nipples small and hard in the weak yellow beam of the flash, had inflamed him.

But the remembered wildness in her eyes turned him off. She had looked as if she could kill him. He had seen a girl look like that once: she had just thrown her baby out a window. Virg shuddered and pressed the back of his right hand to his mouth and found a gouged place with the tip of his tongue, tasted his own blood. Crazy bitch. He wondered if Buffalo was going to be any different, any better than what he'd always known.

The narrow street was filled with water so she walked beside it; there was no sidewalk, just cold mud. A random hazy street-light to show the way. The darkened houses were frame and shingle, small-town ghetto houses. The rain fell needle sharp. She was not aware of it. A dog barked from a porch. She walked slowly on, limping, not looking around, mud splattered as high as her waist. As she walked she shuddered, but the shuddering didn't cause her to stop.

When the street ended she went to her left. Half a block away was a narrow three-story house with a neon tavern sign in one window. She stopped then as if the pale artery of neon had intrigued her, gazed up at the tavern for three or four minutes. There was no sound on this new street except the thinnish rain, no movement. She walked up the dozen steps slowly and then without hesitation opened one of the doors and stepped inside.

It was a warm and beery nest with a neatly blocked ton of smoke sitting low on a margin of light. There was a long bar to her right, tables to the left. In back a lighted shuffleboard, booths. The jukebox was off. Only a few faces at this hour. A bartender in silhouette against a blue-toned mirror.

There hadn't been much noise when she walked in, but it was deathly still now. Rain dripped from her face and fingertips. She looked around but not as if she was terribly interested. Her attitude was one of patience and resignation.

"Livia," the bartender rumbled; a black woman with broad shoulders, African jewelry and a natural emerged from the shadows at the back of the tavern and approached the girl, not believing half of what she saw. The girl stared somberly back at her.

"Yes?" Livia said sharply.

She was surprised when the girl spoke—just something about her, as if she didn't speak at all, or couldn't.

"Where is this?" the girl said, in a guttural whisper. She had to strain to get that much out. She lifted a hand to her collared throat. "This—town?"

Livia glanced at the bartender, then back. Behind them a man got up, laid a five-dollar bill on the table, reached for his hat and went through the door like a cat through a hole in a fence.

"Nyack, New York," Livia said, moving a step closer, frowning. "What's that around your neck?"

The girl didn't answer, only shuddered. Her eyes were abnormally wide, pure agate. The bartender thumbed a dime out of the cash register and put it in a pay phone.

"Honey—you're wet and you're cold," Livia said. "Why don't you come back here and sit with me, and we'll get you something warm to wrap up in." She held out a hand coaxingly. The girl looked at it and went as rigid as a stork.

"My name is Carol Watterson," she said, "and I want to go home." She showed her teeth and Livia prudently decided not to try touching her. Something bloody and wild about this one, she thought. There was a long silence. Nobody seemed to know what to do.

At length the girl spoke again, in her raw whisper of a voice.

"My name is Carol Watterson—and I want to go home."

"Sure, honey," Livia said soothingly. "Don't you worry about a thing. You can go home."

Chapter Eleven

SPECIAL AGENT GAFFNEY PLACED THE MICROPHONE where it would pick up both voices, then turned on the big tape recorder. "I hope this won't bother you, Carol," he said.

She smiled fitfully and shook her head. They were alone: Gaffney had patiently insisted on that. She sat on the regency sofa in the library with her bare bandaged feet tucked under, a cigarette with a long tail of smoke in one hand. She wore a Cardin shirt, striped bell-bottom slacks. She'd made up her eyes heavily so the puffiness wouldn't be obvious. Her hair was clean and newly brushed and it curled to a fall over her left shoulder. It partially obscured the bad bruise on her throat, which was like a deep-purple egg surrounded by a yellowing nimbus.

"But I don't think I can remember anything," she told him apologetically, in her whispered voice.

Gaffney said, "I know it's very difficult right now. As we talk details may come back to you. The blood sample your doctor obtained yesterday may give us an idea of what type of drug, if any, they were using on you. In the meantime—"

"I'll do the best I can," she promised, and yawned. She caught the yawn with the back of her hand, looked guiltily at the FBI man. "I'm *sorry!* I don't know what the trouble is. I couldn't be sleepy. I slept all day. I feel like I'm under glass. I can't—I'm not in touch with anything yet." She stared at him. "Did we meet Friday night? To be honest, I don't remember that much."

"We met. And you'll never know how happy I was to see you, Carol."

"I was given up for dead, wasn't I?" She fingered the bruise on her neck.

Gaffney stopped the tape, reversed, listened, was satisfied with the quality of the sound. He erased what already had been said, paused with his finger on the *start* button. He looked at her sympathetically. "That was one alternative we had to consider. Suppose we get started? We'll make this as brief as possible. To begin with, Carol, why don't you just tell me about last Sunday afternoon?"

She put her cigarette in an ashtray. "Well—Sunday Kevin and I played tennis most of the afternoon, then went down to Jake's in the Village to get something—you know all that. OK. So we were sitting inside and this man came along and told me something was wrong with the Sting Ray. A fire, he said. I was panicked, of course. I went outside with him—"

Gaffney opened his attaché case, handed a photograph to her. "Carol, I'm showing you an artist's sketch of this man as your brother described him."

She pondered the face. Then she put the photo down, face down, on the sofa, biting her lower lip. "That's—yes, that's pretty close; I mean, it's him. The man. His mouth is wrong, and I don't think his nose was quite as long. But you've got him there."

"Would you tell me what happened after you left the restaurant with the man?"

"I had to catch up to him; we were outside by then."

"Did he say anything else to you?"

"I made some sort of rhetorical remark—what could have happened, my car is brand-new—you know, something like that. He tried to be reassuring. He said he didn't think there was much damage—"

"Excuse me. Did you notice anything about his speech?"

"How do you mean?"

"Did he have a regional accent? Yankee? Southern?"

"I was too upset to notice."

"And after you reached the car—"

"Well, the hood was up. But nothing had happened. There were no indications of a fire. I looked up to give him hell. I thought it was a sadistic kind of joke." She gestured with one hand. "He was standing, about here, this far away from me."

"You're indicating four feet, or a little less."

"And on my right. He was looking at me in a—I don't know —frightening way."

"Was there a black delivery van nearby?"

"Oh, I forgot that. Yes. Parked behind us. By that I mean it was between the Corvette and the back door of the restaurant."

"Was anyone in the van, Carol?"

"Driving. I just had a glimpse of him."

"Can you describe him?"

"Not very well. He was dark-skinned and wore sunglasses. I think he had on a blue shirt. Blue like my car."

"A medium blue. There was a man standing to your right, and another in the van. Was the first man blocking you in some way? Could you have run if you'd wanted to?"

"No. I couldn't get around him. But I didn't think about running; that never crossed my mind. I just didn't know what was happening. He had a white can in his right hand. Like a can of shaving cream. He sprayed—sprayed it right in my—face."

"Take your time."

"It was—MACE, I think."

"Chemical MACE?" Gaffney asked.

"I know some kids who were hit with that stuff while demonstrating. It happened before they learned to wear goggles and seal them to their faces with Vaseline, and wear handkerchiefs soaked in baking soda and water over their noses and mouths. Whatever he used on me, it was awful. It almost blinded me. I couldn't get my breath. I was choking and trying to throw up. I knew I was in danger, but all I wanted was to sit down."

"Then he put you in the van?"

"He all but threw me in. And after that—" She closed her

113

eyes and was quiet. After a couple of minutes Gaffney turned off the tape recorder.

"I'm sorry," she said resignedly. "I knew it wouldn't be any good; I knew I'd get that far and—" She touched her throat again, grimaced. "Why do you suppose they did that to me? Why put a—a dog collar around my neck? Was there a chain too?"

"Apparently. The leather was ripped in one place. A chain might have been attached there."

"And how did I get away?" She tilted her head back and sighed in vexation, tensely trying but finding the past week beyond recall. "Did I pull the chain off with my hands—or did they let me go? Or—"

"What, Carol?"

"Did someone else let me go?" She glanced at the cigarette in her ashtray; there wasn't much left of it. Gaffney lit a fresh one for her. He shook his head noncommittally, smiling: he liked this one. She was a little underweight now, tan gone sallow after days of captivity, and the bruised throat probably ached with every word she spoke, every slight motion of her head. But she'd come through in good shape, spirit untrampled. She was a stand-up fighter and had a generous share of the golden good looks he was partial to; abundant sexuality but well grounded in the ego, not running wild and wastefully. This was a woman, openhearted, intuitive, outspoken, and she would only improve with age.

"You'll have to tell us. When it comes back to you."

"*If* it does. But you think they might have drugged me."

"With one of the hypnotics, yes."

"Then I was made to forget. And even if I want to remember, I'll never be able to."

"Depends on what you were given, and how knowledgeable the administrator was. A good psychiatrist using Sodium Pentothal might be able to remove the block." She was watching him, totally absorbed.

"All right, then! I'll take Sodium Pentothal."

"I'm afraid not. It's a tricky area, and there's a possibility that Pentothal treatment, even by an expert, wouldn't be safe for you."

She said, her lip curled in a half smile, "You mean it might blow my mind?"

Gaffney shrugged. "Not my field. But that was the consensus, so we've dropped the idea."

"Now what?" She pointed at the tape recorder. "That won't be any help."

"Well—tomorrow, if you're up to it, I thought we'd drive over to Rockland County."

"Memory reinforcement?"

"Something like that."

"I'm game," she said, not hopefully.

She had awakened at dusk; it was fully dark now and the tennis courts were lighted. Felice and Kevin were playing. She went out the back door and stood in the grass watching them. It was a cool night, not so many bugs, even around the court floods. Riggs wandered over and sat down a few feet away, tongue lolling. She snapped her fingers. Riggs stared at her amiably, then turned his head and began chasing a flea along his backbone.

She heard Felice yell in exasperation at a bad serve. She returned to the kitchen, sat down at the captain's table with her chin in her hands. Dimly she heard Sam's old typewriter clacking away in his room on the second floor.

A couple of minutes later Felice and Kevin trooped in, turning on lights.

"Hi," she said glumly, not looking at them.

"Hi," Kevin said.

"Where's Gaffney?" Felice asked.

"He left."

"Oh. He wasn't here long."

"There wasn't much I could tell him."

"Oh," Felice said again. "Your voice is better."

She straightened, hands slapping the table lightly. "Sure. Now it's like a bad sound track on the late-late show." They were both standing in the center of the kitchen, rackets in hand, faces glistening, looking solemnly and uncertainly at her. She smiled. "Who won?"

"Who *won*," Kevin said.

"Oh, well, of course."

"I think I'll make a sandwich," Kevin announced, dropping his gear on a counter and opening the refrigerator. "Carol, want a sandwich?"

"You must be hungry," Felice said.

"No. I couldn't eat."

"Buttermilk?" Kevin asked.

"No—Kevin, let's go down to Jake's. I'll buy you a cheese-burger."

Kevin pulled his head out of the refrigerator. Felice's expression was peculiar. "Are you sure you feel—"

"If I can walk I can drive," she said curtly, and then her eyes widened and she looked very startled. "I said *Jake's*, didn't I? Oh, Jesus. Take it back, Kevin. I don't think wild horses could get me in Jake's again, ever. We'll try the Baron. If you want to go. I'd love some company."

"Sure," Kevin said. "Let me change my shirt, this one sort of stinks."

Felice poured a glass of buttermilk and sat down, groaning a little from soreness. She laughed. "Kevin's learned to handle my top-spin lob, and I don't have much else going for me."

"Keep him moving to his left; his backhand isn't all that good yet."

Felice listened to the typewriter as if it were Bach.

"Sam's working hard."

"That piece for *Harper's*," Felice said. "It was due last week." She tilted back in the armchair, pulled open a drawer behind her, took out an unopened pack of cigarettes. "Smoke?"

"I'm dying for one, but my throat can't take it."

Felice nodded understandingly, lit a cigarette for herself,

shook out the match, exhaled. She slumped comfortably in the round-backed chair, crossing her ankles. Most of the light from the fixture above the table was in her face. She rubbed a mosquito welt on one arm. Her eyes were half closed, a sheen of perspiration on the dark lids.

"Sleepy, Mother?" There was a smile on her face, thin-lipped, colorless, neutral. Her young hands were clenched on the table as if she were throttling something—her own nerves, perhaps.

Felice said, "Marth Pelling and I are going to an estate sale at the auction galleries in Mamaroneck next weekend. Want to join us?"

"I might. Are you buying?"

"They're offering a Winslow Homer the General wants, so I'll bid for him. And there's a Pollock I'd like, if the bidding doesn't get too steep."

"What would be a good price for it?"

"Oh, seven thousand at Parke-Bernet."

"Twenty-five years ago a junk dealer bought a few dozen canvases Pollock did when he was with the WPA. The dealer paid four cents a pound. He was going to insulate pipes with the canvas."

"Four cents a pound," Felice said wonderingly.

Outside Riggs barked loudly at something and tore off the back steps. They both jumped. Felice laughed at her own fright, then looked concerned.

"*Honey.*"

"No, I'm all right, Mother, please don't—t-touch me."

"What *is* it?"

"T-they had me locked up and wearing a dog collar and a chain. I got away somehow—damn it, *somehow*. But what if they decide to come around and collect me again?"

This time Felice caught one of her hands and held it. "That couldn't happen. There's no danger. If there were, Gaffney would've assigned men—"

"But we don't know what it was all about! Why were they keeping me? It wasn't a—a sex thing, we know that. Why didn't they call? I just don't have any answers. I don't *remember*, Felice. That's frustrating, but it scares hell out of me too—" She leaned into the light, her eyes button wide. "The three of you," she said fractiously. "Sam's the worst, but it's all of you. Trying *so* hard to pretend it didn't happen. You're either too chummy or too too *dear* and listen, I've had all the long thoughtful looks I can stomach! I haven't been resurrected. There's nothing wrong with me!" Her weak voice gave out, ending as a tired squeal; she laughed at the ridiculous voice and was convulsed. She lowered her head almost to her mother's hand and a squeezed-out tear dropped from one cheek.

After a few seconds Felice said tonelessly, "We all took our lumps last week."

"I know," she whispered, disgusted with herself. She sat up, sighed, wiped the leaky eye with the back of one hand, a gesture intact from childhood. "I shouldn't have—I didn't mean to—"

"Better now?"

"Oh, it was just a squall. Ripped the canvas some. But I'm still right side up." She sniffed. "Do I look streaky?"

"Not so bad. You look wonderful to me."

"Thanks," she said shyly.

"Kevin's got a plane to catch bright and early, so—"

"Just down to the Village and back. It's his last night home for a while, and I wanted to treat him. Monday night there'll be people around, there's nothing to worry about."

"We cabled the Dowds this morning, but I think we'll put in a call tomorrow. I know they won't believe you're safe until they hear your voice."

She grinned. "Such as it is." She got up, kissed her mother quickly. "Kevin'll take all night combing his hair if I don't grab him. See you." She went up the back steps, favoring one hurt foot slightly, humming something, and a couple of seconds later Felice heard her croak as loudly as she could, *"Kev-uhhnn! Let's go-oh!"*

Felice smiled to herself, contented. A little of the buttermilk was left in her glass. She snubbed out the cigarette, picked up the glass, decided she didn't want the rest of the milk, carried the glass to the sink.

Sam's typewriter had stopped. It was marvelously quiet in the house now: all sound was external. She heard a barn owl. She listened to the tireless frogs on the shores of the pond. She still felt pleasantly stimulated from the exercise, a shade too tense to settle down right away to a book or neglected letters. Through the six-over-six window above the sink she saw Riggs stride across the lawn, through shadow clusters and cold widths of moonlight, his eyes quick amber, searching idly at every pause.

Felice was about to rinse out the glass when a tremor in her hand caused it to slip. The glass shattered in the sink. She stared at the pieces, feeling a bleak insecurity. Too much demand on the nerves, she thought. Tonight they would all sleep very well indeed with Carol back.

The bleakness settled in like a fog.

Carol was home. But she was changed, had been changed. There was a wrongness in her eyes, trouble there, too deep to see clearly, or to guess at. Simply there.

What had she seen, and could not tell?

Felice trembled. There was blood on one fingertip, running darkly down to the palm of her hand. She washed it off and cleaned up the broken glass.

The tape recorder was turned off after they'd twice heard every word the girl had to say, and for several minutes the two men sat in a smoky contemplative silence occasionally broken by short messages on the Telex.

Pete Demilia yawned. "That blow on the neck huskied her voice up pretty good."

Gaffney said, "Massive internal swelling, some glands affected, according to the examining physician. She'll be speaking normally in a few days."

"What caused that bruise? A fist?"

"No. He was positive about that. She could have been gar-roted a certain way, maybe hit with a club or something." Gaffney frowned, looking at the two-page transcript of a telephone report from the FBI lab.

"Do you think she's telling the truth? Is she drawing a blank?"

"If she's a liar, she's a damned good one." He handed over the transcript. "This corroborates our suspicion that they were doping her—combination of Methedrine, a tranquilizer and a potent hypnotic drug, one so new the lab had trouble identifying the source. The drug is currently being manufactured in small batches for controlled testing purposes. A company in Palo Alto holds the patents and makes the stuff."

"Hey, hey," Demilia said, eyes lighting up.

"De La Cruz will be working all night on the Coast. We should know within an hour if a quantity of the drug was stolen recently. If not—"

"Someone working for the company who has access could have pinched just enough for Carol Watterson. A chemist, maybe? It looks like a break might have come our way."

Gaffney had the habit of smoking every cigarette down to the half inch, but tonight he was so keyed up he stubbed out one only a third gone. "We've had a couple of breaks so far. Keeping the papers off the story was one. Getting the girl back was a colossal break."

"Yeah," Demilia said, and they were both quiet again. Demilia smiled slightly. "Changed your vote, Gaff?"

"No. I still say she escaped. It doesn't make sense otherwise. The kidnappers were thorough. They had a good plan and they stuck to it. They spent money on this snatch. They weren't holed up in a third-rate motel somewhere, bet on that. We won't find them, or find out where they were, by the usual methods, checking the summer rentals and the utilities and so forth. But why should they grab her, then let her go more than five days later, without having made the slightest effort to collect their money?"

"Because they got something they wanted. Something Carol had. It wasn't money."

"It wasn't her beautiful body, either."

"This is far out. Maybe it was an experiment, a dry run. A practice kidnapping."

Gaffney picked up a photograph of Carol, not a studio portrait but a good candid color shot taken by a professional. The photo was a year old. Her face had been rounder then, more youthful. Her gaze was direct, smile expressing a certain optimism and sense of well-being. Not the same girl now, not quite the same face. Tonight the skin of her face had been as taut as a drumhead; she wasn't starved looking but there was no excess flesh, and her expression had changed, subtly. Blame the loss of optimism too, the hard-gained realization that the world was still a hunting ground and anyone could be a victim. Her eyes had looked tighter to him, more sharply defined and barely recessed, but they were still appealing and wise, filled with flashes of warmth and excitement.

"When do you see her again?"

"Tomorrow," Gaffney said, and was immediately aware of how much he was looking forward to it. "She'll help us redraw our suspect. Later we'll drive over to Rockland County and see if we can shake up her memory some."

"That's when we spring the big surprise?"

"That's when we spring it."

Demilia smiled uneasily. "I hope she doesn't have a bad heart to go with her bad memory."

"The doc says she's as sound as a dollar, Pete."

Kevin had turned the bed light out at last but he didn't touch the transistor radio on the pillow next to his ear. It was a bright clear night. He wasn't even a little tired, although the disc jockey had just babbled gleefully that the time was twenty-six minutes to three. Then, with a catch in his voice, he reverently introduced the current Big One by The Doors. Kevin half listened; the radio was for company mostly. He was restless from anticipation, thinking fitfully of the long flight in a few hours, the blue-water cruise to follow. He was a little worried about the fit of the new face mask Sam had picked up for him at A&F. He wondered if Joey Balfour would get bored and goof off in the middle of the cruise and foul up their experiment, which depended upon keeping precise records of water temperature and salinity. He was glad nobody knew about the kidnapping; he wouldn't have to keep talking about it for thirty days. And he was glad he was going away right now, and wouldn't have to see Carol for a while.

If he never saw her again, Kevin thought, his eyes stinging, *never*, that wouldn't make any difference to him.

"Hey, your radio's loud," his mother said from the doorway, and he reached over instantly to turn it off. She came in and sat on the edge of his bed. She was smoking. "No sleep for you, either?" she asked softly.

"No."

"Keep you company for a minute?"

"OK."

"Carol's restless too. I heard her walking around in her room a little while ago."

Kevin said nothing.

"The two of you were gone for quite a while tonight," Felice observed. "Gave Sam and me the jitters." He was lying on his back staring at the ceiling, face immobile, eyes like gray water, like reflecting pools. Plainly he didn't want to talk. He was worried about something, or mad, or both; she could never be sure of his moods. "Where did you kids go after you ate?"

"We drove up the Parkway," Kevin said, vocal at last.

"You must have had a lot to talk about." She looked obliquely at him over the tip of her cigarette and was mildly concerned. "Did Carol—have anything to say about the kidnapping?"

The word acted on him like a prod; Kevin shifted in the bed, acutely uncomfortable; then he sat up, long arms around his knees, forehead just touching. Felice saw that he had failed to get his hair trimmed; it was beginning to get unpleasantly matted.

"Just that she—" He shook his head, not sure of what he wanted to say, or if he wanted to say anything. He decided to plunge ahead. "We talked a lot about the assassinations—about Martin Luther King and the Kennedys. Carol was mad about it. She said all the wrong people were being killed, the world had just gone completely wrong and out of focus and hate was choking us all like smog. She said it would be better for everyone to be on stuff—maybe that was the only way."

"Stuff?"

"Drugs, I guess she meant. Speed."

"What's speed?"

Kevin said impatiently, "It's a stimulant; you know, like bennies—Benzedrine—only it eats your brains up after a while. Gaby Broyer's mother takes them. Everybody says she's a speed freak. Everybody knows it."

"*I* don't know it, pal. What else did Carol—"

"She said that when you're on stuff then you can't hate, you don't want to kill. But the people whose whole life is hating have twisted the drug thing and made it seem evil, because they twist everything that's good into evil, for their own purposes."

Felice shook her head slowly. "Carol has better sense than to believe that."

"We were parked by then. She was shaking. I thought she was just mad. But she said, 'I'm lucky; anything could have happened to me by now. I'm lucky, but I'm scared too.' She asked me if I would hold her, and I did, and then she—sort of laughed and said now that I was getting to be man-sized I would have to learn how to hold a girl better than that."

"Listen to your sister, she knows."

Kevin scowled at her, which surprised Felice. "She held me—pretty tight, for a long time, until she stopped shaking so much. She kissed me too. Twice." His voice had dropped to a low monotone.

"Oh?" Felice said, with a slight smile he couldn't see.

"Then she said thank you Kevin I feel a little better. Then she started the car but we didn't go, she just looked at me sad and said would I do a very—special favor and sleep with her tonight, because she felt lonely and depressed and didn't want to be alone."

"Sleep in the same bed, you mean? How did you feel about that? What did you tell her?"

Kevin said dully, "I didn't know. I didn't say anything. Carol said it would be all right, that brothers and sisters who are close like we are sleep together sometimes and there isn't anything wrong with it."

"Often there isn't. But you felt wrong."

Kevin shrugged, painfully.

"Well, I'm sure Carol understood."

"I guess so."

Felice finished her cigarette and put it out in the ashtray she'd brought along. She stood up. "Everybody but Sam seems to be hard up for sleep tonight. Maybe if I clear out you might get a few winks."

"Maybe," Kevin muttered, not moving. "Good night."

"Good night."

In her own room Felice thought about it, and wondered why she felt obscurely wrong, as Kevin did. She had sensed deep anger in him, outrage, and that troubled and mystified her. Was he so offended because Carol had wanted to be near him? It was not an offensive thing, and he must realize that. Or had Carol said or done something else that—

Felice shied from the suggestion that touched her mind, then returned to it cautiously. Could Kevin have been innocently aroused by an embrace at his age, by a sisterly kiss on the cheek? He was half-grown, had reached a certain stage of curiosity and awareness. Such an experience might have caused guilt feelings, which would explain his present state of mind.

Above her she could hear the give and creak of floorboards; Carol was still awake.

Felice took off her peignoir, turned out the lamp, settled

down in bed, her eyes big in the dark. Her explanation made sense, she thought, still uneasy.

Because the other made no sense at all. Carol would not knowingly try to seduce her brother, degrade them both in such a way. Not the Carol they knew.

Chapter Twelve

SHE LOOKED TIRED WHEN GAFFNEY CAME FOR HER. She was wearing a deceptively expensive sleeveless knit dress in a vivid coral shade with a fabric belt in navy, white and coral, and she had knotted a navy scarf loosely at her throat. The scarf and the casual twist of pale hair over her right shoulder concealed the bruise. She wore French sunglasses with dark-gray lenses. For ornament she had chosen an antique gold bracelet. From what he'd observed so far Gaffney decided that Carol lacked the flair and dedication to costume of, say, a professional model, but she did know style, loved bright colors and dipped sparingly into the fads of the season.

"Carol, we could have put this off," he said, holding the car door for her.

"No point in that," she replied. "Thank you. What happens first?"

"We're still waiting on the man who did the original sketch of our suspect. He should be along in a couple of hours. In the meantime we could drive across the river."

"Cover all of Rockland County today?"

"Just one area we're interested in." Gaffney drove a couple of miles north to route 35, headed west to Peekskill, explaining on the way about the yellow paint found on the tires of the rented van.

"Uh-huh, FBI thoroughness." She leaned toward him to accept a light for her cigarette, sat back. "How many kidnappings does the FBI solve?"

"A high percentage. We're still working on a couple of old cases."

After a few miles she was more at ease with him. The day was a good one, hot but bearable with no humidity to speak of, a low bumpy rim of clouds on the horizon. "I suppose it's an old question, but how did you get into this line of work?"

Gaffney chuckled willingly. "Whores and cops always have to explain themselves. I do this work because I think it's important, and because I'm good at it."

"You don't seem like the type. I mean—it's kind of a grubby organization after all, with a good publicity mill."

He wasn't offended by her outsider's judgment. "We're not perfect. There are internal policies I find hard to live with, but I won't argue the necessity of having them. We have good agents and some indifferent ones; the bad ones are rare and we weed them out fast. The pay isn't good even at my level and the paper work will drive you crazy at times. Overtime can be rough on a man who's conscientious about his family."

"How about your family?"

"We're scattered. My wife died six years ago. I have a boy who'll be finishing up at Notre Dame this year. My daughter is your age, twenty-one. She's married, lives in the city and studies design at the Fashion Institute. She has most of my features so she ought to be ugly as hell, but somehow everything works for her. I'd call her a beauty."

She stared appraisingly at him. "You're a long way from being an ugly man, Mr. Gaffney."

"Thanks. Bob, if you will."

They crossed the Hudson north of Peekskill. "I don't think I've been over this way in four or five years," she said, then added quickly, "that I remember. We used to have picnics at Bear Mountain. A long time ago I got lost in the woods for a whole afternoon. I was about five, I guess. My father was still living then."

At Stony Point Gaffney turned west on 210. "This is the road they may have taken, the evening they kidnapped you or later

127

in the week. We'll go slow along here. Now if anything seems curious or vaguely familiar tell me and I'll pull off, give you time to think about it."

She said hesitantly, "I wish I knew what I was looking for." The road was well shaded by tall trees on either side; she took off her sunglasses. She was absorbed now, concentrating perhaps a little too hard. Traffic was light. They had entered Harriman State Park, a semiwilderness area. They saw boy scouts on a field trip, passed small lakes and camp grounds. It was ten degrees cooler here, and the effect of alternating light and shade caused her to nod sleepily. He reached out and touched her arm and she looked up, wide-eyed, with a guilty smile, then glanced out the window.

"They couldn't have kept me here. Not in the park."

"We're not far from Greenwood Lake. Dozens of likely hiding places along the shore, or back in the woods."

She yawned. "This time of the year Greenwood Lake has bigger crowds than Times Square."

"Maybe the people we're looking for have been part of the crowd for so long nobody notices them. Could you use some coffee?"

"*Could* I!"

They parked behind a frame-and-shingle luncheonette on a graveled point overlooking the narrow lake. Half a hundred sailboats clung like moths to the mild dark swells. On the opposite shore there were fine old summer houses with secluded porches, patriarchal shade trees, lawns that were meticulously clipped to the water's edge.

Gaffney looked at his watch. "I noticed a phone booth by the road. I'll take a minute to phone in first."

"Why not use your radio?"

"No good at this range." He got out and walked briskly away. Tanned kids in skimpy swimsuits and adults in sun-faded tatterdemalion were lined up at the take-out windows of the luncheonette. A white powerboat with a ski tow hurtled by a few yards offshore, bow whapping against the swells, clean-limbed youths indolently taking their summer-bum pleasures. She watched them, then got out her powder and lipstick and opened the compact.

She first saw it coming in the filmy round mirror of the compact. Half puzzled, she was motionless with the pink lipstick poised against her underlip. Then she turned her head to make sure.

A black unlettered VW delivery van. It stopped thirty or forty feet away across the gravel partially screened by a couple of low dusty trees. The man on the passenger side glanced alertly at her, swung the door open, stepped out. He was tall and attenuated and bushy-haired and he wore bulbous sunglasses like the evil lord of the planet Crypto in a children's matinee thriller. He came toward her purposefully, single-mindedly, not hurrying. The effect on her was the same as if a lightning bolt had glanced off the car. She dropped the lipstick. Her throat locked. Her mouth opened in a soundless expression of dismay and her chin trembled for an instant. She opened the door and got out, lipstick squiggle down the front of her otherwise impeccable dress. She took a faltering step in his direction, fists clenched breast high. She could just see the driver of the van. Squat, dark, wavy-haired, wearing a blue shirt.

Her voice was part whisper, part croak as he continued to bear down on her expressionlessly. "Get away!" she said. "Get —" Her eyelids fluttered; a different sort of surprise altered her face like a slap. The bushy-haired man stopped. She whirled and saw Gaffney watching from the telephone booth by the road, the receiver in his hand half lowered. For several seconds they were all suspended. She heard quite clearly the ragged wood-cutting hum of the powerboat, a child whining to its mother, the bell of a cash register inside the luncheonette. Then she threw her hands to her face and sagged against the side of the car.

Gaffney got to her quickly. "Carol—"

"Let me alone. Don't *touch* me! *Who* do you think you are? Just a cop after all, and you're all alike! Brutal, sadistic—"

"Carol, we hoped it would do some good. Help bring it all back, jog your memory—"

She lowered her hands, glared at him with a barbarous anguish. Most of the people queued up in front of the luncheonette had become very interested because of the explicit tension in the air and her undisguised wrath. The fake bushy-haired man was walking leisurely back to the Volkswagen van. Gaffney looked calmly and sympathetically at her, which was more than she could stand. "Get me out of here," she pleaded, sliding down into the car seat. She reached for her sunglasses and the dropped lipstick.

They were on the Palisades Parkway, northbound, before either of them said anything. The dwarf clouds of morning had become thunderheads towering above Bear Mountain.

After glancing at her a couple of times Gaffney ventured, "Still sore at me?"

"I've already drafted three nasty letters to John Edgar."

"He knew about it. We all knew it would be rough on you. There was a good chance the results would be worth the trouble."

"Oh, God," she said bleakly, then gave up a ghostly smile. "Who was he? He looked—damned real to me."

"One of Claude Demkus' cops. Active with the Chappaqua little theater."

"Jolly. I feel all clenched up inside. I may have to have all my babies by Caesarean."

"Look, I'm still good for coffee. We'll skip the meeting with the artist. You've had enough police work for one day."

They stopped at a new place outside Peekskill, took a back booth in the nearly empty restaurant. She dabbed at the lipstick mark on her dress with a napkin and cold water, decided to leave it alone. She looked wan and troubled, eyes darkened to bittersweet chocolate. The air-conditioning was too cold for her. She was filled with yawns and nettlesome fears that occasionally prompted a small sad wince. He felt as badly as if he'd abused his own daughter. But he had to push her just a little farther.

He took the brown envelope from his inside coat pocket, extracted the wire photo, wordlessly placed it in front of her. He was watching her closely. He saw nothing significant—a tightening around the eyes, a thinning of the lips, quickly a stillness that was almost masklike. For ten seconds she stared at the photograph, then glanced up at Gaffney with a sigh he felt rather than heard.

"Who is she?"

"I was hoping you'd know."

She tried again, tapping her forehead lightly with a fist. She shook her head curtly. "I don't."

"You've never seen her?"

"No."

He took the photo back, looked briefly at it himself. A nice cheeky girl with a good-size grin and long tresses, lower jaw and double chin no photographer could minimize.

"Her name is—or was—Barbara Hosker, called Babs. We're interested in her because she worked as a research chemist in a lab which makes a hypnotic drug which your kidnappers gave you. Babs left the drug company a month ago to marry the fellow she'd been living with in Palo Alto, an artist and sculptor named Jim Hendersholt."

"So?" she said.

"The drug has been manufactured in very small quantities so far. Only a few people have had access to it. Apparently it has odd side effects nobody is very sure of, so they're testing it slowly and carefully."

"You think that girl might have stolen some of it?"

"She could have. But we have no proof."

"Where is she now?"

"We'd like to know. She and her husband supposedly are in Mexico. None of their friends knew exactly where. They've had postcards from various places. Mexican authorities are trying to locate them for us. I have a hunch they might not be found right away." He took a second photo from the envelope and gave it to her. This one was of a bony-faced man of thirty or so, with very little hair, a great black moustache, simmering intelligent eyes.

"That's Jim Hendersholt," Gaffney said. "Babs' husband. Shave off the Pancho Villa moustache, clap on a fright wig and dark glasses, he looks like our prime suspect."

"In a way," she said indifferently. "But so did that cop back there. A lot of men in that disguise would look the same." She handed over the photo and sipped at her coffee. "That girl had such a sweet face. Maybe this doesn't mean anything, but she certainly doesn't look like a kidnapper. No more than my brother Kevin."

"She could be an accomplice."

"I wish I could say I knew her. I don't think I was ever in Palo Alto. Oh, once on a frat weekend when I was a sophomore. I had a lousy time." She stared through the tinted window at an expanse of asphalt, scrubby evergreens. "They went to so much trouble," she whispered. "Was it worth it? What did they gain?" She looked inquiringly at Gaffney. "How many of you are working on this now?"

"About a hundred agents on different shifts. It's our baby now under the federal kidnap statute. Of course we get a great deal of assistance from local authorities. Since it happened on his beat, Chief Demkus is still very much interested in the case: he was personally offended."

"That many men. Then you certainly ought to find whoever it is you're looking for." She shrugged. "But I can't bring myself to care. They hurt me, I guess, and caused my family a lot of grief. But I don't know them and I don't hate them. It just doesn't matter." She scrawled through spilled coffee with a fingertip. "You said the drug had odd side effects. Do you know what they might be?"

"I don't have any information. I could find out."

"I guess it isn't so important," she said, smiling, and touched the back of his hand with her fist: a chummy, intimate gesture. "I mean, I haven't noticed anything different about me."

The peregrine waiting on in the high gray sky was only a dot, like a pencil mark on smooth slate, and she kept losing the bird altogether. She shaded her eyes against the mild afternoon glare, maintaining her own watch with a dry mouth, a tense avid expectancy.

The General took a live unfettered pigeon from his falconer's bag and held it in his two hands for a few moments. Then, with a cry, he threw it into the air. The pigeon wobbled momentarily on its wings, circled higher. Almost instantly the peregrine broke her own circle, rolled over, swooped, fell. By the time she hit the frantically evasive pigeon with a closed fist she had traveled close to a thousand feet in eight seconds.

Stunned, the pigeon fell like a loose bundle of feathers tied together with a string. The peregrine, now in an upward trajectory with opened wings, gradually slowed. Then she spiraled downward to her prey. She picked up the pigeon with one foot and severed its neck vertebra with her beak, killing it. The peregrine relaxed her feathers and looked around, eyed them sharply as if expecting approval, then proceeded to plume and eat. The General took the falcon on his fist to finish its meal. "Beautiful, isn't she, Carol?"

Her hands fell to her sides, fingers uncurling. Her palms were wet. She approached the General slowly. The falcon paid little attention.

The falcon was a golden bird, in her prime, lean from the period of training but well-adjusted to captivity. The General called her Rosalind.

"Next week," he said, "with Riggs' help, I'll teach her to hawk game from a point." Rosalind lifted a foot momentarily and the bells there tinkled. "You'd like that, wouldn't you? Time to fly again. Just don't fly too far; I'd hate to lose you."

"How long will it take?" she asked the General as they walked back through the field.

He stroked Rosalind's feathers affectionately. "A day or two.

She learns very fast. Hold her for me, Carol?" She raised her right arm and Rosalind, who had talons that could pierce bone, balanced herself delicately on the offered wrist, stared at her new companion with a full yellow eye, then folded her wings.

The General lit a cigarette. "The only thing to worry about is that she might ride the wind too far for me to recover her. No matter how well-trained she is I can't be sure what'll happen when she's flying free." He smiled. "Even if I lose her one way or another it's been worth it. This is the most effective and humane killing instrument a hunter has at his disposal. If she misses her target she misses clean. When she hits, which is most of the time, she kills."

The General owned thirty acres, not including the pond. Except for Sam and Felice he had no near neighbors. There was a woods on three sides of his property, which was the nucleus of what had been, in the nineteenth century, a farm of over six hundred acres. A couple of the original farm buildings remained, a small tack barn and an equipment shed. There was also a brick tenant's house, in need of a new roof and long disused. The main barn had been hit by lightning years ago and destroyed, although some of the foundation could still be seen, overlapped by the summer tide of the fields.

His house was pure Victorian, a small brick castle of four stories. It had murky windows as big as doors, doors half the size of railroad flatcars, a main staircase with room on each landing for a baby grand piano. There were twenty-six rooms. More than half were not furnished and never would be. The General lived in a spacious apartment on the third floor: bedroom, sitting room, office, eight closets—one of which was stacked full of wood for his fireplaces—two baths, a small kitchen in which he did no more than heat coffee. From his windows he had a fine if somewhat distorted view in three directions. Thirty years ago the house had been misguidedly whitewashed: most of the white had been weathered off but enough persisted to give the house a scabrous ramshackle slightly unsteady look, perched as it was on a knoll.

Between the house and the tack barn stood a trellised grape arbor which the General no longer had the time or energy to tend. Many of the vines still stubbornly bore inferior fruit from worn-out soil; others, thick as cables, lay tight and twisted within the old trellis, matted solidly enough in places to keep out all but a torrential rain. There was a dusty crooked path through the thirty yards of arbor which the General habitually followed from house to barn.

The tack barn had been modified and soundproofed for use as an armory, where he test-fired new and used military weapons and bench-loaded his sporting guns. The adjacent equipment shed he had turned into a hawk house.

He took Rosalind from the girl's wrist, placed her on a hawk block outside the door where he'd been weathering her for the past month. He attached the jesses, leather straps for her legs. The jesses were fastened through a double-eye swivel; a leather leash five or six feet long ran through the other eye, an arrangement which gave her freedom to leave the block, walk around in the yard, bathe in the concrete trough nearby.

While the General attended to his falcon she entered the hawk house.

The floor inside was earth, hard-packed, swept clean. There were two sharply intersecting planes of light from windows at different heights. Ventilation was good but still the air had a taint, a feathery effluence like that from a still-warm nest taken from the hollow of a tree.

On a rail covered with an old tarp another falcon, this one a male and smaller, raised up with a spreading of wings and hissed at her. She paused, watching, then approached slowly. The tiercel's feathers stood out. He hissed again, angry and afraid.

The General came up behind her, put a hand on her shoulder. "You're staring at him, Carol. He thinks you mean to hurt him."

"He looks half starved."

"He is. He won't eat from my fist. I don't think I'll be able to train him. Sometimes you can't overcome what's wild in them."

"Could I feed him something?"

"You can give him a mouse from the cage on the table."

They were barn mice, gray-brown, summer-plump. She opened the top of the cage. The mice were huddled in opposite corners, trembling, intent on her. She swallowed, reached quickly in, grasped one behind the head, lifted it out. The mouse squeaked helplessly, terrified. She carried it back to the tiercel, stopped several feet in front of him. He rose on his perch again, wings opening, watching the struggle of the mouse in her hand. She stroked its backbone with a finger, eyes dark and thoughtful.

Then with a flip of her wrist she tossed the mouse to the tiercel, who caught the mouse neatly with one foot, killed it with a quick jab of its beak, ate it in two gulps, all but bloodlessly.

She wiped her hands on her jeans, staring. A shudder passed through her. Her eyes looked sleepy, her mouth slack. The pulse in her throat beat strongly.

"Carol?" the General said.

He had to say her name twice before she heard him.

Chapter Thirteen

IN THE NIGHT THEY HEARD HER SOBBING. NOTHING WILD
or frightening to mingle with nightmares but despairing, compulsive sobs, then irregular periods of silence.

Felice was up, heart thudding, hands numb, when Sam came
in by way of the bathroom and turned on a lamp for her. "I'll
go," he said.

It was quiet now. "What do you suppose—"

"I don't know. She's been like that for a while." He tried a
reassuring smile which didn't stick. "Why don't you get back
into bed?"

"Leave the light," she asked him. The room was chilly. After
he'd gone she put a pillow at her back and smoked a cigarette.
A minute or more passed; she heard Carol stirring in her room,
as if to answer Sam's tap at the door. The floor overhead creaked
loudly three or four times. Then she couldn't hear anything.
Felice put the cigarette out but continued to sit up worriedly,
until her heartbeat quieted and she began a nodding doze.

A short abrupt cry half awakened her again. It wasn't repeated. There hadn't been anything about it to alarm her, no
particular inflection. She gazed solemnly at the face of the clock
by the bed—it was five after three—then turned over, burrowed
deep under the covers and slept.

When she awoke again it was with a feeling of guilt, muted
dismay. She lay there unmoving, alert, listening; the sky was the
color and texture of crushed ice but the windows had gold in

them and the trees were filled with tuneful birds: wood thrushes, robins, an imperative cardinal whistling like a traffic cop.

She threw the covers aside, got up, found a heavy robe and put it on with uncoordinated haste, anxiety coming and going in her body like the throb of a sore tooth.

She went into Sam's room. He wasn't there. His bed was cold.

Upstairs the door to Carol's bedroom was closed. Felice opened it as quietly as possible. The drapes were half drawn across south-facing windows. There was a good deal of clutter— she was still unpacking trunks, boxing things for storage. A high-intensity lamp on the desk focused its forgotten light on the pale oak floor. The air in the room was slightly soured from too many cigarettes.

She was asleep on her side, covered to her knees, one hand outthrust and holding a pillow as if she were holding some dream beast away from her throat; the other hand was curled protectively between her breasts. She wore cotton pajamas with a couple of buttons missing. She breathed through her mouth, breath catching in places as if she was on the verge of waking up.

Felice smiled with a sharp sense of relief and had to check a motherly impulse to straighten the blanket, give Carol a little more protection against the morning chill. She left the door slightly ajar and went downstairs. There was a light on in the library, voices. She thought she heard the General speaking. It was early, even for her insomniac father, and she shook her head in exasperation.

But Sam was alone. He was standing near his desk, his back to her. The General's voice continued, raspy, disembodied.

"Hello," she said. Sam gave her a wild startled look, then clutched at his chest and pantomimed heart failure.

"I'm sorry," she said meekly. "What's going on?"

"Oh—" He reached low behind the desk, turned off the tape recorder in a bottom drawer, closed the drawer and locked it. "I was listening to some tapes of a bull session I had with the General. I need a quote for the new *Commentary* piece I've been kicking around."

138

"Horrible example?"

"I'm afraid so."

"Lord, when are you two going to grow up and stop—" She gave up when Sam grinned at her. "I looked in on Carol just now," she told him.

He shook his head tiredly. "She had a rough night. I only came down about an hour ago. Is she sleeping?"

"Not too well. Sam, what was wrong?"

"I think it all finally caught up with her. The drugs they gave her have been hard on her nerves. And she's had mild hallucinations—" Felice looked dismayed. "I'm sure it's nothing to worry about, but we'd better check with the doctor; he might want to change sedatives." Sam took a cigarette from a box, scowled at it, decided against smoking. "One other thing: Gaffney's been pressing her too hard. Under the circumstances I think she's been more than cooperative. I intend to ask him to lay off, at least for a few days until she settles down. His turn to cooperate."

"I agree. Did you make coffee?"

"Instant gunk. Terrible. What time is it, Felice?"

"About six."

"Too late to think about going back to bed. I could get an early train into the city, be home by midafternoon. How about dinner out tonight, the two of us?"

"What about Carol?"

"It was mostly her idea," he said, slightly sheepish. "But give me credit for knowing a good idea when I hear one." He put an arm around her waist and kissed her; it was meant to be casual but there was too much tension in him. She had the notion that if she accidentally tapped him with an elbow he might shatter. He yawned hard enough to crack his jaws, smiled. The arm around her waist felt good to her. Felice snuggled a little closer, rested her head against Sam's shoulder for a few moments. Together they walked back to the kitchen. She let Riggs off the porch.

"Baked eggs? Buttermilk pancakes?"

"Wonderful," Sam said. He sat down at the table, looking at

the dark fireplace. Felice went happily to work. "Almost cold enough for a fire this morning."

"Sam?"

"Hmm? Sorry, I was nodding."

"What did you think when you first saw Carol? I mean, when the police brought her home the other night?"

"I remember thinking I needed another drink. My heart kept squeezing up into my mouth like a plastic beach ball."

"How did she—look to you?"

"Terrible. But she was alive, which is all I cared about." He studied her. "Why?"

"I don't know—I keep reliving it. They brought her in, and for a minute she couldn't place us. She tried to smile, but her eyes—"

"She was out on her feet."

"I know. It was just—awful in a way I can't describe. I didn't know what to say."

"You were fine."

"I still feel strange around Carol. I seem to be—fumbling for an attitude. She's aware of that. Either I'm oppressively *Mom* or else I sound as phony as all the bright chattering types at a bridge luncheon. It's ridiculous. What's *wrong* with me?"

"We all have to settle down. Takes a while."

"I guess it does," she said glumly.

It was a big house and it seemed unexpectedly lonely without Kevin tromping around, two or three friends in tow. For Carol's sake Felice tried to be there as much as possible, but there were demands on her time she couldn't refuse: a little charity work, visits to a friend recovering from major surgery in Grasslands Hospital, an afternoon of bridge, some shopping. Sam had his talk with Gaffney: the investigation was plodding, going nowhere. The FBI man agreed that there was very little more Carol could help them with.

Carol went hawking with the General, sunned herself by the pond until she was the color of still warm beer, took long solitary drives in the Sting Ray, glanced restlessly at television, stayed awake half the night playing favorite records—Barber, Shostakovich, Bruckner, Ives, Janis Joplin, Wes Montgomery—and kept the flower beds weeded for Joseph Dowd. She bruised her foot on a stone and couldn't play tennis. Her appetite was uncertain. She lost more weight. The bruise on her neck became less distinct, faded altogether. She smiled readily but there was little laughter in her; she lacked those unexpectedly gay and gabby moments which Felice treasured and desperately missed.

They would sit together, in the kitchen after dishes or on the screened side porch with the sprinklers whirling in the dusk, and talk. Each time Felice would think she had the key. But the key never quite fit and Carol remained locked up in herself, inexpressibly remote.

On Saturday Sam went in to tape a panel-discussion show for National Education Television. Felice picked him up at the station that afternoon. His suit was wrinkled and he looked hot and undelighted with himself.

"Hi," she said, kissing him. "How was it?"

He slumped beside her in the Mercedes. "The infighting got a little bloody and nothing useful got said. We'll see it next week, Thursday, I think."

"Would a gin sour cheer you up?"

"Like nothing else in this wide world."

"I have to pick up a couple of things at the shopping center in Mount Kisco."

"No hurry. How's Carol?"

"The same."

"Oh."

"She needs somebody desperately. Like Dev."

"Has she mentioned him?"

"No. But I'll bet she's thinking about him just the same."

"Somebody else will come along," Sam said. "We could try talking her into a movie tonight. If she can't have Dev maybe Paul Newman would divert her for a couple of hours."

"She's not the only one," Felice said, grinning.

The parking lot at the shopping center was jammed. Sam volunteered to run in for the steaks she'd ordered. Felice circled slowly, waiting for a place to park. Traffic was sluggish, disorganized, slightly hazardous. Ahead of her a woman with too many kids in a gypsy-looking station wagon had fouled herself up trying to manuever into a narrow space. Felice was boxed in. She mentally called out signals to the frustrated wagon driver but the woman hit another car anyway, leaving paint on a bumper and adding a new fender dent to her collection.

She saw Carol.

In a phone booth in front of the Rexall, no more than a hundred feet away.

Apparently it wasn't a happy conversation. She was listening. Her jaw was set. Her back was arched like a combative cat's.

Scowling, she took her turn. She raked at her blond hair with the fingers of her free hand. For a few moments she seemed to be shouting; her face was contorted. Then she turned in the booth and Felice couldn't see her face any more.

The woman in the station wagon extricated herself and took off in a despairing fog of blue exhaust. Felice was able to move ahead a few yards.

When she glanced at the telephone booth again she saw that Carol had emerged and was staring directly at the Mercedes, but the sun was in her eyes. Felice was startled by the look of heavy-lidded hostility and feral outrage on her face just before she slipped on a pair of big sunglasses. Felice watched her jog down a couple of steps and cut across the asphalt, hair swinging, lips pale from some kind of sunburn cream. She was walking at an angle away from the Mercedes. She hopped into her blue Corvette without opening the door, started it, backed out imperiously, roared away, hand on the wheel, hand on the stick. Somehow she found the holes she needed in the bogged-down traffic. She charged through them recklessly enough to scare several people. She caught the light on the highway, preempted a lane, zoomed north.

Sam returned sooner than Felice expected, spotted her, hurried over.

She was going to mention Carol to him; she decided it wasn't that important. But something else had blocked her. There was too much she would have liked to explain to herself, and couldn't. Mostly she wished she knew who had so thoroughly enraged her daughter. She had not liked that look on Carol's face, the brute insensible anger. She had never seen Carol like that and the memory stayed with her, oppressively, most of the way home.

While Sam showered and changed clothes she mixed drinks and carried them to a long porch overlooking a graceful lawn, a variety of flowering trees and shrubs—glossy abelia, Scotch heather, cinquefoil, Japanese tree lilac and a stately golden rain tree. There was just enough breeze to tremble the leaves of the slim birches at one corner of the porch. She sat down in a favorite basket chair to read a dutiful and maddeningly uninformative note on a postcard from Kevin.

Sam came down in a faded pullover shirt and boat denims, the hair on the back of his neck feathery from moisture; he was cooled, glowing, hugely pleased. Without a word he dropped a fat blue envelope with a travel agent's logo in her lap. She glanced at him, bemused, opened the envelope. Airline tickets, hotels, ground transportation in one package.

"Paris," she said wonderingly. "Amsterdam?"

"Rome too if we feel like it. If you get bored with Paris and Amsterdam."

"Sam! When?"

"We leave the fifth of September. Four weeks."

The arrangements he had made were flexible. He'd bought a good guidebook, detailed maps. They spent the rest of the afternoon going over them. They drank several of the gin sours apiece. At five-thirty Sam put the steaks on the outdoor grill. Carol came home a few minutes later, banging the front screen. She came into the kitchen with her shirttail out, waved at them, opened a can of Coke. She kicked off her sandals and joined them outside. She'd been swimming at the Club, she told them. Chlorine in the pool had reddened her eyes.

"Smell that steak! You two look pleasantly smashed. What's the occasion?"

Felice, eyes glowing, told her. She kissed them both soundly and wandered off, whistling for Riggs, who was flipping a turtle over and over at the edge of the dusky pond. Felice watched, sober enough to be impressed by her obvious good spirits but remembering the other face, the look of the savage. But it was a very special day, she was not going to let anything bother her. She got busy with the salad. Despite her protests Sam made off with her half-empty glass and brought her a fresh drink. Felice shook her head in mock dismay, happier than she'd known how to be in months.

They gorged on steak, salad, potatoes stuffed with tiny shrimp and rebaked with a cheese topping. They laughed a lot in the kitchen, which was lighted by the fading sun. Carol laughed easily for once, and it was good to hear. Felice was too happy most of the time to be absolutely sure of what the conversation was about. She looked at Sam often, with an undoubtedly fatuous smile she couldn't seem to get rid of.

"More steak?" Felice asked Carol, who patted her stomach and groaned.

"No, thanks. Oh, I forgot I had some news."

"What, dear?"

"These two boys I know. They're SDS at Berkeley. I heard from them today; they're coming East for—I don't know—strategy meetings, I guess, to prepare for the demonstrations during the Chicago convention. The Festival of Chicago it's going to be called. The boys have had a tough trip and they wanted to know if I could put them up here for a few days before they get down to business in the city."

"A pair of wild-eyed revolutionaries, huh?" Sam said, chomping.

"They aren't just activists, they're egalitarians. They've been

144

known to shave and wear shoes once in a while. And they're fans of yours, Sam."

"Oh, well, that settles it."

"Plenty of room," Felice murmured. "When do you think—"

"Monday, they said." She turned toward Felice; the last direct light of the sun highlighted the planes of her face, turned her eyes to dark crescents. The perfect edges of her teeth were very white against her full lower lip as she smiled.

Felice had a throbbing headache from too much gin. And perhaps she'd eaten too much, she thought uneasily.

Because there seemed to be hidden laughter in Carol's inflamed eyes, a disturbing laughter now, as if she were savoring a mordant joke.

Felice looked away, suddenly feeling drunken and foolish. She was beginning to find it hard to focus.

"Why don't you rest for a while, Mother? Watch television? I'll clean up."

"Oh, Carol, I couldn't let you." The voice seemed to come from somewhere to the side of her.

"I insist," she said, still smiling. "I really do insist, Mother."

Like so many calamitous dreams it began innocently.

A favorite plaything of childhood had been the glass paper-weight.

Shake it vigorously and there was a blizzard inside.

Hold it upright in two hands and the blizzard became a gentle fall of snow, covering evergreens and a miniature cottage with a red roof.

See the lighted window?

Yes, I see it, Felice replied, gazing solemnly into the crystal.

Look close. Do you see the little girl snug in her bed in the cottage with snow on the roof?

Oh, yes!

Time for you to be snug in your own bed, Felice.

Please can I keep it? she said in her dream voice.

Yes, if you want to. Lie down now, and I'll cover you up.

Are you warm enough? Hold the crystal tight and sleep well. Sweet dreams, Felice.

Good night, Carol, she said. Good night, Sam.

Good night, he said, so tall and smiling down from the foot of the bed.

Felice yawned. And in the morning we'll all go to Paris, she said.

Dream Carol reached for the lamp. *Lights out.*

Lights out! Felice repeated, happily.

She clutched the paperweight protectively. And the snow continued to fall all around while the little girl lay secure in her childhood bed.

The shape of her room became the shape of the crystal, expanding and contracting comfortably, like a glass balloon, with every breath. There were no more straight lines, only curves diversely in motion around and above her, responding to key changes in music felt but unheard, shimmering with the incandescence of the moon's track on dark water. At times they assumed vaguely human shapes. This phantasmagoria seemed old to her but it wasn't alarming, no, not as long as the child slept untroubled in her loving hands.

But somehow she'd been neglectful; a change had taken place inside the paperweight. Snow was no longer falling. The glass felt hot to the touch. Felice shook it anxiously. The cottage bloomed with flame.

She stared at it, astounded, frightened. Then she scratched at the impenetrable glass with her fingernails. The crystal grew hotter. A sob hung in her throat. The child would wake, the child would burn—her fault.

She must take it to Carol. Carol had given the paperweight to her; she would know what to do.

Felice slid down the long long slope of the bed to a banked floor, made her way to the door: it bulged wide, like a noose, to let her through. Down a prism hall lined with mirrors of ice and landscapes melting off the walls, up a complicated stair. The crystal burning, burning, inspiring panic. She screamed and heard chimes, ending in a dull cough of machinery: woggle-wogglewoggle, with a tricky echo fading into nothingness. Silence then, except for a little girl crying helplessly.

At her touch the door to Carol's room swung slowly—like a monument falling off its pedestal. There was a roaring-out of light and sound that transfixed her.

Carol stood before her. Naked head to toe. Hair in a love-nest tangle. There were bold finger marks on plump breast hemispheres. The humidity of passion had collected in the hollows of her seething umber eyes. Sexual anxiety: her fingers hooked like claws. Felice felt shrunken before her, craven. The crying of the child had become a thin wail, all but unheeded.

What do you want? Spoken sharply.

What do I want? Felice thought, at a loss. Numbly she held up the paperweight. Surprised to see it was not a paperweight after all. Just a round drinking glass. She held it in front of her face. Carol, seen through the glass, bulged fatly, like an Indian carving of a fertility goddess.

Smell of blood in the room, as vivid as the smell of burning had been to her. Cut at one corner of Carol's mouth, a pink tone smeared on one exposed white tooth. Carol smiling, flat-lipped, not pretty. Music, not meant for her ears, a coarse earthy shouting female voice, a drumming and squalling that lived in the blood. Panic again, electronically renewed. Fertility music. Behind Carol, so far away on the outcurve of the glass, a man was sprawled on the bed. Sam. Startlingly tumescent. What do I want? Felice asked herself, thoroughly dazed.

It isn't snowing any more, she explained humbly.

Carol came closer, looked unlovingly at her: Felice trembled. But Carol relented and stroked her cheek gently with her fingers, quieting her.

She smiled, a benign smile. *Now look!* she said. *It's snowing again.* And Felice looked as she had been told and there was the paperweight, the trim little cottage, everything just as it had been. While Carol stroked her cheek calmingly she continued to gaze at the stylized winter scene. She didn't hear the wild music any more. Carol had mentioned that she needn't hear it if she didn't want to.

I'll take you down, Dream Carol said at last. *There's no reason for you to get out of bed again. Nothing to worry about.*

No reason, Felice repeated drowsily, watching the snow sift down. But she thought she could see the naked man again, and that bothered her. So she did the sensible thing and put him firmly out of her mind.

I'm not worried, she said sweetly, and went down to her bed hand in hand with Carol. Everything was familiar now, in its place. She held the paperweight, which had always been her very favorite, next to her heart.

Chapter Fourteen

THEY PICKED HIM UP AS SOON AS HE ENTERED THE
International Arrivals Building at JFK; he had come in from
Lisbon on Swissair. It was a hot Sunday night and the over-
burdened airport was having one of its classic jams: planes were
landing two hours late from the stacks overhead and customs
was clogged with weary waiting people.

"Dev Kaufman?"

Dev stopped and looked tiredly at the two men. "Yes," he
said.

"FBI, Mr. Kaufman," the spokesman said, showing his cre-
dentials. "My name is Crockett. This is Mr. Hirsch of the Im-
migration and Naturalization Service. If you'll give him your
passport and luggage claim checks he'll clear you through
customs. In the meantime we'd like to talk to you."

"Why?"

"That'll be explained, Mr. Kaufman. We'd appreciate your
cooperation. It shouldn't take long."

Dev studied them curiously and unworriedly, shrugged,
handed over his passport. He was toting an expensive-looking
leather bag with a wide shoulder strap. It was somewhat like an
old-fashioned mailman's pouch, but smaller and more stylish.
Under his other arm he carried an artist's sketch portfolio.

"This is all the luggage I have," Dev explained, slapping the
bag.

"Keep it with you." Hirsch smiled and turned away. Dev

went along with the FBI agent to a small unmarked office in the depths of the building. Another man was waiting there: a homely mellowed Irishman who looked like nothing else in the world but a cop.

"Mr. Kaufman, this is special agent Robert Gaffney."

"Hi," Dev said disinterestedly, shaking hands. He eyed a tape recorder on the desk. The room seemed little used. The floor was dirty. Some sheets of paper were curled and yellowing on a bulletin board. "What's this about?"

"Please sit down, Mr. Kaufman," Gaffney urged.

Dev hesitated, then put his belongings down and took the offered chair. He was tall and lean with a lot of reach, a bright-eyed boy slowly peaking to maturity. His hair was unkempt but not untidily long. He had big ears and a small nose and a look of introverted compassion. He wore the traveling costume of semi-indigent youth—old chinos, scuffed work shoes, a khaki jacket over a blue work shirt. The clothes were clean and he was clean.

Crockett got the tape recorder ready. Gaffney gave Dev a cigarette, sat down to light his own.

"Late last month Carol Watterson was kidnapped," he said, snapping his lighter shut.

Dev looked startled and then as he began to think about other possibilities his mouth opened slightly and he swallowed hard and his bright blue eyes sickened. Gaffney put an end to the reaction he'd been waiting to judge by saying, "She's home now. Either she escaped or was set loose. The kidnappers never attempted to collect the money they were asking."

"She's not—hurt, or anything."

"Carol's fine. They kept her prisoner in two ways: with drugs, and with a rope or chain attached to a dog collar around her neck. She remembers how she was kidnapped, but nothing of the five days that followed."

"Do you know who—"

"We have several leads that may be important. We have a description of one of the men involved. He may have been wearing a disguise. Would you look at the sketches of our suspect?" He took them from his case on the desk and handed them over. Dev stared at the man, with and without his shades and bushy hair. He shook his head slowly. "Am I supposed to know him?"

"We hoped you might recognize him."

"Sorry, I don't."

"Here are two more people we're interested in." He gave Dev the photographs of Jim and Babs Hendersholt.

"I don't think—no, I'm sure I've never seen either of them. I don't know the name. They did it? Kidnapped Carol?"

"They could be implicated," Gaffney said, retrieving the photos.

"Does Carol know them?"

"She says not."

"Where did it happen?"

"Not far from her home, in Fox Village."

"And there was a ransom note?"

"It looked like a legitimate kidnapping in every way. They wanted two hundred twenty-five thousand. But they never followed through."

"Where are those two from? Berkeley?"

Gaffney looked approvingly at him. "A good hunch. Palo Alto."

"But they had to know Carol, or know something about her. I think her grandfather's worth a lot of money. Why didn't the kidnappers grab Carol on the Coast?"

"Apparently the plot took months to develop. They might have decided it would be simpler to take her in Fox Village."

"They doped her so she wouldn't know what was going on."

"That's the way it looks."

"Then how could she have escaped?"

"One of the drugs they gave her was experimental. They may have misjudged its potential."

"Good God," Dev said, shaking his head. "You're sure she's all right now?"

"Why don't you go see her?" Gaffney suggested.

Dev was silent for a long time. "That's what I—came back for," he said in a low voice. "I wanted to see Carol again. It took time to decide that."

"How did you two happen to break it off?"

"We had fundamental differences. Maybe I didn't react well to the domestic situation we created. At the same time I felt—locked into the scientific establishment. Into subtle patterns of personal betrayal. I wanted to grow in other directions before I made the major decision about what to do with my life. She couldn't accept that I might still have doubts about what was right for me."

"Where have you been all this time, Dev?"

"Here and there. Spain; Portugal. Little villages mostly, places I doubt you've heard of. Most recently I was in Portimão; the Algarve's not so crowded now, you can still sleep on the beach. In another five years it'll be like the Costa del Sol." He dropped his cigarette on the floor, stepped on it. "Loafing's not my style anyway. I can't pretend I'm working while I try to learn how to put a painting together. Maybe I'll give Central America a try. I've got the language. I'll build something for somebody, teach school if I can."

"Taking Carol with you, Dev?"

"I'm going to give it a damn good try," Dev said seriously, and then he let a smile slip. "When I get up the nerve to go crashing in on her. Is that all you need from me?"

"That's all. Thanks."

Dev picked up his things. The reluctant smile appeared again, with subliminal speed. "In the beginning you must have thought I did it," he said. "Made off with Carol, I mean."

"In my line of work I have to think of everything."

"It isn't a bad idea, if that's the only way I can convince her she ought to be with me."

"Let me know first so I don't lose sleep over it, Dev. Lost too much already."

"Fair enough. So long."

"Luck," Gaffney said, shutting off the tape recorder.

As she usually did, Felice packed Sam's suitcase for him. She wanted to drive him to La Guardia but Sam gradually discouraged her, pointing out that it would mean two tedious round trips in three days.

He put in a couple of manuscripts he was working on. "Hey," he said. "No shirts?"

Felice smacked her forehead lightly with her open hand and selected four shirts from a drawer, hesitated over a fifth. "Do you want this Gant with the clubby stripe?"

"Sure." He put his arm around her, kissed her glum face. "That's a long-range case of the blues you're working on. All that booze I fed you Friday night?"

Felice pressed a cheek against his shoulder. "No, I'm over that. I've never had such a depressing hangover. Ughh, two days of it was—a bit much." She closed her eyes and sighed. "I guess I'm a little blue at that. I'm going to miss you, that's why."

"I'm sorry to leave you stuck with a houseful of company."

"I don't mind. And it'll be good for Carol to have chums around." She left him, packed the shirts, checked items off a mental list, closed and locked the case and then stared at it, hands on hips, preoccupied.

Sam was watching her with a faint concerned smile. "Tell you what: Fels Whitlund isn't using his place at Fire Island much. We could borrow it for the weekend. Good clean sand and ocean and blue sky and food when we feel like it. No company. No TV. Just good music on that huge damn tape machine of Fels' and some competitive games if we're in the mood. A real throat-cutter, like Monopoly."

"And time to read a book or two," she said, brightening. "Oh, Lord! Wouldn't that be a miracle? I get so starved for books, and it's been such a mixed-up summer I haven't—"

"I'll call Fels right now," he promised.

She stopped him and fixed him with a fierce eye. But her tone was gentle. "You have been so awfully damned thoughtful and good to me lately."

"There's a lot of neglect to make up for," he said, properly contrite. "I'm tryin'."

"And you love me?"

"I love you."

Her face softened. "And do you still want me, Sam? Do you still want to make love to me?"

Sam was surprised, then shook his head chidingly. "What makes you think I've ever stopped wanting you?"

"Because we haven't made love. Not in weeks. And it bothers me when I want you so very much—"

He kissed her, not to quiet her but as if it had been on his mind for a long time and he didn't care to wait any longer.

"One more like that," Felice told him, heart unsteady, "and you don't go anywhere today."

"That's a thought."

"No, only kidding. It'll keep for the weekend. We'll keep. I think. Won't we?"

"Just barely," Sam said, as awed as she was.

Felice kept a lunch date with an old school friend who lived in Greenwich, then did some hasty gift shopping at Altman's in White Plains on her way home. It was five-thirty when she turned into the birch-lined drive. There was a dusty dark-blue Pontiac Le Mans in front of the house. Two boys were sitting on the top step of the porch as if they didn't know what to do next.

The drive wasn't wide enough for her to pull around the other car. She parked and got out. "I'm Felice," she said. "Hello. I don't know where Carol could be."

They were quite different from each other and not what she had expected. The big one looked as if he had come of age by being banged around a lot. He had the kind of sloping powerful shoulders and muscular neck and close-cropped smallish head that reminded her of mountain cats. He had casual ways and a grin that was easy to take. He looked too old for college, perhaps ten years older than his companion, but it was difficult to tell. The second boy was, perhaps, Mexican, with a skin that was the color of old redwood in the dimming light. He had his share of Indian blood, apparent in the bones of his face and the impenetrable eyes, but his mouth was full, with an unexpected softness that was not womanish but graceful and appealing. His hair style was pure mod. He seemed shy and not at ease. Felice liked him instantly.

"Hi," the big one said. "Rich Marsland. This is Arturo Regalo."

"Turo," the boy murmured, with a nod of his head that was close to a bow, and he waited with an attempt at nonchalance he might have copied from his friend, who clearly would be at home wherever he happened to be standing.

"I hope you boys haven't been waiting long."

"Not long," Rich said. "We walked around. You certainly have a beautiful place here."

"Thank you. Was Carol's car in the garage?"

"A blue Sting Ray?"

"That's the one. She couldn't have gone far; she's probably next door at the General's. You boys look as if you've had a long drive, so why don't we get you settled in? I'm sure Carol will be along in a few minutes."

They had three suitcases between them. Felice gave them the largest of the guest bedrooms on the second floor. In her own room she changed, went down to the kitchen. She hummed to herself as she put boned and breaded chicken breasts into a glass dish to bake. By the time the boys came down the back stairs she had completed her other preparations for dinner.

Rich drank Southern Comfort neat. Turo liked B and B. Felice fixed a brandy for herself and took them to the side porch, where it was already dark enough for lamps. Even before they settled down she saw Carol coming, the General towering and gimpy beside her.

She was carrying a falcon on her wrist, a thin and misbegotten-looking bird who appeared to have accidentally flown into a fan. He sat docilely enough on the falconer's glove the General had provided, but he had a fevered murderous eye, which made Felice distinctly uneasy. She hoped the two of them knew what they were doing. Wild hawks never bothered men; only the ones trained to be unafraid sometimes turned disastrously on their captors.

"He's mine!" she said jubilantly to Felice as they came up to the porch. "He ate for me, and he's mine. I'm going to train him myself. Hey, now, Rich! Turo. Good to see you. Sorry I'm late. Let me put Bird here on the back porch."

"On Riggs' porch?" Felice said doubtfully.

"Oh, Riggs won't mind, he's entertaining an elegant bitch on the other side of the pond. Excuse me! Rich Marsland, Turo Regalo, this is my grandfather, General Henry Phelan Morse, you es ay ret."

"You're the revolutionaries," the General said, offering his knobby hand.

"But soft-spoken," Rich said. He had an inch or two on the General—also a good crushing grip, as Felice was pleased to notice. The two men looked each other in the eye like strategists.

"Where are the love beads, boys?" the General said, just managing not to sound nasty.

Felice saw Carol compute his mood with a dark glance. "Now, don't start," she said. "You promised."

"That's not my style," Rich told the General, with an imperturbable smile.

Felice glanced at Turo Regalo. He was on his feet, looking stiffly correct in fussy modish clothes. His lack of expression was nearly deathlike.

"Got any pot on you, Mr. Marsland?" The General was still in Rich's grip, or perhaps it was the other way around; Felice didn't know. She knew this sort of confrontation was childish of her father, and that annoyed her. A couple of significant

156

clues she had learned to look for confirmed that the General had begun his cocktail hour about eleven that morning. It had been happening too frequently of late. Something was bothering him, then. She had no idea what it could be.

At this stage he could go either way: he could settle down and taper off and be amiable company, or he could start drinking in earnest and be a bastard.

"I don't believe in grass, General," Rich Marsland explained, making the vernacular correction. He was as comfortable as if he'd been coping with the old man all his life. "I think it may be a dangerous drug. Anyway I know it's bad for the system."

"That Southern Comfort you've got in your hand can be dangerous if you're not accustomed to it," the General observed, in a voice that told its own story about Southern Comfort whiskey.

"Well," Rich said easily, holding the glass up to the light, "this is the kind of danger I like to be in."

The General stared at him, lower lip protruding, eyes hooded, spectral, unreadable; then he bellowed a laugh. As if by mutual consent they let go of each other. Felice glanced at Carol, who had been waiting uncertainly; now she turned and rushed off with her bird. Felice smiled as indulgently as she could.

"Can I fix you something, General? We'll have dinner in half an hour. I hope you're staying."

"Sure. A little whiskey. Don't overdo me, honey. Boys? Sit down. I'm going to tell you why I damn well don't trust anybody under thirty."

Dinner went smoothly. Everyone had an appetite except Turo, who sat next to the General and seemed to regret it. He picked at his food but drank two glasses of the Rhone wine. He said almost nothing, deferring to Rich. In a complex way he seemed to be dependent on Rich without actually being a satellite or psychologically in debt to him. Felice saw that he stared often at Carol, who was at her best, stunning in a simple beige dress she'd put on for dinner, her skin honey-dark and her eyes large and lustrous, lips a pale frosted pink, hair very pale and pulled back, loose over one bare shoulder. She joked and laughed a lot. Felice felt very proud of her. Naturally she had eyes for Rich. Turo seemed to know and accept this. Felice wondered if Turo had a crush on her daughter. He was so serious and poignantly reserved, and she felt a tender sorrow for him.

They took their coffee to the porch.

"Leeches," the General said, in what for him was a jovial tone of voice, "nothing but a pack of goddam leeches and jackals sucking at the vitals of this nation! None of you has what it takes to rise up on his back legs and say, By *God* I'm a Red and I'm proud of it!"

Arturo grimaced. Felice regarded her father with a mild glower. Rich, as usual, was smiling nervelessly. The General had badgered him all through dinner, ignoring Felice's efforts to get him off The Subject. Rich had, with deftness and subtlety, badgered back.

"We're a mixed bag, General, in the hip sense of the word. We all have our particular bags, our beliefs, our plans for a better world. Maybe there are some hard-core Marxists involved in the Movement, but a very few. Because the young are idealists, not dogmatists. A good many of us are sentimental and elect heroes like Che. That's harmless as far as it goes; don't label us or write us off because of our need for heroes: who has the Establishment provided lately? I dig Che and I dig Billy Graham, for very different reasons. Just say revolutionaries, General. That's what we are. And as activists it's natural that we do some belly-biting in our confrontations, because that's what offends us most—the gross, self-satisfied, swollen underbelly of the country we were born in, and would like to find a home in if it isn't too late."

"Revolutionaries? You don't even know what you're doing most of the time. All we get from you is provocations and platitudes. Now, those boys in Paris knew how to pull it off. Barricades! Siege. Diversionary tactics. Of course they went to a good school, I have to admit it; they learned their tactics from the pros in Moscow."

Rich said, impiously but perhaps seriously, "Maybe what we need is a pro to help our take-over, General. Someone with your savvy."

"Help you pull this country down into the muck? Pull it down where every bloody-minded little anarchist can piss on our heritage and our institutions?"

"Now, General," Felice said, because it did sound as if he was going to get genuinely wrought up instead of pleasantly fervid.

"Yes, we could use your help, General. I think you're an honest man, and we need an honest man to tell us the truth, help us search out what is good and usable and worth preserving in our society. You can't be all that satisfied with things as they are. Help us. If a few institutions should tumble in the process, well and good. Institutions aren't necessarily valuable, General. Only ethics have lasting value."

"We're learning a new set of ethics, and adapting them to our requirements," Turo said gravely, and everybody was a little surprised that he had spoken.

The General studied him with a thoroughness meant to be intimidating. "You're not an American, are you?" It was rude but not cutting. Arturo Regalo swallowed and there was a flash of temper in his normally placid eyes: Felice decided that he hadn't participated before because he was mortally afraid of being offended and disgracing himself with his temper.

"I've always been an American," Turo explained. "Since the age of fourteen I've been a United States citizen."

"Do you have any love for this country?" the General demanded.

"Yes, sir. I have a great deal of love for it."

"Señor Regalo, an honorable man doesn't kill what he loves."

159

Turo flinched slightly from anger but held the General's gaze. It was quiet on the porch. Rich was not smiling now; he looked intent and possibly displeased.

Turo said in a dry controlled voice, "An honorable man kills only what is degenerate, and wanton, and destructive. He kills when he has no other choice but to kill."

The General sipped his after-dinner coffee. "You've given that a lot of thought," he said at last.

"I've given it a lot of thought," Arturo replied, and he was trembling.

"Arturo's a killer, all right," Felice heard Carol say good-humoredly. "With a pool cue."

"That so? Fancy yourself pretty good with a stick, Turo?"

Turo looked confused, then abashed. He glanced at Carol, who grinned reassuringly at him.

"I play a little pool myself," the General allowed.

"Oh-oh," Carol said in a bantering tone. "*Now* what have I done?" But she looked relieved; the tension was going.

"For money," the General said. "I'm strictly a money player. That's not your game, probably."

"I've been there," Turo told him, with a quick glittering smile, and nothing at all in his eyes.

"How about you, Rich?"

"Count me out. Not when the sharks are in the water."

The General did something very unusual, for him. He put an arm around Turo's shoulders, squeezed affectionately. Turo looked slightly shocked, then felt compelled to relax and accept the embrace.

"Let's move the party over to my place," the General suggested.

Chapter Fifteen

SAM CALLED THE NEXT AFTERNOON.

"How's the conference going?"

"Like most of these things," he grumbled. "Nobody can agree what we're here for. Are you OK? What are the boys like?"

"Well-mannered and no trouble at all. Naturally the General came for dinner last night, and he tried to tear up the pea patch, as my Aunt Myra used to say. But Rich handled him well."

"Who's Rich?"

"Rich Marsland. Carol's not saying but I think she has more than a casual interest in him. He's big and confident and talks well. He can be glib. He smiles too much. I don't know."

"Don't you like him?"

"I don't think he's right for Carol. There's something very calculating about him. The other boy is Turo. From Central America originally. He's a treasure. I'm mad about *him*."

"Sounds like I'd better not stay away too long."

"Purely maternal, Sam. But please hurry home anyway."

For dinner the women prepared baked spaghetti, garlic loaves and a huge antipasto, the General's favorite meal. There was plenty of wine again. The General had established a testy rapport with Rich. Turo, having done very well at best-ball the night before, seemed more easily able to accommodate his deep-seated dislike of the General; he had his passions in balance. He wasn't talkative but when he weighed in with an opinion the General listened with rare respect, and never chopped him off before he could finish, as he often did to Rich. Turo was young and not aggressive; even so there was a sureness about him, a level dignity that a sensible man would not want to abuse.

Carol seemed very tired; Felice was sure that she hadn't anticipated the strain of entertaining so soon after her ordeal. But she was determined to carry it off. She hadn't mentioned the kidnapping to Rich and Turo, and she was not likely to.

The weather turned as they were sitting at dinner; all day it had been dead calm and sullenly hot, the sky massed into gray-tinged clouds going nowhere, cutting the sun to a rim, a biting glare. Now the air was cooling. They heard the effect of the wind before the wind itself, leaves slapping furiously together, showing their pale-green undersides in a gale, in vivid storm light. Leaves were torn from limbs and pressed eerily against the glass of the dining-room windows like the whitened hands of the dead. The lights dimmed a couple of times. The house was brought to creaking life by the brute insistence of the wind. Thunder was anticipated, a kind of dismal pressure on the sub-conscious, on full stomachs.

Conversation became difficult, dwindled. Felice saw Carol wipe at a dribble of red wine before it could fall and stain her dress. She looked a little tight and her hands were unsteady. She had done her hair a different way tonight and Felice, who had enjoyed the wine herself, sometimes found herself staring, as if at a total stranger. Felice had a headache and a gritty sense of being distracted by shadows, by spirits massed and willing to announce once the banging of an upstairs shutter ceased and the air was properly charged for their performances.

Only the General seemed unimpressed by the threat of heavy weather.

"Let's move the party to my place," he said ritualistically, lighting a cigarette. "Turo, I've got some evening up to do."

Carol tried to beg off to clean up the kitchen but Felice shooed her out with the others, then settled down for aspirin and a stabilizing cup of coffee. From where she was sitting in the kitchen she could see them hurrying in the direction of the

General's scabby castle, braced against the wind and ducking flying leaves, Riggs tagging along like quixotic fire.

He does enjoy them, she thought. How long since he'd had this much fun? The boys had been good for him. Too bad they couldn't stay much longer.

Her head felt a little better. Why did she have this mad impulse lately to drink everybody under the table? She smiled and nodded to the music of the wind chimes on the back porch. She felt a slumberous sense of brick and hearth and solid homely containment. She dozed.

Someone knocking at the back screen awakened her, scared her. Felice sat up and saw him dimly, waiting on the porch steps. She went and turned on the porch light but still couldn't see him well enough. It wasn't raining yet. The wind chimes tinkled pleasantly.

"Yes?" she said from the kitchen.

"Mrs. Holland? I rang the front doorbell. Nobody came, so I thought it might not be working."

"Who are you?"

"It's Dev, Mrs. Holland. Dev Kaufman. We met once in San Francisco."

She recognized his voice then. "Dev? Good Lord, what are you doing here? We'd heard you were in Europe."

"I was. I got back Sunday."

"Well—I think you'd better come in." She unlatched the screen door and the wind almost took it out of her hands. He ducked inside. He wore a pale hat and a poverty-stricken raincoat coming apart at the seams. "I'm sorry about the bell; sometimes it conks out on us. How did you get here, Dev? Why didn't you call?" She didn't mean it as a rebuke, but he seemed to take it that way.

"I didn't want to do that; I thought—" He looked away from her, around her, as if expecting to find Carol in the kitchen.

"You thought Carol wouldn't want to see you? Of course she would, Dev. Let's don't stand out here. Have you eaten? We had spaghetti; it's still warm."

"Thank you, I'm not hungry."

"Some coffee, then." She took him firmly by the elbow and he came along, hunching his shoulders, looking hounded and worried.

"Just barging in this way—" he muttered.

"Dev, it's perfectly all right, we're very pleased to see you. Where are you staying?"

"No place. I mean, I spent last night out by the airport—"

"Then you're staying with us," Felice assured him. "I hope you brought your clothes with you."

"In the car. But I couldn't—"

"You won't be any trouble. There are two other boys staying here for a few days. Friends of Carol's from Berkeley."

That startled him. "Who?"

"Rich Marsland and Arturo Regalo."

Dev shook his head. "I don't know them; they must have been after my time."

"Everybody's next door at the General's. I'll phone Carol."

He stripped his coat and slumped in a chair and looked at her almost pleadingly. "Could I have that cup of coffee first?" Felice found his state of nerves appealing, and, although she was not altogether sure why, she was very grateful that he had come.

Dev sat with the cup of steaming coffee in both hands, long fingers overlapping. His dark sideburns curled downward to the angle of his jaws. On the slightly overfleshed face he'd had just a year ago they might have seemed childishly opulent, too contrived. But he looked harder and sun-cured now. Wisdom had made unkind demands on the will-o'-the-wisp boy, slowed and deepened him. So he was here to claim Carol, she thought, and felt a chill of affection and pleasure.

"I heard about the kidnapping," he said, looking up.

"You did? How?"

"FBI. They took me in hand as soon as I stepped off the plane from Lisbon. They must have had some idea I knew what was behind it, since Carol and I—"

"What next?" Felice said, sounding indignant.

"How rough was it for her?"

"You wouldn't believe how she looked the night the police brought her home. She'd been wandering for hours. She knew her name; she didn't remember much else. But she's fine now. See for yourself, when you're ready." Felice favored him with an advocate's smile; he replied with a shrug but he looked competent. She picked up the phone.

There were floodlights in aluminum shells on the property, two on poles beside the tennis court, two more high in the trees where the General's land adjoined, and they provided enough illumination so that there was no hazard in the walk between the two houses, even on the darkest nights.

Felice waited on the porch. She deliberately hadn't mentioned Dev to Carol. When she came she was alone.

"Who is it?" she asked, grimacing. "Gaffney? What do they want this time of the night?"

They went in together. Dev had been washing up in the closet-size lavatory under the back stairs. He returned to the kitchen rolling down his sleeves with an air of having tentatively settled in, offering himself to Carol with a self-conscious nod that Felice disapproved of: he could have used a touch of arrogance, she thought.

"Hello, Carol," Dev said, looking closely at her, appearing badly startled. Felice saw her blink inquiringly at Dev as if he was only slightly familiar, like the newspaper delivery boy. Astonishment quickly altered this initial mild reaction; she tried to smile at him.

"Carol?" Dev said again, and seemed to want to touch her. She gingerly moved a step away and glanced at Felice, still smiling; but her eyes looked grim and there was no pleasure in her manner.

"What are you—where did—"

"Dev just now came," Felice said gently.

165

Her lip curled disapprovingly. She faced Dev. "You just came?" She struggled to keep her anger at a proper pitch. "After all this time? You show up here? Well, I hope I don't sound ungrateful, Dev, but I don't care to see you. I don't want to talk to you. Please go."

Felice said quickly, "Carol, you can't—"

"I am not going to argue with anyone," she said, raising her voice imperiously. Her cheeks were burning. "I *mean* what I say. You finished us, Dev. It's over."

He was unprepared for this, for curt dismissal. "Not yet," he said, in a low voice.

They stared at each other, clenched and indecisive. "Put it this way," she said. "You're a *little* late."

"Somebody else?" Dev asked, finding his own anger.

She looked away. "Yes."

"Who?"

"Listen, Dev, this is humiliating. I'm not going to stand here and—" She stopped for breath, losing impetus and emotion rapidly; when she continued her head was bent and her tone was glum. "I suppose you thought catching me off guard would be a good idea. Well, it worked, but it's a bad idea. Be sensible for once, Dev. I don't need you. I don't want you. Now, how blunt do I have to be before you're satisfied?" She gave him another look and then in a parody of exasperation said, "You really want to hear it? All right, Dev: Fuck off." She walked by him without haste or loss of dignity, barely brushing against him, her hands limp at her sides; she left the kitchen.

Dev spoke through the lingering chill. "What's the matter with her voice?"

Felice said, "She was hit in the throat, or half strangled. They made her wear a dog collar. There was a terrible bruise. I thought she was speaking normally again."

He shook his head. "She doesn't sound like herself."

"Drink your coffee," Felice suggested.

"I did."

"There's more on the stove. I'll pour you another cup."

"I was told to go," he said, as if he might laugh, but his eyes were utterly barren.

"It's my house," Felice said toughly, "and nobody gets booted out unless I say. I'll talk to Carol."

Felice found her in the dining room, looking dispossessed and at odds with herself, gazing at a vast and sternly bucolic Hudson Valley landscape by John F. Kensett. They had been hearing thunder all evening; now it was closer, within their sphere, visceral.

"That boy—"

She gritted her teeth but didn't turn on Felice. "Oh, Jesus, Mother, really! He doesn't have the judgment or common courtesy to—"

"He wanted to tell you he loves you, and not with a telephone in the way."

"I got thoroughly fed up abiding by his whims. I don't care if he loves me. I don't love him."

"Are you in love with Rich?"

"I *like* Rich. I'm not making any commitments for a long time to come."

"Then you shouldn't be afraid of hearing Dev out."

All the light in the room was reflected from the glazed surface of the painting. She looked toward Felice, her face falling into shadow. "I suppose that means he's staying."

"Yes. And you shouldn't try to run him off. He looks as if he could be stubborn."

She laughed derisively. "Stubborn's not the word. I lived with him, if you didn't know."

"I knew, Carol."

She chewed avidly at a thumbnail. Thunder seemed to press them closer together, an intimacy which Felice, who was not happy with her daughter, resisted.

"Mother, you might be making a mistake if you let him stay," she said unexpectedly, in a softly belligerent voice.

There was a lick of lightning on the opposite wall, by the windows. The long withheld storm was threatening again.

"It's settled," Felice said shortly.

"You'd better put him in the cottage. I don't think he'd be happy sharing a bath with Rich and Turo. And I don't want him next to me." She walked away. "I'm tired; I'm going up to bed. Would you leave the door unlocked for the boys? The General may keep them up late."

"All right."

She paused in the doorway, head inclined and pressing against the jamb. "You sound cold. I'm sorry. I'm so tired—my knees are like rubber bands. Please understand, I just couldn't be love and kisses and how *are* you, Dev? He put me over the jumps, Mother. I don't like being reminded so soon, by good old Dev in person."

"Give him a chance," Felice suggested.

"Of course," she said, politely ironic. "Good night."

Dev had moved out to the back porch. The wind was trying to snatch the screen door off its hinges.

"Going to rain."

"Dev, I'm afraid she doesn't want to see you tonight."

"No kidding," Dev said calmly.

"I know she'll be more reasonable tomorrow after a decent night's sleep. She really hasn't had much stamina since we got her back."

"Well, actually, I think I'd better be going."

"Oh, no, I wouldn't turn a knight out on a dog like this."

Dev chuckled dutifully. "How does that joke go? I've forgotten."

"Too involved for me to remember. I can't remember the one about Herman's berry, either. Look, I'm going to put you in the cottage out there. Ordinarily it belongs to the Dowds, but I don't think they'd mind."

"Well—"

"The other boys will be gone in a couple of days. And there isn't anybody else, Dev, if that helps."

He came back into the kitchen looking thoughtful. The

168

knuckles of his left hand were scraped and bloody, perhaps from being rubbed over and over against the screen.

"It helps," he said, with a vivid kind smile. "Thanks for wanting to help."

In her room Felice wrote letters while waiting for the thunderstorm to develop. Twice the lights receded to a dull yellow glow, sprang on again almost at once. Finally she grew tired of postponing her bath. Before filling the tub she looked out the streaming windows: the western sky was boiling, illuminated by broad flares of lightning that held no immediate threat. Thunder was nearer, deflected by the shivering glass. Apparently there were several storms in the area tonight. The rain continued soft, soporifically steady. Felice added a measure of oil to her bath. The warm oiled water clung to her skin and she felt pleasantly enclosed, embryonic, untroubled. She soaked for a quarter of an hour, until the water was tepid, then toweled herself until her skin glowed. She put on an expensive layered gown that was as light against her body as a cloud.

She turned back the covers on the canopied bed, smiling to herself. She hoped the storms would miss for the remainder of the night, but she welcomed the rain, the drugging rain. She yawned and remembered to go down the hall to Kevin's room to see if any of the rain had come in around a sash window that wasn't watertight.

She found some leakage, which she wiped off the sill and hardwood floor.

Kevin's windows overlooked the back yard and the Dowd cottage. As Felice was resetting the blinds she saw a figure below: Carol, slanting through the wetness, holding a slicker above her head like an awning. She ducked under the eaves of the cottage, shook out her slicker, knocked on the door. Felice studied her, speculative, amused, hopeful. After Carol entered the cottage she returned to her room, where she read herself to sleep in five minutes' time.

The thud of a car door awakened her a couple hours later. She sat up feeling numb across the shoulders and looked hazily at the ornate antique clock on her dresser. It was nearly two. She closed the volume of Marianne Moore's poems which she had been reading and groped to the front windows. It was now raining much harder. Lightning seared the black sky, close enough to make her flinch. She saw Dev standing, trancelike, in the drive below, his back to her. He was wearing his now soggy raincoat and hat, holding his leather bag by the strap. As the fierce light waned and thunder cracked, Dev tossed his bag into the front seat of the rental Ford, got in quickly himself. Felice was wide awake now. She hadn't seen his face but because of the abruptness of his movements she sensed that he was angry. He drove away, tires slicing through mirror pools of water.

She wondered what had gone wrong. What had Carol said to him, to send him off this way, in the middle of the night?

A jolt of lightning turned her, trembling, from the windows. Felice sat on the bed and reached for her cigarettes. Before she could light one she heard another car. She returned to the windows in time to see the car, obscure in the torrent, turning into the road, highlighted briefly as it passed the lamppost. The car was Rich Marsland's Le Mans.

Felice doubted if it was a coincidence, both of them driving off at the same time. It occurred to her that Carol might have ordered them all to pack up and leave, but that made very little sense.

She knew that she wanted to talk to Carol. She smoked half her cigarette, put it out, selected a robe and went upstairs. Carol wasn't in her room.

The house was silent, silence felt as a tension emphasized by the momentary pauses in the wind-driven rain, the brilliant sledge blows of lightning outside. Felice went numbly down to the second floor and into Kevin's room, opened the blinds there. The cottage below was dark, shrouded, shrunken by rain. A caustic burst of lightning half closed her eyes. Felice swallowed a taste of something bitter and retreated from the window, trying to think. Had Carol gone with Dev? She tried to recall if there had been anyone else in the car, but she'd had only a brief look.

A good night for an elopement, she thought. But she couldn't make herself believe it. Dev had not looked like a man on his way to a hasty wedding. And Carol would never—

She drifted out into the hall, chilled, and closed Kevin's door behind her.

The hall lights went off suddenly, without a preliminary flicker, leaving her in blackness. She had been half expecting this but she shuddered just the same.

The lights came on within a few seconds.

And went out again before she could adjust.

Then they blinked to life and glowed dismally, precariously low, so low that she scarcely cast a shadow as she walked toward her room.

There was a forceful easing in the storm, a taut suspension of the rain. Felice looked at a high window, reflectant, rain trails like molten metal upon it. In the lull she found it hard to breathe. She was aware of a fury above her, of the worst of the storm to come, and she wanted to be in her bed.

Someone came in downstairs. She heard the whack of the screen door on the back porch, a sweet tinkling from the wind chimes.

Felice turned and went to the head of the stairs. As she reached them the weak lights gave up and it was black again. Her eyes smarted; she saw an afterglow, a metallic oscillating rainbow.

"Carol?" she inquired, listened. No reply. But she heard—

There was no way to be sure; the rain was hitting again. A kind of snuffling groan, then labored effortful sounds. Then she couldn't really hear anything through the rain hiss and cataract. The long silence scared her.

"Carol!" she said. Hall lights flared on, hurting her eyes. Felice squinted at the floor of the center hall below. No one there. She went down, a slow step at a time. She could see that the front door was closed.

The lights flickered just before she reached the first floor. *Stop it!* she thought irritably, as if someone were playing a demented joke. She could feel the beat of her shocked heart in her throat, in her fingertips. She was fainting cold.

"Carol?" she said, demanded. *"Please?"*

From a glint the lights failed completely. Felice froze to the banister. She was listening, listening, but there was nothing to hear. She descended the last three steps. Living room to her right. Windows a torrid whiteness, walls richly blacked with enlivened shadows, but nothing human discernible there.

"Where are you?" Felice asked, in a voice too choked to be audible more than a few feet away. She heard the back screen, clapping in the wind, the glassy notes of the wind chimes.

Perhaps, she thought, perhaps someone had gone out and left the door unlatched.

The lightless seconds dragged on; Felice stood rigidly in the center hall, slowly turning her head. A bolt paled her face to the color of mercury. She caught her breath and became, very gradually, sensible and voluntary. She forced herself to go toward the kitchen.

It began again, somewhere in front of her.

Hah—huh-ah. Breathy, explosive.

She whirled and ran for the front door. Outside something heavy, like a tree limb, crashed, its shadow in glissade across the wind. Felice turned again, seized a metal vase from a table. The weight of it kept her from bolting into hysteria.

"Carrrrrr—" she screamed.

Hah, it said to her, grisly, expectant. It was not Carol, she knew that. It couldn't possibly be Carol.

Huh, it pleaded.

Felice beat against the oaken front door, wrestled with the lock. The overhead light came crisply on, throwing her antic shadow to the ceiling. Behind her, in the kitchen, the thing dropped with a clump and a clatter, as if overwhelmed by the presence of light. It groaned.

Felice set off down the long hall to the kitchen, momentarily impelled by terror to find out what was possessing her.

She halted in the doorway, saw it lying near the sink. She didn't hear her own sucked-in scream.

There was a muddy track on the vitreous tiles. He had been drenched by the rain. His hands and feet were lumped with mud. He sat up with a gruesome strained elegance like an aged man welcoming sickroom visitors. The rain had partly cleansed his face but there were dark gobbets of blood everywhere. Blood had come from the ear suspended Dali-like and obscenely auditory by a scrap of tough gristle; from the steep gash which exposed pearly teeth deep in his jaw; from multiple stab wounds and a cut throat. He tried valiantly to speak to her. But obviously his vocal cords had been severely damaged, or sliced in two.

"Dev," Felice said, in a small absolutely toneless voice. The lights glistered sadly.

Hah, he breathed, and fresh blood welled from the stab wound in his throat. With his knees under him he was able to get to his feet. When he had made it there was a look on his face similar to joy. The lights faded and faded until Felice couldn't see his face any more. She sobbed for him.

"Dev, I'll help you!"

The back screen plopped open. Felice turned dumbly at the sound. Hurt as he was, Dev caught it too. There was a suppurating sound of terror in his ruined throat.

Kitchen lights surged and flagged in a confusing flicker. A bedraggled figure stood on the back porch, peering in at them.

"Carol," Felice said, gladly. The kitchen went dark.

She came toward them, breathing hard. Felice heard her wet shoes squeaking on the floor, slowly at first, then more urgently. "Carol," Felice said again, "help us! Dev is—" The lights flashed around them. She was almost there. Her eyes were lidless, sharp-edged. Her face was half masked by wet tendrils of blond hair. She looked like something drowned and washed up by the sea. She had a butcher knife in one hand.

Dev raised a protectionless hand. She stopped, just beyond his reach, totally intent on him. His own eyes were mad with fright. She gathered herself, made a clean decisive lunge with the knife, putting muscle into her attack. His head was nearly severed by the blade. As he fell grotesquely, leaving a bouquet of fresh blood on her blouse, she slashed a second time at him. Then she turned and calmly threw the knife into the sink. The metal vase which Felice had been holding dropped and rolled aimlessly on the floor.

She glanced once at Felice. "Get back out of the way," she said, preoccupied.

Felice, no longer thinking for herself, obeyed.

"That finished him," Felice heard her say grittily. Blood was pooling on the floor. Dev's head was at a terrible angle. She looked up, trembling, with an air of casual lunacy.

"I said he's dead, Mother. I've killed him." Her lips turned up rather slyly, but she was too inflamed by the act of killing for laughter.

"Now I expect you'll have to help me get rid of him."

Chapter Sixteen

BABS HATED THE STAIRS AND WENT UP THEM AS SELDOM
as possible, but sometimes, when Jim left in the early morning
for the prearranged place to await the call from the boys, she
had to take the breakfast tray up herself. It also had become
necessary at other times—more frequent lately—during the tedious afternoons and evenings when Jim was working and
couldn't be bothered. She would begin to feel lonesome because
it was contrary to her nature to forgo company for so long a
time. What she craved and needed was girl talk. When the craving became a misery she would make the considerable effort required to climb the stairs again.

Babs was five feet eight inches tall and she weighed two hundred and eighty pounds; most of the excess poundage was in her
hips and butt. Her hips were three-quarters of an inch wider
than the walled staircase, so she was forced to climb sideways,
inching up with her back pressed against one wall. That made it
awkward for her to lift the lead foot to the next riser, and there
was always a dangerous moment when she was tilting downward, unsure of her balance. Because of its narrowness the staircase lacked a railing, which would have given her something to
hold onto. When she had a loaded tray in her two hands she just
held her breath and prayed that she wouldn't fall, because she
had a very weak back and once down she couldn't get up without help.

On the morning following the storm which knocked out the
lights and the TV in the middle of *Woman of the Year*, her

favorite Tracy-Hepburn flick, Jim left in an easter-egg dawn and she made the trip upstairs to the white bedroom, crabwise, not spilling anything this time, and said hello as cheerily as always.

Only a burning silence from the bed. Babs, although she didn't show it, was crestfallen, because she'd hoped to sit awhile and visit and catch her breath. Jim had groceries to buy and wouldn't be back for at least an hour. There were still FBI men in the area (although probably the number became less each day) so the route had to be changed each time. Each disguise was different. This morning he had created jowls for himself by packing Silly Putty into his cheeks, padded his belly, tackied up his eyebrows and bulbed his nose. He had driven Uncle Webb's jaunty Triumph, and he looked like a thousand other slightly disgruntled upper-ech executives off a little early to the suburban offices of the corporations across the river in Westchester.

Babs was dying to tell all about the disguise; obviously, though, she was not going to be welcome this morning, and she never lingered when she wasn't welcome. Rule Number One in Babs' book.

With a smile she set the breakfast tray down, opened the windows several inches. The air was cool and windless. She admired the view for a few moments, then returned to the bed.

"I fixed currant buns this morning," she said. "And plenty of poached salmon. We're all out of English tea, I'm sorry to say—" She was still hopeful of a friendly visit. But she wasn't encouraged so she stopped talking and shrugged, as if she were slightly embarrassed by Carol's obstinacy (what was the point of being chummy one day, and enemies the next?) but still gracious in defeat. She set about unlocking the chain at one end so Carol could get up from the bed and go to the bathroom.

The arrangement which Jim had decided upon, after Carol had tumbled out the window and nearly broken her neck, was simple and effective. Carol now wore a cyclist's leather support belt with buckles and a steel ring at the back. At night when she was ready to sleep a chain was passed through the ring. The chain bisected the bed lengthwise and was locked to the frame at either end. There was enough play for Carol to sleep on her side if she felt like it: she was really much more comfortable that way, although she complained often about the wide close-fitting belt, which she said made it difficult for her to breathe. Once the chain was fastened she couldn't leave the bed, or even sit up.

Her wrists were always manacled now, with eighteen inches of chain between the bracelets so she could feed and clean herself: she wore the stainless steel manacles even when bathing. Jim had provided manacles for her ankles as well, but they were used only on occasion.

When Carol was to be taken downstairs for sun on the sky-lighted porch she was made to step over the wrist chain. Then her hands were drawn up behind her back and the chain fastened to the ring with a small padlock. Jim had explained to her that any attempt to escape meant the drugs would be resumed, with a needle if necessary. Carol had no idea of what her captivity with the drugs had been like; only a stubbornly sore throat remained as a memento. But that, along with what she had been told of the near hanging, was enough to frighten her into obedience.

After the accident they'd given her no drugs except a necessary pain killer and, later, when it seemed that she might be developing pneumonia, Babs had used antibiotics freely. For four days Carol had had someone with her constantly because of sporadic, potentially fatal hemorrhaging in the throat. Each time she awakened she was sick to her stomach from the swallowed blood. She was often delirious and dangerously weak; Babs, the little doctor, was glumly afraid they would lose her. It had been so close anyway; another half minute of hanging by her neck and she surely would have strangled. But Jim had risked his own neck and averted a terrible tragedy and now Carol was recovering. Her throat was still in poor shape but not abscessed. When her appetite improved she would gain strength. At Babs' insistence she was doing simple exercises to maintain muscle tone.

Mentally she was better too; although she still had her confused and depressed times. Babs wondered what kind of day this would turn out to be. Maybe, she thought, an extra treat would be good for Carol's morale.

As soon as she was freed Carol walked slowly and wordlessly to the john. Babs busied herself at the chifforobe and selected new lingerie, a clean shirt and a pair of slacks for her, arranged the things on the bed. Carol came back with her face washed and glistening and looked hollowly at the clothing.

"You don't have to do that, Babs. You're not my maid."

"Oh, that's all right, Carol. Don't let your breakfast get cold."

Carol sat down on the bed and uncovered the food. The rising sun had filled the room with a golden light that was very flattering to Carol, Babs thought. But she wished with all her heart that there was something they could do about those bronzy circles under her eyes. Probably Carol needed shots of B_{12} and iron. Babs had been tempted to give her a rejuvenating shot, the whole works, including ACTH, Demerol, Dex, vitamins, calcium gluconate and gamma globulin, but she doubted if Carol's system could stand the "buck," or abrupt acceleration. Let mother nature take her course, Babs decided. Good food, fresh air, sunshine. Carol's tan was coming along: a couple hours on the porch this afternoon and she would be almost as dark as the day she arrived.

Carol ate only a little breakfast but drank all of the orange juice Babs had painstakingly squeezed for her. She seemed listless and yawned a lot, as if she hadn't slept. No wonder, with that king-size storm banging around God's heaven half the night. Babs told her how scared she'd been: "I would've hid in a closet if I could have found one big enough to fit me." Carol nodded thoughtfully, as if she hadn't noticed the humor in that remark, and asked what day it was. Babs told her. Carol tried to figure it out.

"That makes—eighteen days, doesn't it? No, nineteen."

"Twenty," Babs said apologetically. "It'll be three weeks tomorrow." She laughed; she had a happy little girl's laugh. "We'll have a cake," she said. "With candles on it." Carol didn't seem to be listening. She was staring out the windows at the muted blue sky and a milky cloud.

"We ought to put some curtains over those windows," Babs said. "I'll bet you didn't get a wink of sleep."

"I don't know," Carol said indifferently. "I wouldn't have slept anyway. I was thinking. I wished—"

"What?" Babs asked, after a wait.

Carol looked patiently at her, then through her. "I wanted one of those bolts of lightning to come through the roof and strike me dead. So it would be over with." She spoke slowly and with a slur. But every day her diction had improved; for a week following the accidental hanging she hadn't been able to utter an intelligible sound. "I can't understand why you worked so hard to keep me alive." Her eyes were fuming, exhausted. "You'll just have to kill me anyway."

"*Kill* you?" Babs said, appalled. "Oh, Carol, what put an awful idea like *that* in your head?"

Carol's expression altered gradually; she looked stricken, as if she were being mocked, and then hideously angry—anger paralyzed every muscle in her face. She raised her manacled hands deliberately, shook the chain until she couldn't catch her breath and all but fainted from the exertion.

Babs was grimacing. "I told you I was sorry about the chains! They're just to keep you from, you know, running off until—until after—until it's time to let you go. Carol? Please! My Lord, we're not—we wouldn't *think* of—Jim's a *pacifist*, you know that! He's nonviolent. Look, I was almost a doctor. I believe in the Hippocratic Oath, that oath is as sacred to me as the Lord's own Prayer! I mean, I don't go as far as Schweitzer: sometimes there are good reasons for letting a spirit out of a body that's corrupting it, but—"

"Oh, Babs, shut up," Carol said ruthlessly, and sat down on the bed to cry.

Babs felt vulnerable enough to cry herself, but she controlled the wobble in her big chin and said in an injured tone, "You're safe with us, Carol. Gosh, you're just as safe as you'd be in a convent, and boy, I can tell you about convents."

"Maybe," Carol gasped, "you d-don't have anything to say about whether I live or die." She stopped crying as abruptly as she had begun, looking dewy and overheated. But the hiccups happened on schedule. "Whup-whup-whup what abou-bout the rest of your gang? Huc! What about Handsome Dan, or whatever his name is?"

"Turo? Turo certainly wouldn't hurt you. He's got the biggest crush—"

Carol dabbed her wet eyes with a tissue. "He does?"

"He's flipped over you! Gosh, how did you miss that?"

Carol said in a pathetic little voice, "I've been sick." And she laughed, a bawl of laughter that brought fresh tears. Babs giggled along with her, holding her belly with both hands, like Santa Claus in children's Christmas books.

"That's—uh—an interesting piece of—huc!—news," Carol said, stopping the flow at last. She had a long drink of water. Her ears remained scarlet, but otherwise her normal color had returned. Babs wiped at the tears on her own cheeks and dried her hand on the half acre of gray denim skirt she wore. "Where is Turo?" Carol asked. "Haven't seen him—huc! oh, shit— lately."

"Oh, he's—" Babs clammed up rather obviously and snitched the breakfast Danish which Carol hadn't wanted. When she'd eaten it she licked her fingers and said, "I'm going to ask Jim if you can come down the rest of the day. Do you want me to help you change clothes now?"

"In a minute. Babs?"

"Yo."

Carol was looking very seriously at her, with just a trace of sternness. "I'd say we were friends, wouldn't you?"

Babs' face took on a shine. "Gosh, I hope so. After what we've been through together."

"If it wasn't for you I wouldn't have survived. I owe my life to you, I know that, and I'm sorry I said—what I said about being killed; it was finky of me and I didn't really mean it. I was just depressed. I think I'm about ready to start, or something. I needed a good cry."

"Sure," Babs said, nodding. "I understand. If I were you—I mean, I just hate it, the chains and all. I'm really sorry."

"Well, it's better than being doped out of my skull."

"Oh, sure, lots better."

"Why did you use the drugs in the first place, Babs?"

"So you'd be easier to manage, that's all."

Carol thought it over and said in a remonstrative tone, "I wouldn't have been any trouble." She lit a cigarette with shaking hands and looked again at Babs, neutral, perceptive. "Three weeks. And you don't have any idea how much longer before I can go. Another week? Two weeks?"

"I hope not," Babs said insecurely.

"Why so long? Can't you get the money?" Babs scratched behind an ear and looked distant, uncomprehending. Carol said quickly, "That isn't what we're waiting for, is it? Not for ransom. That's what you'd like me to believe; but you don't want money."

Babs turned and walked to the windows: a labored stride, as if she were wading through snowdrifts, or her own suet. "Gosh, Carol, don't start again. There's no reason for you to worry. I've told you and told you."

"You haven't told me anything," Carol replied, insinuating cruelty, her tone bleak. She looked at the chains that had made her wrists sore and then at the dark staircase and thought, as she had thought before, of running. Babs, who still considered her an invalid, had been somewhat careless again, letting her loose with only her hands bound. Carol was still weak and unsure of her wind, but she knew Babs couldn't hope to stop her. Big Jim had gone out; Carol had heard one of the cars earlier. But perhaps he'd returned when she wasn't listening for him.

Of her three captors she was afraid only of Jim Hendersholt. Not because he had tried to frighten her; he wasn't crudely menacing or sadistic. But he had engineered her captivity, first the kidnapping, now the system of locks and bright chains. Sometimes he came to look at her, wordlessly, with a dark mulling speculation, a watchfulness that distressed her. He had quiet ways and the artist's or physician's talent for analytical observation. She felt, ultimately, that he was inside her mind. His psychological pressure was unnerving, it caused her to mistrust the recurrent impulses to escape, mistrust the limited freedom he was allowing, which could turn out to be a trap. She was afraid of attempting her escape and running afoul of Big Jim or some fail-safe he had devised, of then having to face his clinical disapproval. She was afraid of the oblivion he had promised.

She was afraid because she didn't understand him: his cryptic humor, his odd sculpture, most of all his marriage. She wondered if he was a potential murderer. Babs had protested and protested —too much? Carol pondered the reaction she had provoked and concluded that if eventually she was to be killed then Babs hadn't yet been informed. She just wasn't capable of concealing such knowledge.

Carol's head and throat ached and she felt nauseated from apprehension and lack of sleep. But she was determined to keep after Babs, sweat her down, render her evasion and sunny rationalizations into a hard lump of truth.

"Babs, after you let me go I'll have to tell the police everything I know about you and Jim and Turo."

"Sure," Babs said, unconcerned. "We know that, Carol. It's all right."

"*Why* is it all right?" Carol persisted, talking to the girl's Olympian back. "Because you don't think the police will be able to find the three of you afterward?"

"No, they won't find us."

"How can you be that sure? Babs, don't you ever think about what will happen if you're caught? You'll spend the rest of your life in prison." Babs folded her arms and continued to gaze, perhaps serenely, at the morning woods and the brightening hills. "Don't you know what prison is like? I was in one, on a criminology field trip. A women's prison. It was—"

"It was full of dykes and brides," Babs said curtly. "I know. You don't have to tell me what prisons are like; my mother was a guard in a women's prison. They caught her in the laundry that one time. Four dykes. They didn't kill her but it would have been better if they had. She started drinking after that. She died about a year later. She didn't want to live after what those dirty butches did to her."

Babs left the window and came back to Carol, a young fair tidy girl with a gross and inappropriate body, a glandular accident. What, after all, could prison mean to her? Carol thought, perhaps unfairly. Babs was smiling, but it was a smile of undirected hatred which Carol hadn't seen before.

"Before I'd ever let an old dyke touch me I'd kill myself," Babs vowed. "If they catch up to us—which is practically impossible, we've worked it out so well—then we'll take cyanide. We've all got cyanide."

"Cyanide?" Carol repeated, in horror, and this desperate solution made her own predicament seem clearer, her fate undeniable. "Oh, God, you couldn't—"

"It's just part of the plan," Babs said, sounding bored. "We planned for everything. Look, I'd better help you change clothes now. I've got a terrific lot of stuff to do downstairs, Carol."

"All right," Carol said numbly. She unbuttoned the Levi's and worked them off, pulled the nylon pants to her ankles and stepped out of them. Momentarily she was naked from the waist down. Babs, as usual, looked the other way. Carol dressed in the things that had been provided for her. Babs knelt to attach an ankle chain, growing red in the face, then struggled to her feet with Carol's help. She undid the buckles and removed the cyclist's belt. Carol rubbed her welted stomach and ribs and breathed as deeply as she could without making herself dizzy. Babs unlocked the manacles, put the key back into her shirt pocket. Carol took off the shirt and bra she'd been wearing and finished changing. She sat down on the bed and rubbed emollient cream on her tender wrists.

"The plan you were talking about. Is it Jim's plan?"

183

Babs was using the pillowcase as a laundry bag. "Everybody had something to contribute," she said. "Everybody but me. Jim had the best ideas, though. I'd better take those sheets too, Carol."

"Let me help you."

"No, no, listen, enjoy your smoke, girl." Carol stood aside while Babs stripped the bed.

"How did you get mixed up with somebody like Jim?"

"What does that mean?" Babs said, her eyes getting frosty.

"He's—"

"Jim is a very sweet guy. You don't know him. Basically he's a shy person who doesn't happen to talk much. I'm not mixed up with him, I'm married to him. *Married.*"

"I didn't—"

Babs looked contemptuously at her. "You think the way everybody else thinks. How did I get him? How do I hold on to him? The same way *you* get a man. The size of my ass doesn't mean anything."

"Babs, you don't have to jus—"

Babs pulled fresh linens from a drawer of the chifforobe. She banged the drawer shut. "I do anything he tells me to do. I do everything he wants. He doesn't have to say it twice, either." She stopped to get her breath, shoulders back, gasping. "I guess you think something's the matter with *him.* Some hang-up or something. Wanting to be married to me. Listen, I keep a good house. I'm a damned good cook. Beautiful girls can be absolute pigs; don't tell me, I've been around enough of you to know!"

"Please don't be mad at me, Babs."

"It doesn't take anything special to be married to a fat girl." She paused, and then, with a charmingly impudent grin, her face terribly red, she concluded, "It helps to have a long prick."

"*Babs.*"

Babs lunged past her with an armload of sheets. "Just let me get finished with the bed here. I've got a million things to do downstairs. Look, if you want to think we're a bunch of criminal psychopaths, go ahead. We're not. We're like everybody else. We just take our responsibilities as human beings a little more seriously than most."

"Babs, let me go. Now. Today. And I swear I won't tell the police anything. I'll say that I wanted to disappear and so I faked—"

"Oh, come on, Carol," Babs said, almost rudely. She tucked the sheets in on one side and walked around the bed, hands on hips, breathing hard.

"I'm going crazy here!" Carol screamed, and Babs looked at her, startled and worried.

"Hey now, shhh, no yelling, you know what that'll mean," she cautioned.

"I swear," Carol moaned, as if her nerve had failed, "I'll never say a word about—"

"Too late," Babs muttered, frowning, and bent to her task of making the bed.

Carol faltered in her lament, looking vague and off balance. "*What* is too late?"

Babs gave the pillow a punch and put it down. "Oh, hell," she said, as if she might be angry at herself, or circumstances. "Carol, for the last time. We can't let you go, not for a few more days anyway. There's a good reason: right now you'd be one Carol Watterson too many. If you don't want the rest of your coffee I'll take the tray down now. For lunch we can have a nice *dubujike* or *chanbuktang*, except I don't have the abalone so it wouldn't be quite right. Or if you'd rather I'll fix—" She had to sneak a glance at Carol, whose expression was disturbing. Babs sighed, feeling uncomfortable.

"You're being impersonated," she explained, as if she were explaining a great deal. She tried to get to the breakfast tray. Carol, chain rattling, blocked her. "Now, Carol," Babs pleaded, "it's part of the plan, an important part, and I absolutely can't tell you any more."

"Babs, you're going to," Carol said, in an unearthly voice.

"Absolutely, I can't," Babs said, backing up.

185

"I think you're lying to me. I didn't know you could be that hateful!"

"I'm not being hateful," Babs protested, seriously wounded again.

"Tell me!"

Babs took another step and almost backed off the bed platform. Carol caught her before she could fall. Babs, deathly afraid of falling, even from a height of eight inches, blanched and swallowed hard. She had nowhere to look but at Carol.

Carol discovered something in Babs' ferny eyes, badly concealed. Babs loved secrets, but, quite naturally, she loved telling secrets even more.

Carol squeezed a little harder, not trying to hurt her. Babs attempted a smile.

As if their roles had become logically reversed at that moment, Carol was able to guide the fat girl to the bed. She sat her down gently. And sat next to Babs, close enough to feel an anticipatory tremor in the soft ballooned body.

"I just don't want you to think I could lie to you," Babs said earnestly.

"I know," Carol said, holding her hand comfortingly. "I know."

Chapter Seventeen

SAM, REACHING HOME AT FOUR IN THE AFTERNOON, saw Felice and the two boys sitting peacefully out under the trees in the side yard. Riggs was lying a few feet away chewing on a bone. Sam slowed and honked the horn twice. They all looked at him. Because of the distance he couldn't see their faces clearly. He had expected a wave from Felice, but she was unmoving.

Suddenly she bobbed up from the tubby white chair. Sam saw the big blond boy reach lazily to one side and seize her. For four or five seconds he held her by the wrist; she was steeled against him, arrested in her angle of flight. Then apparently he decided to let her go. Felice stumbled, almost losing her balance, gained momentum and plunged toward the drive. Riggs followed, happy to have a chance to romp.

Sam was puzzled and angered by what he'd seen. He stopped the Mercedes and got out. Felice ran hard across the patterned lawn, crazy-legged like most women, while Riggs loped erratically around her and at a slant across her path.

"Hi," Sam said pleasantly, an instant before he recognized the panic in her sharply creased face. He caught her in his arms. She lay against his breast, heaving and winded, fingers digging into his back.

"Sam—Sam!"

He looked at the two boys over her shoulder. They had risen and were coming.

"What was that clown trying to do to you?" he said indignantly. "Are those Carol's—"

Felice pushed away from him and looked into his face. She shook her head once, fiercely, to regain his attention.

"They—Sam, they're murderers—they killed—"

He gaped at her and pried himself loose, held her at arm's length, visibly alarmed by her.

"True!" she gasped. "Believe me! They have Carol. They've come to kill the General!"

"What in God's name," Sam said slowly, "are you talking—"

Felice looked back and all but turned to stone. Riggs licked at her legs and looked eagerly up at her, then cut away in a wide circle to invite her back to their romp.

"Sam," she whispered, "I don't know what we're going to *do*."

He let go of her and stepped to one side as the boys ambled up. The big blond one was smiling.

"Howdy, Mr. Holland. I'm Rich Marsland. This Latin lover is Turo Regalo. Did you have a nice trip for yourself?"

"Dev," Felice said, eyes on Rich, her teeth bared in a sickened way. "Dev—in the pond. Oh, God—I saw it—"

"Now, Felice," Rich admonished, "you promised you weren't going to get all worked up about that again."

"What are you talking about?" Sam said furiously. "What the hell is happening here?"

Rich scuffled at the grass and squinted at the low-lying sun and at a boy in the road peddling along on a bicycle. He said in a low voice, his smile still comfortably fixed, "Maybe this isn't the proper place to discuss it. You look like you could use a stiff shot of something, Mr. Holland. I'll call you Sam if you don't mind, since I think we ought to get well acquainted in as short a time as possible. Call me Rich. Let's all walk along together now, folksy and happy-talking. You tell your husband why it has to be that way, Felice."

"They have Carol," she said, as if by rote. Rich beamed and beckoned to her. She looked at him with blind abhorrence but joined him, falling in at his side, her head bent. The one called

Turo walked slightly behind Sam, his face damply expression-less. Sam was sweating too, although it was a mild summer's day.

"I want to know—" Sam began.

"Don't get hasty, Sam. And lower your voice. This is really a fine antique house you have here, sound as a vault. They don't make them like they used to, do they? The front porch seems a little weathered, though; Turo and I were talking about giving it a coat of paint tomorrow, as long as we have time on our hands. Pay for our room and board sort of thing, you know?"

Beside a thicket of young birches Sam stopped; Turo bumped into him and stepped back quickly. "Listen, you miserable idiot," Sam said to Rich, "tell me what's happened to Dev, and Carol; where's Carol?"

"Listen yourself, Sam," Rich said, turning, his shadow cutting sharply across the grass, across Sam's body. "If you don't care to cooperate I'll make a little phone call, a little arrangement right now." He nudged a clump of freshly turned earth back into a bed of multicolored begonias, looked up quizzically at Sam. "I mean I'll arrange it so Carol wakes up in the middle of next month so relaxed and happy she'll have to take toilet training all over again. Do you follow me?"

"Carol isn't here," Felice said dully. "Sam, after the kidnapping they put somebody else in her place. It wasn't Carol we got back."

A door of the porch opened and Sam looked up, stared, looked again at Felice disbelievingly.

"Who is that?" he said. "*That's* not Carol?"

"No," Rich said, smiling at the girl. "Come here, love. Have a good nap? Her name's Lone," he explained.

"Lone Kels," she said, joining them, slipping an arm around Rich's waist. "Now, forget you heard me say it, because as long as we're together, Sam—it's all right if I call you Sam, isn't it?—I'll be Carol to you."

Sam studied her face—nothing could have diverted him at that moment. She was Carol, and then again she positively wasn't. Feature by feature the likeness was good, almost uncanny. But the girl wasn't posing now, she was still tousled from a hard sleep, one cheek welted by a pillow or cushion. There was no appersonation, and the specific gravity of her face, the sum of what she was emotionally, made her far different from Carol.

Felice, her eyes curiously bland, one hand tugging and tugging at the short culotte she wore, said, "I knew she was different. I must have known."

"You were fooled," Rich said. "No shame in that. We went through the motions of a kidnapping so you'd trick yourselves into believing Lone was Carol. Give Lone credit for a damned good job of acting."

"But I couldn't *stop* it, Sam," Felice said more shrilly. "I didn't realize she had the knife until it was too late. Don't you see? She cut Dev down right in front of me—"

"Shut her up," Lone said viciously, and Sam put his arms around his wife. She didn't move or cry or seem to breathe.

"Let's go inside," Rich said. "Turo, get her something to drink."

"Brandy," Sam instructed. He guided Felice onto the porch. Her feet moved clumsily. She sat where he put her with her head sharply bowed, clinging tightly to one of his hands. "I'm all right," she advised him in a weak voice. "Don't go away, Sam."

There was a drink cart on the porch. Turo brought a brandy in a large snifter and Felice cupped it with both hands, drank. The pungent brandy resulted in tears. She lifted her anguished face.

"Poor Dev," she sobbed, heartbroken. "They just threw him in the *pond*, that's all." She hurled the snifter the length of the porch, curled herself tightly into the chair to weep. A fly buzzed over the shattered glass. Nobody said anything. Sam's face was contorted by his wife's grief.

"How did Dev Kaufman get involved in this?" Sam asked Rich. "Was he one of you?"

Rich lifted a bottle of Southern Comfort from the drink cart and poured himself a shot. Turo, like a compulsive house-keeper, silently picked up the fragile pieces of glass and swabbed the brandy off the tiles with a cloth moistened in the ice bucket. Lone Kels leaned against a post with her arms folded and her blond hair celestial in a ray of sun, watching Felice with eyes narrowed and tarnished like slots in neglected armor.

"What's yours, Sam, gin over ice?" Rich dropped a cube into a glass, milked the gin bottle, pinched two beads of lemon oil onto the surface of the gin and handed the drink to Sam. "No," he said, "Dev wasn't one of us, but in a sense we were expecting him. He was the X factor, I guess you'd say. The unforeseeable complication in an otherwise mathematically exact plan. He blew in with the rain last night ready to take up where he'd left off with Carol. Lone tried to ease him out of here before he got suspicious of her, but she had only a little background on the relationship; it was just a question of how soon he'd catch on, and what we could do about it when he did. We had a meeting and decided to level with him immediately. Lone thought she could handle it by herself. Unfortunately when Lone explained that we had Carol safely tucked away and required his co-operation, Dev lost his head. He was a one-man wrecking crew. Lone doesn't like being hit; she had too much of that when she was younger. When someone hits her she's not responsible for what happens."

Felice was no longer crying but she remained painfully fetal with a cheek pressed against the soft vermilion back of the chair, her eyes slitted and apprehensive, a kind of pallor just beneath the skin of her face, as if the bones were showing through. Sam, flushed with dismay, looked at her, swallowed a lump of his gin.

"All right," he said, the taste citric on his tongue. "What happened?"

"She didn't have much to defend herself with. A pair of sewing scissors left out on a table. She kept jabbing until one of the blades hung up in his rib cage, but he wouldn't go down.

Lone was in a state of shock by then, Sam. She hunted up a knife in the cottage kitchen and used that on him. A dozen times or more. Lone doesn't remember."

"It was a dull knife," Lone commented, not moving her lips, seeming not to be very interested.

"Nightmare, nightmare," Felice said, quietly.

"We honestly thought he was dead. We found an old awning and carried him in that to the potting shed and left him there while we cleaned up the cottage. I put his hat and coat on and drove his car to La Guardia and turned it in. Turo followed in my car. We weighted that satchel of Dev's with a building block and threw it off the Whitestone Bridge. While we were gone Dev made the best of a spark of life we overlooked and crawled out of the potting shed to the house. Felice found him on the kitchen floor. Lone was still in the cottage. When she heard Felice scream she ran to the house with the knife and finished him."

The fly that liked brandy buzzed around Lone's head and she waved him away impatiently. Turo sat down at the far end of the porch with his hands clenched between his knees and stared at the sun-blazed tile.

"The body's in the pond?" Sam asked.

"We added his weight in stones and sewed him up in the canvas with an awl and rowed him out to the middle of the pond in that leaky boat of Kevin's. The time comes, Sam, when you want to raise him up to ship him home for a proper burial, remember that he's as close to the middle as we could figure in the dark, with all that rain."

"Good Christ," Sam said, and finished his drink in two swallows.

"We're sorry," Rich said. "Lone did her best. We thought he'd be sensible. You never know how a man's going to react under stress. It was just one of those unpredictable accidents. It shook us some, but we're all right now. Could I fix you another drink? No? Carol, isn't it about time you got dinner started?"

"Don't call her that," Sam rasped.

"He still doesn't catch on," Lone said, with a glance at Rich and a shrug.

"We have to give him time," Rich explained. "He just got here. It takes some getting used to."

Sam said carefully, "I think I've heard enough to know what you're doing. You elaborately faked a kidnapping so you could substitute this girl for Carol. You depended on the fact that we'd be so happy to have our daughter back we'd ignore minor differences. By continuing to hold Carol you had control over us, so if we did become suspicious it wouldn't matter. With a substitute Carol in the house you invited yourselves as guests. You came prepared to stay awhile if necessary. You're a cold-blooded bunch of killers and it's the General you're after. God knows why."

"Good so far, Sam."

Felice lifted her head and looked hopefully at her husband, as if the sound of his voice had convinced her that somehow he'd be able to reason with their captors.

"I object to the part about being cold-blooded killers," Lone said, sulking coltishly.

"I was going to correct him on that," Rich assured her.

"Good."

"One of our objects is the General, Sam. The other is his friend and associate Vernon Metts. We plan to kill both of them as efficiently as possible, without warning, without ceremony or unnecessary suffering on their part. Once you're familiar with our motives and procedure you won't think we're so cold-blooded."

"Vernon Metts," Sam mused. "Now I see why you need us, and the house. It makes a little bit of sense now."

"Well, the General is always accessible, killing him wouldn't be a problem. Metts is much harder to pin down. When we began a feasibility study we realized it would be best to let him come to us. Metts customarily visits General Morse three times a year. His last visit was in late February. The General tells us we can look for him any day now. The General has made our work a lot easier by giving us the run of his house. We didn't expect that."

"Why kill them? No, I don't have to ask that question. You're eliminating someone's competition, aren't you? Who's behind it? Who sent you?"

Rich laughed. "You took a wrong turn, Sam. No one sent us. We're not part of some sinister international conspiracy. Nothing melodramatic like that. We're just a little group of friends who share a moral concern, a founding concept."

"Concept?"

"Ethical murder, Sam. Do you know the term?"

After a few moments Sam said worriedly, "I've written about it."

"That's right."

"As a matter of speculation, not advocacy. If you take the trouble to read carefully what I write."

Rich said with apparent seriousness, as if he were addressing a mentor, "We read you carefully, Sam. We hold you in high esteem. I hope, when time permits, that you'll be proud of us."

Sam didn't reply. Instead he looked helplessly at his wife.

"What's he talking about?" Felice asked. "What does he mean, ethical murder?"

"It would take an hour—"

"Let me try, Sam," Rich said enthusiastically, and addressed himself to Felice. "This is a time of revolution, moral and political revolution, as anyone who reads a newspaper knows. Most people associate revolution with violence and a period of total anarchy. We've already had a little violence, which is probably necessary to earn recognition, but this country is well organized against the revolutionary impulse, so a major and bloody upheaval is as unlikely as it is undesirable. For one thing, there would have to be an economic basis for it, another Great Depression, a worldwide economic collapse. I think we can rule out that possibility. Therefore the revolution now taking place

194

will remain youthful, a student revolt; the working class won't be involved at all. In fact this class is the greatest enemy the revolution has because the values of the proletariat are, as Elijah Jordan proposed, the values of institutions, not individuals."

Felice looked uncomprehending. "Who is Elijah Jordan?" she said.

"An American philosopher who deserves more of a public than he has."

"And does he say it's all right to murder whomever you feel like murdering, as long as you're sincere about it?"

"No, he hasn't said that. I've mentioned him and one of his major precepts so that you'll better understand what the revolution is about. It's not happening just because we're all tired of school and war or because we want to embarrass Mom and Dad for not toilet training us properly. It's happening because only the young mind seems to grasp the essential tragedy of this country: the values of its institutions are self-serving, masterpieces of cynicism and duplicity. It's happening because we reject cynicism and the unscrupulous ways of government; we have to assert our own values if we're going to survive, if there's to be meaningful change."

Sam said, "The premeditated murder of someone you barely know but still condemn is the most cynical act I can think of."

"Not when corrupt institutions permit the immorality of men like General Morse and his partner. In a half-crazed and volatile world they're allowed to sell arms and encourage aggression by doing so. If it's in our power to eliminate, completely, a source of human suffering, then we're justified, we're compelled to do it. The act of murder then becomes ethical. In a religious sense, it's holy."

Felice came up out of her chair and was stopped by Sam's warning hand on her shoulder. "They're all insane," she said, fevered but calm. "Sam, they must be." She looked uncertainly at Turo; he didn't raise his head but seemed to feel the heat of her eyes. To Rich she said scathingly, "You'll just shoot the two of them down? For *God's* sake—the General's an old man. He's crippled."

"Bang, bang, bang," Lone said softly. "He's lived his three score and ten. Three score too many if you ask me."

Rich quieted her with a disapproving look. "We have guns," he admitted to Felice, "because we'll need them at first. But we don't plan to do any shooting. We'll use gas to kill them. It's quick and it eliminates suffering."

"Gas them? Like dogs?"

"Exactly like dogs," Rich told her. "Believe me, it's the best way. A long time ago I worked at a humane shelter. It was my job to put to sleep the strays and mongrels nobody loved and wanted. I know how effective gas is. Do you have any idea how many sick friendless dogs I put away over a two-year period? Make a guess."

Felice's eyes were rounded in horror. "I don't want to guess," she whispered.

"Four hundred and twenty-four," Rich said proudly. "And not one of them suffered."

"I suppose we won't suffer, either," Sam said with an angry tremor. "It's going to be cyanogen for all of us, isn't it?"

Turo sprang to his feet. "You won't be harmed in any way," he said, too loudly, anxious to be reassuring. He looked around, startled, and sat down again, like a schoolboy who'd had a piece to recite but couldn't remember any more of it.

"Listen to Turo," Rich said. "Now that you know just how serious we are, we shouldn't have to force cooperation from you. I apologize again for Dev Kaufman; we didn't come here to kill innocent people. When we've finished our work you'll be given a drug that will make you sleep a minimum of two days. After you wake up it'll be another two or three hours before you're tracking well enough to get your story told. By then we'll be long out of the country. Where we're going, of course, is privileged information. We expect to be very comfortable

196

there. Eventually those of us who want to will come back to the States."

"If you have Carol," Felice said, "then I want to talk to her. Right now."

"That isn't possible," Rich replied. "But we'll have her write you a note tomorrow. I don't want you worrying about Carol. She's fine now."

"What do you mean, *now?*" Felice said ominously.

Rich smiled. "She had a little cold, nothing serious."

Lone spied the General a long way off, headed for the house. "Guess who's coming to dinner?" she said, with an ugly delight.

"Sam," Felice groaned. He looked silently at her, lips compressed, and shook his head.

"Carol's fine as long as you're cooperative," Rich said. "Make our work harder and she'll be permanently regressed to infancy with a combination of drugs. Think about it: is there a choice? Turo, let's have some drinks. We're all too damned tense here."

Lone pressed against him. "Rich," she said, wheedling. "I'm way down again. I do need a jolt."

"Love, I'm sorry. We're almost out."

"Out? I've only had two good jolts since I've been here."

"Sorry, Lone. Babs spoiled a batch."

Lone pouted. "Honest to God, she's got the touch of a blacksmith. Some chemist. Straight speed, then. I can get by on that. Never mind the gamma glob and the monkey balls."

"Get back into character," Rich said fondly. "You'll be rewarded."

She turned her glossy eyes on his amiable face, stung the end of his nose with a playful fingertip slap, sighed, composed herself, lowered her head in concentration. Sam watched her, fascinated, as she filtered out dissonant elements of her own personality, the cruel and concupiscent, allowing the nuances and complexities of Carol Watterson to emerge without effort. She blinked owlishly several times, sighed again as if refreshed. Turo at his bartending popped cubes into a glass. Following the chilly musical sound of ice in crystal her head bounced up and she gave her blond hair a settling shake across one bare shoulder and surveyed them, with a Carol look and a Carol smile that was hauntingly precise. She let herself off the porch and ran to the General's side and put an arm around him; they could see her smiling again, smiling up at her favorite man in the whole world. The General's pleasure was obvious.

Felice leaned against Sam, nails biting into the flesh of his thumb.

"Stop them, stop them," she begged, in a tenuous voice that Rich overheard. He turned to gaze chidingly at her. Felice shrank closer to Sam, avoiding Rich's eyes. Rich presented her with another brandy. His hand shook a little; it was the first indication of how keyed up he was. It was the first time he had really seemed dangerous to Sam, despite his Nazi technician's talk of the goodness of gas and of Dev slashed and bloodless deep in the pond.

"Last one until bedtime," he said. "You know the drill: now be good." Felice looked at Sam once more, quickly; when she saw no hope there all expression drained from her face, leaving it as desolate and impoverished as a mud flat. She accepted the belled glass and drank deeply from it, and shuddered.

Chapter Eighteen

"SHE MUST BE GETTING AWAY WITH IT," CAROL SAID vexedly, "but I don't see how. Granted she's a good actress; but Lone just doesn't look anything like me. You swear she hasn't had plastic surgery?"

She was sitting on the bed in the upstairs room, one ankle and her wrists in chains. Her newly washed hair was wrapped in a towel. There was a summery breath of air in the room, green and rye. The windows of the white room squared a depthless portion of black sky, turning it into artifact. Below them Jim Hendersholt chipped and chiseled relentlessly at stone.

Babs had pulled up one of the white sling chairs and she occupied it to the bursting point. She was eating an apple with gusto, little finger poised to scoop the clear juice from her chin. She reached over the side of the chair with her free hand, sorted out the reading matter there and picked up a recent edition of *The New York Times Magazine*.

"She's much more like you than you think," Babs said, leafing through the magazine. She stopped at a full-page color advertisement for a synthetic fabric and nodded. "Here, look at these three girls." Carol leaned over and took the magazine. "At first glance they're completely different, but the difference is basically in hair style and dress. Study their faces." She crunched into her apple. "See? The girl in the middle is slightly lantern-jawed but otherwise their faces are shaped the same. Their eyes are alike in color and shape but each girl draws her eyes differently. The other features are very close. Lighten the hair of the middle girl, change the style and redefine her eyebrows, she's the twin of the blonde on her left, *n'est-ce pas?*"

"Maybe," Carol admitted. "This is a photograph, though. Makeup can do a lot, but there must be a hundred subtle differences that aren't revealed."

"True. That's where impersonation becomes a high art. Lone is great, believe me. She slaved to get you down cold. It helped that she had plenty of time to study you."

"All those 'accidental' meetings my last semester at Berkeley —Lone was stalking me."

"Lone took a lot of photographs too. Just like a secret agent. She recorded your voice. But there's something about your voice —a timbre that's hard to duplicate. That wasn't important. Lone bruises real easy, she's almost a hemophiliac, so Rich decided she should fake a throat injury. It went with the dog collar anyway. That gave her an excuse to whisper for a few days until everyone was used to the sound. Then she gradually worked up to a normal speaking voice. There's a funny coincidence: you almost lost your voice for good."

"Funny," Carol said dispiritedly, lighting a cigarette. She closed the magazine and watched Babs polish off her apple.

"They give me the farts but it's worth it," Babs said, happily licking her fingers.

It was difficult to think of hapless Babs as part of a conspiracy to commit murder. That part of the story—the reason for Lone's long and difficult impersonation—hadn't been easy to pry out of her. She'd stoutly defended the incredible murder plot. ("We're saving human lives, Carol, for goshsake can't you understand that?" "I suppose my grandfather isn't human." "His soul has been corrupted by the body it's in. It's an act of kindness to let his soul out of a body in which it's suffering so it can return to the Beautiful Country." "That's a pretty weird philosophy, Babs." "Weird? For goshsake there isn't anything weird about reincarnation. It's the only answer that makes sense in this miserable world. We've all lived before. I know I have.") But after exhausting her store of secrets Babs had been depressed and uncommunicative all afternoon. Carol believed that she was truly appalled by the whole business. She went along with Jim because, married to him, indebted, she had no real choice. Belonging outweighed guilt, and what fear there was. Carol could understand that much. Perhaps Babs was as serious and dedicated as the others, appreciably mad, but Carol preferred to think that she retained most of her innocence. Otherwise she wouldn't have been able to talk to Babs any more, as friend and confidante. And as long as innocence persisted, Carol thought, there was hope she could persuade Babs to let her go. For her part she would see that Babs was protected, no matter what.

She unwrapped the damp towel from her head, picked up a fresh towel and rubbed her hair vigorously for a minute. It was dry enough to brush. As she worked with her hair the fact of the impersonation, the audacity of it, continued to pique her. After all, she was an individual, one of a kind in habits, mannerisms, intellect, abilities. Riggs was a mutton-headed dog who accepted everybody. But how could Sam, Kevin and the General have been fooled this long? How could her own mother have failed to recognize an impostor? Even though they had seldom been together during the past four years Carol felt especially resentful because her mother had been fooled; it gave her an odd panicky feeling that except for her captors she no longer existed, that Felice was oblivious, and content with her substitute daughter.

"What about fingerprints, Babs? What about my handwriting?"

"Fingerprints didn't matter, since neither of you is on file with the FBI. Handwriting? She spent a couple of days learning to forge your signature to sign statements and such."

"I suppose she's been driving my car," Carol said petulantly.

"Sure. Lone's a crack driver, don't worry."

"How did she learn the roads around Fox Village?"

"She had two weeks to go over the whole territory before she changed into you. She drove by your house dozens of times."

"What about people I've known all my life? She couldn't possibly have a file on everybody."

"Well," Babs said guardedly, "she was prepared to finesse any accidental meetings. Old school chums and so forth. But the plan called for her to stick close to the house and not socialize."

"But Lone must have made slips. I can think of a hundred things Kevin or my mother might ask her that she couldn't possibly answer."

"She's clever. Don't underestimate Lone."

"I don't," Carol said grimly. "I just hope we meet again someday. I want five minutes to tell her what I think of her." She continued to brush her hair; short, fierce strokes. A hard-shell beetle soared in through an open window and landed in Babs' lap. Babs flung it away moodily.

"The General's not well known," Carol said. "He's always been publicity shy. How did you—I mean, how did Rich and Jim happen to choose him?"

"Rich heard about General Morse and was curious. He has his sources and the money to pay for information. He found out everything there was to know about the General before they decided to—to go ahead. And of course you were handy at Berkeley, which gave the boys an idea of how to work it, you know, so they'd be sure to get both men at the same time. Otherwise they wouldn't be stopping anything, the arms trade would go on like before." Babs stirred in the chair as if she wanted to be free of it, but she couldn't budge without Carol's help, and Carol didn't make a move. Sweat appeared on Babs' forehead. "It's almost eleven. Why don't we go downstairs and watch a movie. *Sayonara*, with Brando? Did you see that one? Gosh, I cried all the way through it the first time."

A shadow intruded at the foot of the bed, startling them. Jim Hendersholt, in his superquiet way, in dust-whitened Hush Puppies, had come up the stairs and was regarding them with a faint sardonic grin. There was marble on his face and forearms; he looked quaint and crusty except for the red-traced eyes, a cool dark omniscience impacted there.

"What are you talking about, girls?" he asked.

"Oh, clothes and movies," Babs said uneasily. Carol wondered how long he'd been in progress on the stairs, listening all the while. After her initial reaction she didn't look at him again. "Are you all through for the night?" Babs asked.

Big Jim yawned. "I've done enough. How about fixing me a hamburger?"

"Sure! Right away. I just mentioned to Carol about coming down to watch a movie—"

Jim said with a sympathetic grimace in Carol's direction, "She looks tired to me. She might want to go to bed."

"Well, yeah, I didn't think about that. Do you want to go to bed now, Carol?"

Carol lowered her hairbrush and stared with a touch of hostility at Big Jim. "If he says I do."

Instead of replying Jim crossed to Babs, held out his hands, leaned back tautly as she pulled herself from the chair. "Upsy-daisy," he said genially. Babs giggled and tugged her clothing into place, looking flustered and adoring.

"You go on down," he said. "I'll get Carol squared away for the night."

It took Babs three or four minutes to descend. Big Jim stood by the windows looking out, hands clasped behind his back.

"My uncle is an early-to-bed, early-to-rise type," he said. "That's why he never installed shades or curtains in his bedroom. He likes to paint early in the morning, first light."

"Where is your uncle now?" Carol asked.

"Greece. Hydra, I think. The light is supposed to be exceptional there."

"Is he a good painter?"

He turned and shrugged too elaborately, lips upturned in a good-humored acceptance of mediocrity. "He has a following. He sells."

"I don't suppose he knows what you're using his house for this summer."

Big Jim chuckled. "No, he doesn't. He'll be surprised. But I expect he can turn the publicity to good advantage." He came back to the bed. He walked like a duck and his arms were too long, Carol thought, bristling at the pincer of his eyes, afraid as always of a lethal nature prudently concealed, of megalomania.

"You'll never be a good sculptor," she said, wanting to wound him. "You'll never have a following and you'll never sell a damned one of your blobs."

His expression was saintly soft, indulgent. "I don't crave recognition," he said.

Big Jim's imperviousness angered her even more. "What do you want," she said, almost sobbing, "besides blood on your hands? I never liked Rich, I knew there was something wrong with him, but you're worse, because you're dragging poor Babs down with you." She heard herself say too much, and was dimly shocked by her betrayal. She closed her eyes in despair, unable to look at him.

After a while she heard his knees pop when he hunkered down, felt his fingers firm on her ankle as he unlocked the manacle there, releasing her. "Go brush your teeth," he said. Carol got up trembling and stepped down from the bed platform, linked hands low in front of her, and went to the bathroom. When she returned Big Jim was turning down the covers on the bed. Carol had a last hurried smoke before he confiscated cigarettes and matches; she was aware of his eyes on her back. When she finished he passed the long chain through the steel loop on the belt she wore and, as she stretched out in the bed, he locked the chain to the frame.

He turned out the light but Carol didn't hear him go. After a minute or two she rolled onto her left side and perceived him against the background of the windows, which in contrast to the room held light now, like a ghosting of silver on a photographic negative. Her vision blurred quickly and tears spilled over; the wrist chain was as cold as a serpent across her throat. His presence, apocryphal, continued to diminish her.

"So our subterfuge is discovered," he said mockingly from the dark. "Thanks to dear Blabs. Notice I've called her *Blabs*. A little humor there."

"Amusing," Carol said, as if she had lockjaw. She lay on her back, bisected by the other chain, knees drawn up, hands pressed against her mouth—inevitably she had the hiccups.

Big Jim sat down beside her. On the surface he smelled dry and powdery. But his breath was rank, like a marsh, as if the manifold excitements of murder had now begun, in their pitted locus, to turn blackly against his system.

"Go away," Carol said harshly, regretting the intrusion; it meant a marked change in procedure, in his previously sterile and professional approach to her.

"Now that you know we're not kidnappers for fun and profit, that we have a serious motive, I expect that puts ideas in your head, lots and lots of brilliant ideas."

"Hic!"

"Do you want a drink of water?"

"No!" Carol moaned. "Just get out of here."

"One idea you may have, since you've discovered how to turn Babs' mouth on and off like a faucet, is the idea that her heart like her head is just a big baked marshmallow. But it's no use appealing to her to unlock the chains that bind so you can sneak away from here sometime when I'm not around. Soft and squishy as it is, Babs' heart belongs to me. A disloyal Babs is a sorry Babs indeed."

"I—huc!—don't have any ideas like that."

"That's not very truthful. It may not be a big bad lie, but it isn't altogether a truthful statement. Of *course* you think about getting away. Particularly with all the freedom you've had lately, the run of the house. But Babs and I knew you weren't strong enough to run a dozen yards without fainting, so we didn't worry." He picked up the chain between her wrists, lifting her hands. "Maybe some idea about saving the life of the Great Old Soldier might give you the extra strength for an escape," he mused. "What should I do, double the chains? Stand vigilant all day and all night? What do *you* think?" He let go of the chain and with one hand companionably fondled a breast. Carol writhed, cold with loathing.

"Cut that out!" She suffered a new spasm of hiccups, which caused the blood to pound in her temples until she felt giddy.

Big Jim took his hand away. She lay panting. "Or would you prefer something from Babs' little black bag instead? Babs has all kinds of treats in her bag. I'll bet there's something that'll make it next to impossible for you to have any more original ideas."

"No," Carol said. "I'll be good. I won't—try anything."

He leaned over her, and she felt that she would suffocate. "Is that a definite promise? Can I really count on you?"

"*Yes.* Now get off the—hic!—bed. It's *my* bed."

He sat upright. "In a minute," he said. He reached out, fumbling in the dark, and loosened the side zipper of her slacks.

"What do you think you're—huc!—doing? Do you want me to holler rape?"

"I don't want you to holler anything," Big Jim said severely, peeling the slacks down her thighs. "If you do, I'll just have to come back up here with a needle full of treats for you. And believe me, after a liberal dose of treats you'll be living with the squirrels and liking it." He hooked his callused fingers inside her panties and yanked them down to her knees. "Now be still. I'm going to cop a feel."

Carol resisted until the pressure of blood in her brain almost knocked her out. She caught the wrist chain between her teeth as his violations of her became increasingly gross and seductive and ground the chain: if her teeth had not been strong she would have broken several. She learned it was easier not to resist. Big Jim was at her, inventively, for a long time. "Groovy," he mumbled, time and time again. And, "Oh, man." Her throat felt scalded from swallowed tears.

When he had finished he dressed her and she felt his hands trembling like those of an impotent old rogue. She spat out the chain with a bloodied tongue and cursed him as he lifted himself

206

from the bed. She knew exactly what names applied to Big Jim.

He said wanly, not offended, "But it cured your hiccups," and left. She lay burning, humiliated, hating. She heard Babs laugh downstairs, and imagined she was the inspiration for this laughter. Ultimately she arrived at a fine passionless urge to murder them both, and slept on it.

Chapter Nineteen

TOWARD DUSK WITH DINNER OUT OF THE WAY SHE HAD gone alone to the sedgy perimeter of the pond, driven from the house by the General's huge laughter, by Rich's nonchalance and the brazen death's-head merriment of Miss Lone Kels. She felt poisoned; the crimson air, sluggish from the day-long heat and rot at the water's edge, was scarcely an antidote. She threw up into the weeds. It was no relief to her. Tears ran freely down her cheeks but she continued to feel gorged and glumly horrified, committed to returning and committed to betraying her father as long as it was demanded of her.

Sam found her there, staring at the darkened pond.

"How are we ever going to tell his family?" Felice said, choking on her remorse.

"I don't think it'll be up to us. Let's go in now."

"Oh, no, Sam, I *can't* go back to the house."

"It's all right. Rich and Lone took off with the General."

"Where did they go?" she asked, frightened.

He put an arm around her shoulders. "To buy booze, I think. It's inexcusable, but we ran out of Southern Comfort."

"Sam, there has to be a way to stop them!"

"We'll talk about it."

Turo was playing the piano in the living room, making the best of some difficult Chopin although the piano was long out of tune. They paused in the kitchen to listen.

"He's very good," Felice said with a reluctant fascination. "I mean, it's obvious he's studied."

"Yes," Sam said.

"I don't want to stay downstairs. Is there brandy or anything?"

"A full bottle of Martell."

"Would you bring it?"

She sat by the small cold fireplace in her bedroom while Sam opened the cognac. Turo continued to play for several more minutes, his passion for the music overcoming the deficiencies of the instrument. As she drank Felice found herself thinking of him, and when he quit she said, "Turo isn't like the others, Sam."

"I've seen that."

"I don't know how he got mixed up with Rich and that girl. He's not a thrill seeker or a bogus intellectual. No, and he's not pathological. I don't think he really understood what he was getting into until Dev was murdered. I watched him today. Turo is as terrified as I am. I think we can change his mind."

"Maybe."

The liquor gave her a fiery confidence. "Go and get him, Sam. Ask him to come up. He must know where Carol is. This may be the only chance we'll have, with those other two out of the way for a little while."

Sam winced, skeptically, polished off his cognac, gave her a smile and went to find Turo.

While he was gone Felice refilled her glass. She was restless, in her mind already meeting with Turo, appealing to him, swaying him—she liked Turo, had liked him from the first minute. Lone was evil, a bloodied succubus, and Rich was artfully mad; in Turo's presence they seemed slightly less murderous because there was a distinction about him, if nothing else a lack of eccentricity. The cognac, which she was sipping almost as fast as a soft drink, warmed her affection for Arturo Regalo. At the same time she felt less aggressive, she felt a loss of fire, a diffusion of purpose. Her throat constricted. "Just let me have Carol back," she whispered to herself. It was Carol for whom she was most afraid, and she recognized this without a qualm. After all, she thought, temporizing, the General was a brave man, an experienced soldier. Were Rich and Turo a match for him, despite his age? *Think about that, Turo. Save yourself while you can. Save us all.* The room swarmed before her eyes. She bumped against the porcelain eagle at the foot of her bed, stared at it wearily as if trying to recall the mood which had prompted her to buy it. She emptied her second glass of cognac.

Sam didn't come back. Someone had left the television on downstairs. Frantic laughter. She stretched out on the bed with the glass in her hand, feeling humid, sustained, a little dizzy. Think what to say to Turo. Manliness there. Sense of honor. The General respected him. In your hands, Turo; Carol helpless. You can't let anything happen to Carol, no matter what you believe. Dear God, this house. Always wanted it. Old and elegant. Two-hundred-year-old trees. Sanctuary. After all this time it has to become haunted. An ordeal to go into the kitchen now: Dev lying there on the floor. You're staying with us, Dev. Wouldn't put a knight out on a dog like this.

"Felice?"

She opened her eyes, feeling thick and stupid, and abrasively guilty. Sam was standing beside the bed; he looked thwarted. His eyes were chrome. "I couldn't find him," he said. "I guess he went out for a walk or something."

"Oh, no."

"Still, it's a good idea. We'll have to talk to him. Lean on him— What did you do with the cognac?" She pointed out the bottle and Sam poured a shot for each of them, carried his own glass into the bathroom. He took off his tie and shirt, put his glasses aside, bathed his face for several minutes. Felice watched him, drinking more slowly, craving the full power of the cognac, not wanting to sicken herself as she had done before. After a while, with her eyes on her husband, she felt mildly, agreeably erotic. Sam was well muscled for a man whose occupation was basically sedentary, reflective: tension and a finely adjusted metabolism kept him trim. She thought of how his hands would feel on her face and body and smiled eagerly at him when he came, as she hoped he would, to sit on the bed beside her. His hair was wet around the ears. He wore glasses well but without them his face had a certain masculine bleakness Felice admired. She sat up and kissed his cool forehead.

"I'm going to get undressed," she said adventurously, a trifle uncertainly; she took off her clothes on the bed while he drank and mutely considered the provocation.

"Are you too tired?" she asked. He shook his head.

"Do I still make you want me, Sam?"

He undressed and came to her, but not in the full-length embrace they were accustomed to. They kneeled facing on the bed as if new to each other, her knees well inside his. They were dumbly exploratory, like sexual innocents. Felice put her face against his shoulder. He was already excited; she grasped him to make the erection even more powerful. Instead he dwindled in her hand.

She looked at his face, saddened, disturbed. There was a look of ordeal in his eyes, an expression of shock and infinite concern.

"Why?" she asked, letting go. He lay back and turned on his side, making fists. "Did *I* do that to you?"

"It wasn't your fault, Felice."

"But that's the third time in the last couple of months. Isn't it?"

"I'll get it back. Don't press me."

He spoke matter-of-factly but she felt a chill. She got up for a robe and a cigarette. He went to his own room and closed the door partway. Felice felt uninvited but she followed after a couple of minutes. Sam looked up thoughtfully when she came in.

"Didn't mean to rush off."

"Oh, Sam." She leaned against him, brushing a kiss against his ear. He held her tentatively.

"Unless I'm just coming unstuck in some obscure way," he said, "the only answer I can think of is Patsy."

"Patsy?"

"Uncle Hat's girl. My cousin."

"You've mentioned her. She was a sexpot."

"At a tender age. When she was about sixteen and I was

thirteen she began to develop an interest in me. Until then she'd either ignored me or made my life miserable. There was no lock on the door to the bathroom we shared. She got into the habit of coming in while I was taking a bath, to brush her teeth or use the john. She'd manage to expose herself in a casual way. But it was all very calculated. She'd come to my room at night in her underwear to borrow a pencil or something. I wasn't too intrigued. I just didn't like Patsy."

"What was the little bum trying to do, seduce you?"

"It was just a pastime for her, another game to play when she was in the mood. I was normally curious, I looked at what I was supposed to look at, but I don't think I was greatly aroused. She gradually got bolder. One night on some pretext she dashed in completely naked. That upset me; I told her to wear pajamas or stay in her own room. She didn't bother me for a while. Then one night when I was half asleep she snuck into bed with me. She said she'd had a nightmare that scared her. She jabbered about a dozen things, but it was impossible for her to talk five minutes without getting onto sex. Dirty talk disgusted me. It still does. I told her I wanted to get some sleep. Patsy said that she'd go back to her room if I kissed her. She turned it into a dare, a challenge. I kissed her to get rid of her. She was all worked up and she was—damned proficient at sex play. I found out I liked it. I halfway forgot it was Patsy I was kissing. In a way I was paralyzed with fright but she kept stimulating me—I think I came sexually of age in about five minutes. It was traumatic and unforgettable. But we were both so excited and nervous it didn't work. Strangely enough she was a virgin.

"Then Uncle Hat came in. He must have heard us wrestling around. You can imagine what he saw, and what he thought."

"That kind and gentle man," Felice said with a sneer.

"Patsy threw a quick tantrum and blamed the whole thing on me. I was in shock. Hat dragged me down two flights of steps to his basement workshop. He locked my arms into vises and spent an hour squatting in front of me in his shabby old robe with this fanatical light in his eyes that was more horrible than cruelty.

He honed a knife until I was chewing my tongue at the dry slidey sound of the blade on the whetstone. I tried to—appease him, but he wouldn't even look at me. 'I better cut it off,' he said. 'If you can't control yourself in my house around my daughter then by God I'll cut it off.' Needless to say he didn't, but he got the reaction he was after."

"Don't tell me." He looked very pale, to the tips of his ears, though he was trying to smile.

"I—couldn't," Sam said wanly, shrugging. He touched her cheek with his fingertips as if to reassure himself about something, and she snuggled against him gratefully.

"What happened to Patsy after that?"

"Oh, well, she stayed away from me, and a few months later she ran off with some boy. Hat held me responsible for that too —for ruining her life in the first place."

"But he never hurt you—physically, I mean."

"I could have taken a beating now and then; it might have toughened me in a useful way. That wasn't Hat's style. He was a master of psychological pressure, an artist at grinding me down, bit by bit. You know all that. I've told you." Sam was uneasy, and cold to her touch. His eyes were hostile, but she knew the hostility wasn't directed at her.

"Why couldn't you make love to me, Sam?"

"No matter how much I wanted you I was convinced that if I tried to go through with it Hat would break down the bed-room door and carry out his castration threat. It's been hanging over my head for a long time now. The sooner that miserable bastard is in his grave the better off I'll be. You realize that, don't you?" He looked at Felice, his eyes unfamiliar now, poorly focused.

"Dear Sam," she said, confused, and with a sigh tried to snuggle again. He broke away from her, preoccupied.

"Don't you?" he said in a gray voice, and went to the window, stood there leaning with his fingers splayed on the sill, seeming disappointed and terribly anxious.

"Hat died a long time ago, Sam."

He began to breathe again. "Yeah," he said wearily, thankful. He located a cigarette, snapped his lighter. "Just in time too." He blew smoke, smiled at her. "I couldn't have withstood him another year. Jesus."

"Feeling better now?"

"Some." He thumped his solid chest with a fist, somewhat derisively.

"I think it's good we talked about it."

"Sorry I—flopped."

"You'll get me mad. Stop it, Sam. You're no flop. We've been married nine years and I could recite you chapter and verse. I just picked a perfectly lousy time. Soon we'll—" She winced and shook her head slowly. Tears stood out in her eyes.

"I'd better get dressed," Sam said, "and find Turo. Do you want to come down?"

"I was thinking about a bath. Another drink. Don't stay long. Sam, I love you."

"That's all I really give a damn about," he told her.

He was sitting in the library downstairs listening to tapes when he heard them come in by way of the back porch. He walked through the living room and down the center hall to the kitchen. Lone was laughing. He saw their shadows on the kitchen floor. He saw the blackened beat of wings and heard the hissing of the bird on Lone's wrist. He came to a stop in the doorway and turned his head, hands grabbing for his face. He saw the blue Pacific sky and gulls wobbling in the air and heard them scream for his liver. They descended like sharpened bones. He saw the ocean sweltering and the sun rain down. He saw dreadful shapes pressing landward from the sea. He pinched at his cheeks and eyelids, inflicting pain, forging a semblance of reality.

They stopped laughing when they saw him and heard the sob of breath in his throat.

"What's the matter, Sam?" Rich asked.

"The bird," Sam gasped.

"Captain Midnight," Lone said proudly. "That's the name I picked for him, Sam. Captain Midnight. Look how he's filling out. A few more days and I'll be able to fly him."

"We don't have a few more days, love," Rich reminded her.

"Maybe I'll take him along," she said. "Nobody to miss him. Would you like that, Cap'n?"

Sam's vision failed gradually, leaving him with a heavy breath and the specific muscle memory of kneeling in cold sand, a glare of winter light in his eyes as he methodically and resolutely beat a crippled gull with the clumsy ax of his hand, beat it until it was pulp and feathers. "Get that bird out of here," he said thickly, glancing at it, at the perfect round of a yellow eye and the sharp curved beak.

"That old phobia still bothering you, Sam?" Rich asked, concerned. "I guess it is, you look mighty pale. Porch, Lone." She scowled mock ferociously at him and walked away, gurgling to her half-tamed pet. In the dark of the porch she tethered the falcon to the high back of a wooden chair.

Sam turned abruptly and went back down the hall, heart pounding, breathing through his mouth.

"Hey, Sam," Rich said softly, following.

In the library Sam opened a bottle of Scotch, a drink he disliked, and poured a shot of it. He was drinking when Rich sat down on the sofa.

"What happened back there, Sam?"

Sam stared at him, drank a little more of the Scotch, squeezed his temples between thumb and forefinger. "A little side trip," he said lethargically.

"Oh, yes? Remember, I warned you that could happen. Even months after you stopped dropping acid. How long did the reaction last?"

"Too long. But it was mild compared to a couple of others I've had. There was one about a month ago, while I was flying from Minneapolis to New York—" He drained the whiskey from the glass but continued to swallow hard after it was gone.

"I thought I was going to have to get up and leave the airplane. At thirty thousand feet."

Rich said judiciously, "Still, it's not such a big price to pay. You can put up with a few unexpected trips. You owe your sanity to acid. Your life."

"That's right." Sam heard a sputter of voices on the tape recorder in his bottom desk drawer and went to turn the machine off.

"Good news, Sam. No need to monitor the tapes any longer. The General heard from Vernon Metts a little while ago. Metts is flying in late tomorrow afternoon. The General expects him around eight o'clock."

"God. After all this time. *Finally.*" Sam locked the drawer. "One of you will have to remember to pull the bug out of his telephone. We overlooked that."

"I'll make a note of it, Sam."

Lone slid the library doors open and came in. "Where do you suppose Turo is?"

Rich said, "He might have gone to Mother Church. After last night he needs Her."

"Just so he doesn't drag his troubles into a confessional."

"He knows better."

Lone took off her butch trench coat. She was wearing a horizontally striped shell and indecent red shorts that left two firm crescents of her behind bare. She was flushed but the whites of her eyes were startlingly clear. She was glossy, electric, at the peak of health and good feeling; she laughed, making a drink for herself. "I don't really need this, but I hate to see you drinking alone, Sam-the-man. Do you want another?" To Rich she said, "Has he heard the latest?"

"I told him."

Sam said, "I'm worried about Turo."

"Why?" Lone asked. "He wants this more than any of us. He's waited half his life for this chance."

"Felice has an affinity for Turo. She seemed to have reason to think we could crack him if we tried."

"Well," Lone said, stirring the drink with a finger, "then we'd better keep the lady away from Turo. That shouldn't be hard. I'll stay very close to her tomorrow."

After a few moments Sam said, as if the fact had been weighing on his mind, "She doesn't like you."

"No surprise. She's scared to death of me. I tell you I could have stuck that knife in her just as easy as Dev, and she knows it. Don't know what stopped me." She gave Sam's ashen face a sly close study and said pleasantly, "Only kidding, Sam-the-man. But I don't like *her*. I never have. She's made this thing twice as tough for me as it should have been. Every day I expected her to come out with 'You're not Carol!' I saw it in her face two or three times. But she never quite let herself believe it." She made a seat for herself on the edge of his desk. Rich lit a thin cigar and watched the two of them with great enjoyment. Lone clinked her glass against the empty glass in Sam's hand. "*Salud.* I think you're making a mistake. I think you really ought to come with us when it's over. Could be you'll miss your true friends when you're way up here and we're way down there."

"I doubt it," Sam said, with a leaden smile.

Lone pressed a hand to her heart and pretended to swoon over the side of the desk. "Sam, you put the hurt on me! I'll miss *you*. After all, I nursed you at my own breast in this your second life."

"Sam's tired, love. Don't badger him."

"Well, just you remember, Sam. After the old man's dead, if it isn't good with Felice the way you think it's going to be, we'll be happy to see you any time."

"I love Felice," Sam said, looking at her, grim in a manner she found mildly distressing. "And nothing had better happen to her between now and the time you leave here for good."

Lone wagged her head. "Sam," she said reprovingly, "I'm surprised at you. I don't like Felice. But I'm not *mad* at her." She got down from the desk and walked around the room tippytoe, humming to herself. Sam stared at her, then glanced at Rich.

Rich was watching Lone too, and he looked as nearly worried as he ever could.

"Tomorrow night can't come too soon," he said, "for all of us."

"I'm going to bed," Sam told him.

"Send Turo in the morning?" Rich asked.

"Send him in the morning. It'll give him something to do."

Chapter Twenty

MORNING LIGHT. MORNING OF THE TWENTY-FIRST DAY. That called for a little celebration, Carol thought, remembering Babs' remark about the cake and candles. She didn't smile. She had slept poorly and there was an ache in her lower back she couldn't massage because of the constraining belt and the manacles.

She'd heard the car, heard someone come in downstairs. Voices, subdued and unintelligible. Rattle of cutlery in the kitchen. She wondered who had come. Turo? He hadn't visited for about a week. The last time she had been groggy, scarcely aware of his presence, unresponsive. By experimenting she found a position that eased the strain on her back. She waited. She did her yoga breathing exercises. Breathe in for a count of four. Hold for a count of four. Breathe out slowly one-two-three-four. In her condition it was hard work, but she had to build lung power. She felt stronger this morning. Not exactly full of fight, but no pushover, either. She hoped it was Turo, and that he would bring the breakfast tray. She did not want to see Big Jim. If he had the gall to come near her today she would spit in his eye.

When she began to feel light-headed she stopped the exercise and closed her eyes. Presently she heard the breakfast tray on its way up.

"Hello," Turo said.

Carol turned her head quickly. "Turo! I'm so glad to see you!"

219

Her enthusiasm was real, unexpected. He smiled bashfully as he approached with the tray. "Babs said you're feeling OK now."

"Yes. How have you been?"

"Oh—" he said vaguely, "fine." He put the tray down on the small table and took a key from a pocket of his sand-colored Edwardian jacket, reached behind her to unlock the big padlock that held the chain to the frame of the bed. Carol sat up thankfully. He pulled the rackety chain through the loop, then undid the several straps on the belt, releasing her.

"Please stay," Carol said. "I'll be right back."

When she returned from the bathroom he had uncovered the dishes on the tray: corn cakes and molasses, a small breakfast steak, a three-minute egg. "Babs always fixes too much," Carol said. "Why don't you share breakfast with me, Turo?" He declined with a shake of his head. "Some coffee, then? Believe me, there's plenty. And Babs sent two cups along. She never fails to be thoughtful, that Babs."

Turo looked uncertainly at her but her smile was brisk and uncynical. He accepted the coffee and stood nearby drinking with the saucer beneath his chin. His hands were shaking. He was nervous this morning, and Carol was sympathetic. She ate half her breakfast but the pain in her back finally made it impossible for her to sit without fidgeting unendurably. She got up and paced. Turo watched her with a heavy-lidded admiration and despair, and nibbled at a fingernail between drafts of coffee.

"What's the matter?" he asked finally.

"I've got this bad back."

"Oh."

"If I could just get the blood circulating—Rub it for me, will you, Turo?" She didn't look to see what he thought of the suggestion. She kneeled on the polar-bear rug and eased flat onto her stomach, joined hands outstretched. Turo put cup and saucer on the tray, clattering them. He came over and stood looking down at her blond head and then kneeled astride her and began to massage. He had strong hands but he was deft and careful and seemed to know the musculature of her back.

"Ummm," Carol said. "Heavenly. It feels all right now." Turo got up and she turned over on the soft rug. "You must do that for all your girls," she said, kittenish, curious about him. She knew so little. Two years ago at Berkeley they'd attended lectures together, a poli-sci section with two hundred students. Occasionally they passed on campus, smiled and nodded to each other. He always seemed to be alone and in a hurry, profoundly occupied. Before Dev she'd been tempted a couple of times to stop Turo and get acquainted. Now they had a little time, and she was surprised that she still cared. But he had touched her and been gentle; she knew the reason why.

"Do you have anyone special?" she asked. The sun had fully risen and she felt it warm through the windows; sun touched his face and favored it.

"A girl? No." He raised a fist to his mouth but he had no nails left; he'd chewed them all to the bloodied quick. Instead he mauled his knuckles and looked remotely ashamed of his nerves.

"Once I nearly elected myself. You were somebody I wanted to know. I always looked for you first when I walked into old what's-his-name's lecture."

The confession prompted a strained smile from Turo. No skepticism. His reaction gave her a reasonable idea of his feelings for her. She felt delighted and forlorn. "I was always late," he said.

"It was an ungodly hour of the morning." Carol sat up, chained hands on her knees. He looked at the chain and then away. The fact of her captivity disturbed the mood of intimacy so easily created. Sensing this, Carol said ruefully, "Always trust your instincts. If I'd chased you when it occurred to me I probably wouldn't have been interested when Dev came along."

Mention of Dev offended him somehow, or disturbed him; she wasn't sure which. "Finish your breakfast," he said, not unfriendly but with the severity of a jailer. Carol felt crushed. He walked to the stairs.

"Please," she said, getting up, "I have to talk to you, Turo."

He didn't want to stay but something, a chivalric impulse, a dim sense of obligation, turned him back. Before he could reconsider Carol went to the breakfast tray and poured the last of the coffee for them, an awkward business with the chain in the way.

"I know what's happening," Carol said. "I know why I'm here. I know about your plans for the General. Babs told me everything."

Turo looked at her without comment and chose one of the sling chairs. His cordovan face was hard and he looked unreceptive. He turned his head toward the windows and closed his eyes wearily to the sun. Carol sat cross-legged on the tufted skin, facing him. She wondered about the small eggshell scar on his chin, and was diverted by the tarry length of his lashes. Momentary relaxation had loosened his mouth and his breath broke from the throat with a sibilance that startled him.

"I can't defend the General's morality," Carol said, conceding everything at once, hopefully to engage Turo despite his seclusion. "For a long time I've been determined to change his thinking. We've had some bitter arguments, gone weeks without speaking to each other. But he can't be argued with. He can't be changed. He's just a soldier, an old warrior. I've called him terrible names but still he's my flesh and blood and I'm fond of him. I don't want him to be killed. I don't want you to have to kill him."

"Well," he said, after a long painful silence, "I have to, that's all."

"You don't."

"Listen—" He turned his head slightly and regarded her with a scorn he might have shown for a younger sister: he had found an attitude and was secure. "We can argue, but I can't be changed, either. It isn't something I decided to do yesterday. I decided twelve years ago."

"Oh," she said softly, disappointed in him, "Turo, I don't believe that. When you were a *boy?*"

"When I was a boy your grandfather was selling guns in and around my country. He sold a few thousand dollars' worth of automatic rifles and light machine guns to a mountain gang in our province, a collection of killers who had no politics to speak of and not much ambition. The weapons made them brave and a threat to the stability of the province. Two villages were shot up. Federal troops had to be sent in. The capital of the province, where I lived, where my father was mayor, had the worst fighting. I lost my father and relatives on both sides of the family. It wasn't difficult to find out where the sophisticated weapons had come from. But no protest was ever made. General Morse sold to everybody in my part of the world. Even to the government."

"Turo, I'm very sorry about your father."

He nodded and got up from the chair, drank a little coffee, carried the cup to the tray and left it there.

"But the General isn't consciously evil. You won't settle anything by driving a stake through his heart. You'll just be throwing your life away."

"What is your conception of evil? He's still selling guns. And I have a debt of honor to satisfy."

"I see. A debt of honor. That's—very serious." She walked over to Turo and stood beside him. "I'm sure your father was a good man. But he's dead. The General's not a good man, but he's old and he'll die soon enough. Maybe he'll go to hell; I don't know, I'm not theological." Her voice rose a little as she became more aggressive, anxious to seize responsibility for his fate. "I don't care what happens to him, but I do care about you. Turo, why don't you get out of here? Leave this house and just keep going. Turn yourself in to the police or FBI. They'll know what to do."

"That would really be throwing my life away. Kidnapping. Conspiracy to commit murder. Accessory to—" He checked himself and glanced at Carol with a bewildered smile and said, half seriously, "You know something, you could get me in a lot of trouble with suggestions like that."

"Turo, what were you about to say?" He didn't reply. Carol seized his arm, her chain rattling. "Accessory to *what?*"

"Oh, *chica*," he mumbled.

"Murder?" She shook him. "Turo," she said wildly, "has anything happened to my family?"

"No."

"Don't tell me lies, I wouldn't lie to you!"

"They're all right! Nothing's happened. Your mother—guessed."

"About Lone, you mean?" Carol let him go and collapsed on the bed. "Oh, God, for a minute there you had me scared. How did she catch on, do you know?"

Turo looked paralyzed. His lips barely moved. "Lone—lost her self-control."

"Oh," Carol said, sighing. "So she couldn't carry it off after all. I didn't think it would work. A ridiculous idea."

Turo reached into an inside pocket for an index card and his pen. "Your mother's worried about you," he said. "Could you write her a note so she'll know you're OK?"

Carol pondered an appropriate message for several minutes and then wrote:

I wish I could tell you where I am, but I don't know myself. It's no fun, but they treat me OK and the food is good. I'm very homesick and I

She paused, about to weep, but controlled herself and determinedly wrote:

224

miss you all
very much. Please don't worry, I'm
really fine. So you'll know this is me and
not a fake — Felice, do you remember
what I said to Miss Watkins at school
when she told me I had to be a frog
in the second-grade play?

When she had finished Carol read it over critically. Trite, she thought, but since no masterpiece was called for she signed and handed the card over to Turo, who stuffed it away without a glance.

"Turo, don't go now," she begged. But he had what he'd come after and during the interval of note writing his morale had gradually improved. He studied her composedly, without reluctance, but there was a lack of recognition in his tribal eyes that inhibited her. He seemed possessed by an epic fatalism.

He hauled the ankle chain from beneath the bed. Carol jerked her foot away when he tried to attach the manacle. Turo looked up with an expression of forbearance until she submitted. She tried earnestly to hate him, and couldn't; the effort and misspent emotion made her cry instead. She spilled tears, her throat full of glue.

"Don't go." She stared brightly at him, cowed by misery, by his youth and his tragic, priestly gloom. "I'm afraid. I'm afraid. Huh. I'm *so afraid!*"

He touched her hair absently, as if the gesture was one he had become used to during the nights she had lain purple-eyed and semiconscious with fever in the white bed. He began to rearrange her hair to suit him, with a furtive reverence that dismayed but spookily calmed her. She hushed; he smiled for her.

"Soon you'll go home," Turo said. "Very soon. That I

promise." Then he left as fast as he could, slipping once, unseen, on the stairs as he went down.

Babs went all out for dinner that night: interesting hors d'oeuvres, *salade Babs* with the freshest, tastiest lettuce Carol had eaten in months, *foie de veau sauté aux raisins,* a cheese platter that featured a delectable Brie. There was *poire cardinal,* served in a coffee cup. Babs apologized sincerely for this lapse in etiquette, but still it tasted pretty good.

Carol was reasonably sure that it was a farewell dinner. For all of a sultry afternoon she had been hearing distinctive sounds from below, sounds of packing up and closing up that indicated leave-taking. Big Jim had made many trips from the back door to the shed where he kept his car, which he hadn't driven locally because of California plates. Babs, despite her habitual chatter, had a highly colored distracted air of holiday, of imminent release. It greatly depressed Carol but she tried not to be sullen. Babs had washed and trimmed her hair. She was wearing eye makeup. She tended to become tearful whenever Carol offered a compliment.

So the murder of her grandfather had happened, or was going to happen very soon, Carol thought, desperately chewing her way through the gala meal and keeping an eye on restless Babs, calculating what it might take to pry this last and most important secret from her.

Before long she began to sense that Babs was not going to talk to her tonight. Babs would talk at her, talk circles around her, but she was trying hard to push something unpleasant to the back of her mind. The *veau* began to stick in Carol's throat and she couldn't wash it down with wine. She put her fork aside, looking at Babs with an edgy fascination. They had spent the long day packing, tidying up loose ends; it was eight-thirty in the evening now, the sky had begun to turn from a silvery apricot shade to a midnight blue agleam with constellations, and the only loose end remaining before their departure was Carol.

Despite all of Babs' protestations and the plaintive reassurance she had seen in Turo's eyes, were they simply going to kill her? For half a minute she lived with this belief. Babs was describing something she had winnowed from the newspapers or seen on television. She made neat gestures with her fat, hard hands. Carol couldn't make much sense of what she was saying, or even hear very well: something was happening deep in her ears, a ringing, a cold fibrillation. Babs wore tiny gold beads for earrings. Her long hair was tied at mid-length with a ribbon, exposing the tender broad root of her ivoried neck. Her throat swelled and bobbed with incomprehensible speech. Odd that she couldn't hear any more, Carol thought, when she was perfectly lucid on another level. But she couldn't feel anything, either; she existed in a state of numbness beyond panic. Babs flashed a smile. Unlike most fat girls, she had healthy even teeth and healthy eyes, somewhat pinked by tears tonight. She kept her distance and wiped her tears surreptitiously, thinking Carol wouldn't notice. A very emotional girl, Babs, and considerate to the end: she would maintain the pretense of friendship until the last good night, see you in the morning! And later she would be sitting in the front seat of the car in her traveling togs listening to something well modulated and schmaltzy on the radio without a sniffle or a regret in her head while Big Jim came cat-footed up the stairs one last time to say *his* good night, a needle loaded with a dose of treats gleaming in his fist.

"Is that all you're going to eat, Carol?"

She had come closer to the bed and was peering dubiously at the dishes on the tray. She had dabbed perfume on her wrists tonight: Babs' physical presence affected Carol as the moon affects the tides and the scent of perfume roused her more completely. Her skin continued to feel iced and she was sweating alcohol in all the hollows of her body, but she smiled.

"Oh, I— Babs, it was delicious, but so filling, you know? I'm absolutely stuffed."

"Do you feel all right? You look sort of white."

"I'm fine, Babs," Carol protested, concentrating on a parody of cheerfulness. "A little tired—a backache kept me awake most of last night."

"Your period's late, isn't it?" Babs said, frowning: always the little doctor.

"Well, I could be skipping this month. You know, because of the fever."

"Oh, sure." Babs appropriated the wedge of Brie and nibbled at it like a vast bucolic mouse. "Scrumptious," she said, dribbling crumbs.

"Out of this world," Carol agreed, certain that she was going to vomit. "Babs, would you mind? The chain. I'd like to go to the bathroom."

Babs crammed the last of the cheese into her mouth and searched herself for the appropriate key while Carol stood haggardly by with her throat locked. She made herself walk to the bathroom and turn on the faucets. Then she was privately sick. She felt as if she were trying to throw up everything she had been fed during the term of her captivity. She expected to be quite frail after it was over, bleary and palpitating. Instead, after splashing her face with cold water for a couple of minutes she felt revived, precariously calm and operative. Her hands trembled but they trembled almost continuously these days, and her grasp was adequate.

"Oh, Babs! This is going to take a while. Could you bring me a smoke?"

Babs, who was strictly rationed by Big Jim, handed a lighted king through the door space.

"Thanks so much," Carol said, closing the door.

"*De nada*, girl."

"Why don't you finish the *poire cardinal* for me?"

"Oh, God, I've already had three glasses of it! But, if you insist—"

Carol sat on the john seat while she smoked two-thirds of the long cigarette. Then she set it aside and took two squares of toilet paper, folded them into a loose pad which fitted the palm of her left hand. She lifted the lid and flicked the ash of the cigarette into the bowl. There was about an inch and a half of the cigarette left. She clamped the butt between the third and fourth fingers of her right hand with the smoldering tip sheltered in the hollow of her palm. She flushed the toilet and went out into the bedroom, chained hands held close together in front of her, palms in, so that Babs couldn't see she still had the cigarette. It had started to blister the wet skin of her cupped hand but she ignored the pain and worked up a convincing yawn.

"I think I'll turn in."

"So early?" she said. But it was clear that Babs approved. She swigged the last of the wine from the bottle, leaving a prim red crescent on her upper lip, put the bottle on the tray. She began to fold the covers back. While she was engaged, facing away from Carol, Carol squatted at the foot of the bed, placed the cigarette stub between folds of tissue, separated the mattresses quickly and unobtrusively and stuck the wrapped cigarette between them. She stood up and licked the burn on her palm and smiled guilelessly when Babs turned around, plumping the pillow.

"It's supposed to be not quite so humid tomorrow."

"There's good news."

"The last couple of days I was so damp all the time I thought I'd sprout mushrooms."

"Babs, you're droll."

"Well. Time for the belt, I guess." She strapped Carol into it. Carol sat down on the bed and Babs ran the chain through the eye. She was more than a little damp now; a rivulet of sweat ran from one temple to her chins, and her dress was splotchy. Carol lay back. Babs secured the chain to the bed frame with the big brass lock.

Carol smiled up at her, but it was an artificial, ill-meant smile that caused Babs a certain amount of puzzlement. "I'd say I'm suitably restrained."

"Gosh, Carol, you know how I feel—"

"That bores me, Babs. That really bores me, to hear how you feel."

Babs wiped uneasily at trickling sweat. She licked her lips, trying to think of something pleasantly equivocal to say. Carol didn't alter her smile, but after a half dozen seconds she abruptly switched it off; then her face was stone. She lay there accusing Babs with her eyes, and on occasion her peculiarly lidded brown eyes could be reptilian, cold as a mongrel whore's.

"Well, I d-d-don't know what else—" Babs fumbled, overwhelmed.

"Oh, shit," Carol said, flicking the epithet at her with a deadly aim.

"—*tell* you!" Babs concluded, eyes squeezed shut. Her features had lost their customary wise and cheeky definition, and her face was a watery pudding. She found her normal voice but kept her eyes shut. "You have every reason to hate me," she said stuffily.

"Don't I, though?"

"But I hoped—"

"I'm trying to get some sleep here, Babs. Turn out the light."

Babs stood there a dismal minute longer, melting in the glare of Carol's displeasure, gradually bringing her eyes to bear on her tormentor: her eyes seemed smaller in the pudding face, reduced by a greeny haze. Somewhere inside her head something difficult and chancy was going on. Carol felt a swift return of fear. But Babs simply turned and stepped down from the bed platform and went to get the light.

In the dark Carol heard her breathing. A little moonlight defined the windows. More light filtered upward through the curtain over the doorway below, a dull ocher shading on the wall above the staircase.

When she could see to find her way Babs returned to the bed. Striving for balance, she kneeled and captured one of Carol's hands. She pressed a wet inflamed cheek, then her lips against it. Apologetically, with a birdlike grace, she kissed the hand. And still she was speechless.

Carol snatched her hand away and the chain caught, pulling Babs' face roughly awry. Babs gasped, and her eyes gleamed like pools in the insubstantial light from the sky.

"Get out of my bed, you sewer rat."

Babs, on her knees, sat back. She was quite motionless for a while. Carol felt Babs studying her. She couldn't quite will herself to turn her back.

"Babs," Big Jim called from below. Babs trembled. She put both hands on the bed to brace herself, raised up. She picked up the supper tray from the table, hesitated again, her great bulk blotting out the windows. Carol feigned sleep, or indifference, but her heartbeat seemed shockingly audible to her. At last Babs went away. Carol heard her descending, breathing anxiously, her back sliding against the wall, dishes jarring on the tray at each down-step.

The smoldering cigarette, feeding on the tiny amount of oxygen trapped between layers of the toilet tissue, quickly burned holes the size of horseshoes in the ticking of both mattresses; the fire spread quite slowly after that, and unpredictably, through the densely packed stuffing, flaring briefly in minute air spaces, settling down to a slow but inexorable charring. An hour passed and Carol, glumly certain that her scheme was a failure, dozed off.

She stirred and shifted position from time to time as the burning mattress became warm, then hot. The fire ate its way to the surface in an hour's time; it broke through at last at the foot of the bed, and a sheet, turning brown, suddenly burst into flame. She smelled the smoke in her sleep, awakened to the puff of flame. She screamed, forgetting momentarily what she had done. Forgetting the chains, she tried to leap off the bed.

"Help! Oh, God, it's burning!"

Screeching in panic, she kicked at the burning tattered top sheet, trying to get it off the bed. Sparks and flecks of charred cloth alighted on her bare legs. The mattress had begun to burn through in other places: little puffs and jets of flame surrounded her. The room was filling with a noxious yellow smoke. Carol arched her back in an effort to get as much of her body as possible off the hot mattress. She smelled her hair as it began to singe and beat at it with her linked hands. She screamed.

Big Jim charged up the stairs and turned on the lights. For several seconds he stared in disbelief at the flame and the wildly writhing girl. Then he grabbed the pitcher of water from the little table beside the bed and doused Carol with it.

"Babs!" he roared. "Get up here!" He went to the bathroom and refilled the pitcher, came back and dumped the water on the hot spots in the mattress. Babs' head and shoulders heaved into view. Carol sobbed and strangled on a thick wad of smoke. Big Jim yanked Babs up the last two steps, a feat equivalent to squat-lifting an antique safe.

"Where's the key? The key, damn it!"

"I don't know!" Babs wailed, frantically searching. "It must be in my other—"

"Throw some more water on that mattress," he said, shoving the pitcher at her. "And douse the sparks on the floor." He slapped her, not hard, to be sure he had her attention. Then he ran down the steps.

"Babs, Babs!" Carol moaned. "I'm burning up!" Babs, a ghastly white except for Jim's finger marks on one cheek, hurried to the bathroom and stuck the pitcher under the flowing tap. She came back and stood too far from the still smoldering bed and threw the water more or less blindly.

"Babs—the mattress—pull the mattress out from under me!"

Babs groped closer to the bed, holding her breath. She took a purchase on the mattress and tugged. Nothing happened. "Harder!" Carol sobbed. Babs, bulging with determination this time, tried again. The mattress slipped sideways several inches. It proved to be a mistake. Air fed the fire that had been eating through the mattress below and a picket of bright yellow flames

232

penetrated the dense smoke, endangering Carol. Babs backed away from this new misfortune with a blood-curdling shriek. She was still retreating when Big Jim returned with a pair of long-handled bolt cutters and freed Carol in two snips.

Carol tumbled to the floor and lay there gasping with her cheek pressed against the cool wood. Jim dropped the bolt cutters and began to stamp out burning remnants of linen. He retrieved the porcelain pitcher and dashed into the bathroom for more water. Carol got to her hands and knees and saw the bolt cutters handy. Jim appeared, murkily, and laid careful arcs of water along the sizzling mattresses, his eyes streaming tears from the heat and smoke.

Carol picked up the bolt cutters and stood. She made a clumsy rush at Big Jim and, just as he was turning, she swung the cutters savagely and crushed his left temple, opened his forehead to the bone in an angular slash that extended to the tip of his right eyebrow. He crumpled in a dark gush of blood, the pitcher bounding away across the floor. Carol dropped the bolt cutters and ran.

She ran right into a shrieking Babs.

"What? Jim! Carol, you—"

"Babs, let me go!"

"I'll *kill* you!"

Carol dropped a shoulder into her imposing breasts and rammed her back a couple of inches; she was almost able to slip away to the steps but Babs, reaching frantically, grabbed the wrist chain and jerked it, upending Carol.

"You hit him. You hit Jim! And I'll killll youuuuu!"

Carol, on her back, kicking with a bare foot, found nothing but substantial blubber. Babs was coughing and trampling with an elephantine instinct, still holding fast to the chain. She stepped ponderously on Carol's stomach and stepped on her face. Carol pummeled the girl with both feet, still screaming. A heel in the groin undid Babs and she tottered backward to a wall. Carol lunged for the steps, a second too late.

Babs rebounded from the wall and lumbered toward her with arms opened wide for a pulverizing embrace. Carol ducked and tried to evade her charge but Babs hooked a solid arm around her throat. Babs took two more flatfooted steps to slow her momentum and the last step found nothing but air. She howled at this essential miscalculation and toppled down the stairs, pulling Carol along. Carol's head glanced off the wall, then struck a riser. She was only distantly aware of the great tumbling mass of Babs rolling over her like a warm wave of the ocean.

She was restored to full consciousness by the terror of being crowded upside down in a small space, by the more specific sensation of being casually and meatily pressed to death. She gasped for air and tried to wriggle free of her burden, but her skull was achingly wedged against a step and she wasn't quite sure where her hands were: there was no feeling in them. Dimly she heard a burning crackle, a gusty explosion. The mouthful of air she had taken was spoiled by smoke.

Her bare feet were planted against something solid. She heaved again, increasingly frantic, and the hill of flesh above her shifted a little.

Babs, she thought, recalling now what had happened to her. She felt more irritated than frightened.

"Babs, damn you, get off!"

The wall against which her feet were braced had become hotter. Carol ground her teeth and hoarded her strength and bucked again. This time she managed to change position, freeing her hands and turning her face to the bad air. The space above them was filled with orange-tinted smoke. Babs, the ninny, was just sitting there on top of her with her ample chins on her breast and her greeny eyes wide, a kind of elongated foolish grin on her face. She seemed to be having a damned good time in perilous circumstances. Bits of glowing wood were falling like meteors. Babs' soft pink sweater was already charred in several places, and smoking.

"Babs!"

To Carol's horror Babs' hair suddenly lit up in a frowsy nest of flame, casting a sullen light on her wide face, on the expression of goony passiveness.

Carol reared with all her might and Babs was dislodged from her seat on Carol's back and shoulders. She keeled over in a buttery sprawl to the floor inches away. Carol followed her, tried to beat out the flames with her hands, but in seconds it was too late. Somewhere above there was a resounding crack as some vital part of the roof structure began to cave in. Carol backed away from the lifeless Babs. There was nothing left of her hair except crispy smudges, a sour reek in the air. Carol, temporarily unhinged, grasped Babs' outstretched hands and began to pull her corpse across the highly polished floor. She stopped with a grimace of anguish when she saw the loose way Babs' denuded head rolled against the boards.

Carol barked and coughed and some dark fluid ran out of the corner of her mouth. She stared at the heavy smoke boiling down the steps. Then she simply turned and walked away from it all, went outside by way of the unlocked back door.

There was no moon now and it was raining, but very softly, an almost unnoticed fragrant summery rain. She walked along a well-trod path with her head high, ignoring stones and ruts, sometimes stumbling but always regaining her balance. When the path cut down a long slope to a woodlot she paused for a moment and looked back at the glary windows and plumed roof of the isolated country house.

She thought she saw something near the house: the tall shape of a man. Perhaps her name was called. She whimpered and spit up more of the bitter liquor and took off in a streaking run with her fists upraised, sawing against the chain at each long stride.

At the edge of the woodlot, away from the light of the burning house, she stopped. She heard her pursuer. Looking over her shoulder, she saw him in a skidding plunge down the loose stony path a hundred feet behind her. She whirled and tripped over a root, fell hard. She sighed in pain and crawled into a scraggly pasture. But she was trembling too violently to go far on her hands and knees.

He seized her from behind and lifted her up. Her head fell back.

"No more!"

"Carol?" he said.

She looked at him then but her eyes were glazed, she couldn't see a thing. Still, there was no mistaking his voice.

"Oh, Sam," she said, "thank God!" and she leaned gratefully against his chest.

Chapter Twenty-One

THE UNLIGHTED DRIVE SWEPT BETWEEN CEDARS THAT seemed Biblical in age; their trunks were as thick as the masts of old sailing ships. At night the massed branches formed a barrier against the sky, obscuring the yellowed drift of moon; they absorbed the silent rain and the sounds of the car toiling without headlights up the low hill to the General's house.

In the loop of the drive Sam parked behind the General's own car, a modest Buick. He looked at Carol. She was curled up in the trench coat he had provided, fast asleep, breathing through her mouth. She had been like that for half an hour and he was confident she would go on sleeping for a while, as long as she was undisturbed. He got out of the Mercedes and closed the door without latching it, turned up his coat collar and walked to the front steps of the General's mansion. On the third floor he saw a lighted window but otherwise the place seemed dark. There was an old-fashioned bell pull beside the door. He tugged at it intermittently for three or four minutes before the General came and looked out at him.

"I thought you'd send Metts down," Sam said pleasantly. "All those steps must be hard on your leg."

"He's on the phone to Cairo. What do you want, Sam?"

"General, you're in a hell of a lot of danger."

The General looked at him as if he were drunl

"Can I come in? It's wet out here."

The General hesitated a full thirty seconds longer, his veined eyelids twitching and crawling like pink caterpillars; then he swung the massive door wide and turned away. He was wearing boots, whipcords with suspenders, an old flannel hunting shirt as soft as the skin of a pampered woman.

"Sam," he said, "I can't recall five minutes I've spent with you that I didn't consider a complete and sinful waste of my precious time. You'd just better not be drunk, that's all I've got to say."

Sam closed the front door and followed the General as he clomped slowly back up the broad staircase to the third floor. There were a lot of echoes in the place: the rooms on the first two floors were as dark and empty as a series of caverns. Each landing was lighted by a couple of bulbs in wall sconces; the bulbs were the size and shape of those that decorate Christmas trees. The carpet on the stairs was in tatters, and they raised unseen dust that caused the General to cough miserably on the way to his quarters.

In the smoky sitting room the General waved Sam to a chair and went to close the door to the adjoining office. Sam had a glimpse of Vernon Metts inside and heard his voice. He was speaking a strange language, Egyptian Arabic for all Sam knew.

The General eased down into his own favorite chair and put his good leg on a hassock made from an elephant's foot. He reached for the tumbler of Southern Comfort whiskey that was never far away, no matter where he happened to be. He didn't offer Sam any.

"What's it about, Sam?"

"I'll try to be brief, General."

"That would be appreciated."

"Well," Sam said, leaning against a gun case with his arms comfortably folded. "Do you remember the kidnapping, General?"

"I'm sure not about to forget it."

"It was a fake, a ruse. The girl the police brought home that night wasn't Carol. We've been living with an impostor all this time."

238

The General's hand paused with the whiskey partway to his mouth and his small-bore, flesh-encrusted eyes studied Sam with a keen flicker of amazement. Then the lower part of his face opened like a clam: he was smiling. "You're crazy."

"Am I?" Sam said evenly. "She looks, talks and acts like Carol Watterson, but it's all an act. Her real name is Lone Kels. She knew Carol at Berkeley. She's part of a plot to kill you and Vernon Metts. Rich dreamed the whole thing up; he and your buddy Turo are the assassins. They're going to take both of you prisoner tonight, then use cyanide gas to finish you off."

The General's face bulged like a mottled balloon as he sought to contain his amusement. Or perhaps it was triumph he was enjoying so vividly. "I've always known, Sam, that you were a bona fide mental case. This, by God, proves it for all time! Not Carol? You think I don't know my own granddaughter?"

Sam fidgeted. "Your eyes aren't what they used to be, General. Neither is your pickled old brain. I'm telling you we were all fooled for a while. They switched girls to give themselves a base of operations close to you. Until an hour ago two other members of their little group were holding Carol prisoner in a farmhouse out in the boondocks of Rockland County."

"Until an hour ago?"

"I went and got her."

"That so? How did you know where to look?"

"I searched their luggage today," Sam explained. "One of them had a map with the location X'd on it. I had to drive around for about an hour before I found the house. You can't see it from any road."

"Then you just walked in and walked out again with Carol."

"It was almost that easy. The house was burning when I got there. Carol set fire to her mattress with a cigarette and when they cut her loose from the bed she smashed one of them in the head with bolt cutters and ran. The other one, a girl, broke her neck falling down some steps. That's what Carol told me, but she wasn't clear about it. I found her wandering around outside.

Except for a bruise or two and total exhaustion she's all right. We got out of there before the local fire brigade turned up and I drove straight here."

The General sipped his whiskey, no longer appearing amused. "Expecting maybe to find us dead, Sam?"

Sam looked at an old Swiss cuckoo clock on one wall: the General's rooms were as disorderly and packed with mementos as a pawnshop. "It's only twenty minutes after eleven. I didn't think Rich and Turo would be in a hurry about this thing after waiting so long for Metts to show up."

"Why didn't you invest a dime and warn me as soon as you had Carol safe?"

Sam grinned edgily at him. He was sweating. "Why, do you believe me now?"

The General ruminated, rapping his knuckles lightly against his artificial leg. "I'm not sure. It's a hell of a story. Still—after we got her back she was all of a sudden fond of my birds. Carol never would go near them before. But she hunted with me, and she took that runty tiercel I couldn't do a damned thing with and trained him herself." He looked up. "Where is she, Sam? Where's Carol? If you've got her, bring her up here. I'll believe what *Carol* tells me."

The door to the office opened and Vernon Metts came in. He was a bony, morose-looking man with a Guardsman's moustache. "Hello, Sam. Didn't know you were here."

"Did you put the screws to that son of a bitch Fouad?" the General asked.

Metts nodded and lighted a cigar. "I was about to place a call to Jean-Claude in Marseilles when something went wrong with the phone. It seems to be dead."

The General looked puzzled. Then he glanced at Sam and at the same time reached for the telephone beside the chair. He picked up the receiver, listened bleakly for several seconds. "Dead," he pronounced, hanging up. "Wires cut?"

Sam said, "They must be in the house already."

240

"Who's in the house?" Metts asked sharply.

The General heaved himself out of the chair. "What's their plan, Sam? Are they coming in together, or did they split up?"

"I don't know."

"What are you talking about?" Metts demanded.

"Not a lot of time to explain now, Vern. There are two punk revolutionaries loose in the house and they're after our hides. They've got guns. What kind, Sam?"

"Automatic shotguns."

"Oh-oh," the General said, impressed at last. He limped to the gun cabinet, took a key ring from his pocket and unlocked the doors, revealing a gleaming row of high-powered weapons. Metts looked regretfully at his cigar and placed it in an ashtray. He took off his Cardin blazer and folded it across the back of a chair, removed the studs from the cuffs of his classy striped shirt, peeled the cuffs back.

"Name your piece," the General said to him with a faint smile.

"Tell you what, Henry, I'll just take that Russian Army assault rifle. I don't want to tear up the plaster any more than necessary."

"Maybe," Sam said, "I could get out of here somehow, get the police—"

"We don't need them," the General said flatly. "Now, do you want to be in on this or do I lock you up in the bathroom until the shooting's done?"

"I can help," Sam said. "Let me have a shotgun. Pump action, please."

The General threw a shotgun to him. "Fully loaded, Sam. Don't aim from the hip, it'll cave your ribs in."

"I know how to shoot."

"By the way, Sam, I don't believe you mentioned what these boys want us dead for."

"It's a raison d'être experiment in ethical murder. Rich and Turo consider you to be immoralists. You sell guns and cause a lot of human suffering. Institutions protect you and absolve you of guilt, so they feel obligated to remove you as a source of corruption to the human spirit."

The General and Metts exchanged amused glances. "Whew," said the General, "I just feel dirty all over, don't you, Vern?" He paused to listen carefully to something, then gestured and whispered, "A little less light there."

Metts turned off the table lamp, leaving the room dark behind them. There were three stout doors to the sitting room. The General's bedroom, a cul-de-sac, was behind one. The office door was directly opposite and it now stood open about two feet. The door to the foyer and steps outside was closed. Metts, moving lithely, his assault rifle at port, crossed to the foyer door, turned the knob, toed the door open a few inches while Sam and the General moved back out of the way. With his body and most of his head behind the thick oak paneled wall, Metts examined the foyer. It was dimly lighted by a high chandelier, the crystals of which were yellow and crusty with age.

"Clear," he said. "Shadowy where the stairs begin, though; one of them could get that far easy, pour a few rounds in here."

"Sam says they want to take us by surprise and then use gas. For humanitarian reasons, I suppose. Open the door a little wider, Vern. That's enough. I'll just sit right here and draw a bead. You and Sam sweep the rest of the apartment. Pay particular attention to the back door into the kitchen and the door at the top of the steps to the servants' wing. Both are locked, but those goddam revolutionaries had the run of this place long enough to get keys made."

"Reconnaissance down below?" Metts asked with a hungry smile.

"Why not? I'd join you except for my leg. You know the layout of this place, Vern. Try to flush them up the front stairs into my gun. Maybe if we pour a little fire into them they'll get discouraged and quit."

"Don't forget the cylinder of gas," Sam warned. "I don't know who's carrying it."

"That does complicate things. We'll just have to try for head shots, then. Sam, you go along slow and careful and do what Vern says or you might wind up getting blown in half. Those automatic shotguns are nothing to trifle with."

"Ok," Sam said, and the General, taking up a shooting position in a chair with his own weapon, a rare custom-made Parker that was the cream of sporting shotguns, waved them off.

Sam followed Metts, who was stalking now with a monkish concentration. They passed through the office. Metts paused to turn out the overhead light, then stationed Sam with a jab of his finger and went through his door-opening routine. Sam's hands were slippery on the shotgun. The outer door of the office opened onto a hallway that was long to the left and carpeted in red. Metts sprang out into the hall like a commando, taking up a prone shooting position. There was a little light, not enough to make him a fat target. But no one fired on him. Sam knew the man was in his fifties, but he seemed to have no regard for his bones. He picked himself up as quickly as he had dropped, the stubby military weapon level in the crook of his right arm, and beckoned to Sam. Sam, breathing through a dry mouth, joined him.

They saw at a glance that the kitchen was empty. A leaky faucet dripped water into the corroded sink and a moth fluttered around the shaded bulb fixed to the greasy plaster near the door to the outside staircase.

Metts turned the kitchen table over. "Stay here, Sam. Nothing to it. Just lay the barrel of your shotgun across the edge of the table and cover the door. Don't open the door for any reason; don't go poking around. I'll sweep the rest of the apartment and drop down into the servants' wing for a look around." He grinned. "Having fun?"

"I don't think so."

"You'll know I'm back when I tap you on the shoulder." He demonstrated, then left without a sound. Sam looked back at the doorway through which he had vanished. His glasses were misting from perspiration. He took them off and wiped them, then put the shotgun over his shoulder and went to the outside door. He slid the bolt back and opened the door, left it ajar.

He looked down the wide and empty stairway. There were small recessed windows at each landing, admitting faint oblongs of light. Sam eased down with his back to the wall. When his chest began to ache he let his breath out. The board steps were loud under his feet.

"Turo?" he whispered.

He waited half a minute and then continued to the landing, revealing himself as he passed the window space. "Turo?"

"Yeah," Turo said at last, from below. "I see you."

"Where are you?"

"I'll come up."

Turo joined him on the second floor. "What are you doing here? What's the gun for?"

"Turo, they've caught on. They're armed and ready for you. Where's Rich?"

"Front of the house, where he's supposed to be. What do you mean? How did they catch on?"

"I'll tell you later. Metts is just above us. Turo, we'll have to use the guns."

Turo hesitated.

Sam said harshly, "Turo, it's kill or be killed! The man's like a cat, and he's a crack shot."

"All right," Turo said. His face was a pale wet gleam in the darkness.

"Give me your gun. Go ahead of me up the stairs. Stop on the landing facing the door. I'll call Metts out. When you see him in the doorway take three steps and then drop. I'll shoot over you. He won't be expecting it."

"What about the General?"

"He's just sitting and waiting for the action to come to him. Don't worry."

"All right," Turo said again. Sam clasped the boy's upper arm briefly: he was like a block of wood. Turo handed over his automatic shotgun. Sam took it in his right hand.

244

"Let's go." He had to push to get Turo started. They walked up to the bend in the stairs. "Metts," Sam called, not loudly. He watched the second hand on the luminous dial of his watch and when a quarter of a minute had gone by he called again.

"Metts! It's Sam. I've got one of them."

The door above was cautiously opened and Vernon Metts appeared, silhouetted against the kitchen light.

"Damn it, Sam, I told you to stay put! All right, bring him up."

Turo didn't budge. Sam prodded him with the muzzle of one of the guns. Turo started up reluctantly. On the third step he threw himself against the wall with a sob, clutching his head with his hands. Sam dropped his shotgun, shouldered Turo's weapon and started pulling the trigger. The muzzle flashes from the shotgun lit up the stairwell like artillery. Vernon Metts disappeared in an explosion of splinters and plaster.

Turo reared up through the smoke after the reverberation from the fourth shot. He tried to tell Sam something, but Sam was too deafened to hear. He was also too busy to pay attention. He put down the automatic, picked up his own shotgun in a pistol grip, rammed the muzzle against Turo's big chest and fired a fistful of choked shot cleanly through him. The blast hurled Turo through the railing and he disappeared. The recoil from the blast sprained Sam's wrist and the butt of the stock almost unjointed his elbow. He fell back to the landing and lay there stunned. Then he slowly got to his feet. He unbuttoned his shirt with his left hand and carefully slid his other hand into the makeshift sling until it supported the sprained wrist.

He walked empty-handed up the stairs and stepped over the body of Vernon Metts, not giving it more than a glance. There were bright splotches of blood on the walls. The air was still dusty. Very little of the door remained on the hinges. The automatic rifle was lying a few feet away from Metts' body. It had been nicked but not severely damaged. Sam stooped for it.

"Metts!" he heard the General cry, his voice muted by the

thick walls and doors of the old mansion. "Sam? What the hell's happening out there?"

Sam shook his head, angry at the intrusion of the old man's voice. He was in pain and somewhat weakened by the shock of having rapidly killed two men. Something in his chest was trying to break loose: a shudder, a peal of laughter that might never end.

The General cried out again.

"Coming," Sam muttered, and plodded through the kitchen with the rifle in his hand.

Lone put the last of the suitcases in Rich's Le Mans and stood for a few moments in the drive with her hands in the pockets of Carol's trench coat, looking up at a misty half moon. The intermittent rain had stopped and there was a tidal shimmer on the broad front lawn. She breathed deeply, taking pleasure in the night and the freshened air.

Everything done, the smallest detail attended to on schedule. It was now eleven-thirty; by midnight at the very latest they'd be on the road. She liked driving at night. She couldn't be very enthusiastic about the boat trip coming up at dawn; it bored her to think of being cooped up for three weeks with the Hendersholts on the fifty-foot motor sailer Rich had bought. But Babs could cook up a storm and Jim was an even better poker player than Rich, so the time would pass. And there were more rewarding times just ahead. Turo had assured her that Caracas was a lively place; when Caracas palled there was always Rio.

Despite her sense of well-being she was bothered by an irritant, a nagging sense of something undone. Lone frowned. What had she forgotten? Felice was fast asleep in her bedroom; she would sleep until the drug wore off or until a stimulant was given her. Little chance of that happening.

No, she hadn't made any mistakes. She'd played her part, played it reliably and damned well, not counting the run-in with Dev Kaufman. And it was over. *Good-bye, Carol. Soon you'll be one big happy family again. If Sam holds together, that is.*

She wouldn't take bets that Sam was going to hold together very long without their help.

Lone made a leisurely last tour around the outside of the house. Through trees the General's mansion was visible against a bank of gray cloud. Only one light showing. They'd been over there for fifteen minutes, she thought. She could expect them soon. . . .

She remembered then the one thing she'd overlooked. Old Bird. Cap'n Midnight sitting over there in the hawk house. Lone smiled, but it was a regretful smile. If he wasn't freed in time, if no one remembered that the General kept birds, then her tiercel might starve to death. A terrible shame, considering all the time she'd lavished on his domestication. The General had been proud of her ability to handle the hunter bird. She had a genuine liking for her tiercel—it would certainly help pass the time if she took him along on the jaunt to South America.

Why not? Lone thought, elated. The falcon certainly wouldn't be in the way on a boat that size. She could teach him to hunt from the deck. It wasn't asking too much of the others: she'd done more than anyone else so far. She'd certainly earned the privilege of having Old Bird with her.

In ten minutes' time she could fetch him and be back ready to roll when the boys arrived.

Lone smiled to herself and took a small flashlight from a pocket of the coat, cinched the belt a little tighter and set off briskly through the noiseless misty night for the General's.

Sam approached the carved door at the end of the red hall. He turned the knob gently and opened the door about an inch, peered out into the foyer, which looked like the abandoned lobby of a once-ornate movie theater. Thirty feet away behind another door the General was waiting, watchful, silent now.

Sam's face was drenched. He wiped it awkwardly on his sleeve and thumbed his glasses up the bridge of his nose. His right arm hurt; shooting pains. *Two down*, he thought. He said in a choked voice, "General."

He heard nothing. He coughed and tried again, remembering to sound weak and gutshot. "General—please—it's Sam." He paused, thinking, listening, then rushed on, "Help me—hurt—I'm hurt. They're all dead. Oh, Christ, do something for me!"

Come on, he thought, his anger so intense that he was afraid of betraying himself by making a foolish move. And there was a remorseless itch of laughter in his chest. He couldn't understand why.

He saw the General emerge, limpingly, from the sitting room with his prize shotgun leveled.

He was unable to rejoice at having tricked the old man; suddenly he was petrified. He forgot that he had a gun of his own. Instead of anger he felt a sense of shame, a persuasive sense of guilt; he felt a buzzing of anticipation in his loins at the prospect of long-deserved punishment. He wanted to fling open the door, exposing himself fully. In confusion he stepped back from the crack of the door.

"Sam?" the General said, his eyes on the door, not seeing too well. His lined face was suspicious. He had come a little too far from the safety of the room. He seemed to change his mind suddenly and, as Sam leaned toward his slit view, the General made an awkward move as if to get back.

Sam threw open the door and stepped out. At the same time Rich Marsland rose from the shadow of the front stairs and blasted away excitedly, knocking a leg off the General, separating him from his shotgun.

Rich ran up the remaining steps and looked down the barrel of his gun at the General, who had recovered very quickly and was dragging himself along the patchy carpet to his own weapon. The General blinked in surprise at Sam and shot a look at Rich. His face knotted with anger.

"Sam, goddammit, he's got a bead on me!"

Rich was confused by Sam's presence and glanced sidelong at him. Sam put the rifle on him. For a couple of seconds Rich didn't get it, and then he flinched.

"Not me!" he bleated, aghast. Sam fired coolly from only five feet away, fired half the magazine, driving Rich flatfooted back to the steps with the uplifted shotgun going off in his hands. The charge ripped the bottom tier of crystals from the chandelier and set the whole thing swinging. Rich went rolling down the steps. Sam went to look, stepping over the General's artificial leg, which Rich had shot off. He spotted the small canister of gas where Rich had placed it for safekeeping. Then he walked slowly back to the General.

The General, who was still lying on his hip, had picked up his valuable fowling piece. Sam tore it away from him and hurled it. The General looked at him in outrage. He started to speak, to berate Sam, but the expression on Sam's face checked him. The General groped for an answer to his puzzling manner and decided that his son-in-law was suffering from a touch of combat nerves. He smiled grudgingly.

"Fine shooting, Samuel. You did fine. Just fine."

"Sure I did," Sam said, laughing at some absurdity.

"Well, damn you, help me up!"

Sam clucked at him, and grinned. "I did it," he said. "I'm the hero. But you know something, General? They got to you before I killed them. Too bad."

The General reached up with a shaking hand and brushed fragments of glass from his shirt. He didn't take his eyes from Sam's face. He looked suspicious again, and worried as well.

"What?" he said.

Chapter Twenty-Two

NOTHING IN PARTICULAR AWAKENED CAROL; SHE HADN'T dreamed. But suddenly she was sitting upright in the Mercedes with her heart thudding, staring through the rain-pebbled side window at the midnight landscape. Convinced she'd seen something or someone out there in the seconds between sleep and full awareness.

She was alone in the car. Her throat was raw and she smelled of smoke. She remembered the burning house and poor dead Babs and—

Sam. Thank God for Sam. He had found her there, and taken her quickly away.

She looked up at a lighted window just below the flèche of the house. It was the General's house. She felt a slight shock. Of course, they'd had to come here right away. Because the General was going to be killed.

Carol reached for the door handle, then held up her hand, shocked again. No manacles, no chain. She rubbed her chafed wrists, then groped beneath Sam's olive trench coat. The cyclist's belt was gone too. Sam must have taken the things off. But he would have needed a key for the handcuffs; where did he get a key?

She rolled back the sleeves of the coat, touched her cold dirt-streaked face. She glanced again at the house; the absence of lights frightened her. But she couldn't accept that they might have come too late to help the General.

Carol opened the door and stepped out of the car. The night

air made her tremble and she turned up the full collar of the coat, feeling frail and slightly ludicrous in it. She went slowly up the front steps and reached for the bell pull. Timidity, or perhaps some intuition of disaster, kept her from ringing. She knew the door was never locked. She had to press against it with most of her weight before it opened on great hinges. There was no light in the vacant chandelier above the center hall, but there was a trace, a sheen on the stairs. Before she could call she heard voices in conversation and identified the General's distinctive rasp. She shuddered and ran joyfully for the stairs.

"And that night in Lubbock when you tried to kill me. You went halfway across the country to take a potshot at me. I recognized you that night, General. Do you deny you were there?"

"Damn right I do; I've never set foot in Lubbock." The strain of not changing his position, of not moving even a fraction, was causing the old man excruciating pain, but he kept any sign of it from his face and voice. To move was to die, as abruptly as Rich had died with a sockful of lead in him, and the General knew it. He had decided that his hope lay in keeping Sam occupied, talking the whole night long if it had to be, until something occurred to change the balance, until some freak of luck gave him a one-legged chance to survive.

"Oh, you deny that," Sam said, shaking his head at the General's obstinacy. He had been pacing some, always keeping the muzzle of the rifle tight on the General's midsection. "I realize now you weren't trying to kill me; you just wanted to shove me over the brink. I'd been under tremendous pressure since my magazine folded, working too hard and abusing my nerves. And I was worried about my marriage. You'd done a thorough job of driving a wedge between Felice and me." Sam paused and wiped his glistening forehead on his sleeve, blinked sweat from his eyes.

"I never realized, Sam," the General said, annoyed but trying to be judicious, "that I've been such a trial to you."

Sam sneered. "You've been trying to—castrate me from the day I married Felice and took your little girl away from you. But I've been too strong for you, General. I admit that after Lubbock I was just hanging by my fingertips. I knew there wasn't a damned thing I could do to stop you once you made up your mind you really wanted to kill me. If I hadn't met Rich and Lone at Big Sur last winter I think I might have just waded out into the ocean and let the waves take me under. But they showed me it didn't have to be that way. They helped me, turned me on to psychedelics. With the help of Rich's therapy I discovered I had the courage to take you on your own terms, and win. I found good friends in Rich and Lone. And the others. We shared a common concern."

"You don't treat your good friends so nice, Sam," the General said softly. "I don't think they planned on getting killed, now did they?"

"I made most of the plans," Sam said slowly. "I knew when it reached a certain point that it would be—awkward having anyone alive."

The General had grown weary of Sam, of waiting to be slaughtered, weary of his own fear. He did not like being afraid under these circumstances.

"All this because you hate me, Sam?"

"I'm just protecting my interests, General."

The General said shrewdly, "Stand to pick up a comfortable piece of change when I'm gone too."

"Four million, six hundred and fifty-eight thousand dollars," Sam replied. "That's comfortable. Yes, I know almost exactly how much you're worth. I've monitored every telephone call you made for two years."

"What about the girl? Lone, is that her name? Are you planning to kill her too, Sam? How in the name of God do you expect to get away with this?"

"I'm the hero," Sam said with a shrug. His glasses had fogged again; he took them off and put them in his pocket. The General frowned, having found something new to worry about. Sam

252

was crazy, of course. But he was unshakably convinced that he could pull it off. And, once the bodies were hauled away, who would be around to doubt his story? Carol, in her innocence, would be overwhelmingly convincing. There had been a plot, and she was proof of it— The General groaned.

"Shut up," Sam warned him.

"You can't go back to Felice tonight, Sam. You'll never be able to fool her. Truth is, Sam, you don't have the guts for murder. You won't survive long with blood on your hands. Believe me, she'll know."

Sam said passionately, "Felice loves me. God, don't think it hasn't been a torture this past year. For months I wasn't able to come but I pretended so she wouldn't know. It just got worse and worse until I couldn't even get—hard any more. But you knew all that, didn't you? You knew how castrated I felt, not being able to perform."

"A real tragedy," the General snarled. "Who are you trying to fool? You never did have much lead in your pencil, Sam."

The General knew he'd bought it then; still he felt vaguely proud of himself. He blinked at Sam, lips still frozen in the snarl. Out of the corner of his eye he saw something stir in the gloom by the stairs. For an instant he thought it must be Rich, who had seemed securely dead. But nothing would have surprised him tonight. He moved his head slightly, trying to focus; his curiosity turned to dismay when he recognized Carol.

She had heard Sam's confession, his lunatic pride in the violence he had committed, and it had not even shocked her further to unexpectedly come across the tumbled corpse of Rich Marsland on the landing between the second and third floors. She had stepped over it more or less calmly and proceeded up the stairs, not knowing what she intended to do or could do, knowing only that she must go on.

The General saw her first and looked so shocked that she had to try to smile at him. But her main concern was Sam.

"Sam," she said, "I'm sorry for you, please understand how

terribly sorry I am! You can't go on with this. Put the gun down now."

He whirled, startled, the muzzle of the assault rifle dipping. Carol paused a few feet from him, her face chalk. There was a thunderous light in his eyes.

"Hello, Lone," he said.

It was ridiculous and unexpected but she said firmly, "No, I'm not Lone; I'm Carol."

"You don't fool me," Sam said, scowling.

Carol swayed, close to tears. "Sam, I absolutely can't stand another second of this. Put that gun down somewhere, please."

He jerked his head a fraction toward the General. "I haven't killed the old bastard yet."

Carol hesitated only an instant, took two quick steps and wrenched the rifle from his hand. He stared at her. "Run!" the General shouted. "Carol, get away from him!" There was fear in his voice and it broke her nerve. She saw a doorway and dodged through it, pausing to slam the heavy door behind her. Sam screamed. She ran witlessly down the red hall, lugging the potent rifle; it didn't occur to her to try to fire it. As she made the kitchen Sam came yelling down the hall. There was an overturned table in her way, then another body, mangled beyond belief. She whimpered and backed around this lump and took to the stairs. When she reached the second floor Sam was following, three jumped steps at a time. She was too shortwinded to outrun him for long: terror cut her flight to a slow hazy stumble.

The body at the bottom of the stairs stopped her for good, and when she recognized the upturned face she cried out. Sam caught her there on the ground floor and flung her against a brick wall with his good hand. She cowered there. He tugged at the rifle but she was welded to it.

Behind them a door was opened and the light of the moon struck the wall, stopping Sam. He turned. A flashlight beam isolated his face, was reflected in his rounded eyes.

He had only a glimpse of the dark falcon before it spread its wings on the girl's wrist, shrieked at him and launched itself.

The hunting bird struck immediately with a sharp curved talon that pierced a transfixed eye and sank deeper still into the brain. It hovered about his head for three swift wingbeats and then disengaged itself and lighted on the railing of the stairs nearby with a gloating hiss. Sam fell heavily forward at the feet of Lone Kels.

"God," she breathed, and turned in the doorway as if to sprint away. But Carol stepped forward, pointing the rifle.

"Wait," she said. "Lone? I don't know anything about guns, but I think I might shoot you if I have to. Do you hear me, Lone? You just wait."

At dawn the dolorous sky had a rusty tinge and there was more rain in the air; a cool wind blew through the lofty branches of the cedars. Special agent Gaffney had switched on the heater of the government car as they sat in front of the General's house. There were still half a dozen official vehicles parked in the drive and a good many others had come and gone during the small hours of the night.

"Don't you think I ought to take you home?" he asked Carol.

"Mother has plenty of people watching over her; she'll be all right until I get there." She sipped the black coffee that someone had provided and kept her eyes determinedly on the door. She looked awful, Gaffney thought: there were great tarnished circles under her eyes. Not a dab of color in her face, which resembled a carved bone mask more than flesh. But she had lasted splendidly through the night and too much questioning; he was not about to deny her the satisfaction she might get from a confrontation with Lone Kels.

Within a few minutes the door opened. Lone, platinum, tigerish and poised, came out in the company of two FBI men. She wore handcuffs as if they were high fashion. Carol went to her, a wraith in a baggy trench coat, and they met on the steps.

After a few moments Lone smiled.

"You have to admit," she said to Carol, "that I was awfully good."

Carol said nothing. She trembled delicately. She showed no anger but nevertheless she took a step up and cracked Lone across the face. Neither of the FBI men did anything. Lone just shrugged.

Carol looked curiously at her hand. "I'm sorry," she said.

Lone smiled flippantly. "Don't worry about it." She glanced at the two men and they took her down the steps to one of the cars. Carol stayed where she was, the wind tangling her hair, until Lone had been driven off. Then she came back and got in beside Gaffney.

She sat looking at him as if trying to comprehend something she was never going to get remotely close to.

"I always felt," she said in a small voice, "that Lone had been badly used. And I was sorry for her."

Gaffney saw tears forming in Carol's eyes and he wondered self-consciously if she was going to break down then, as she certainly was entitled to do. But her emotion passed. She clasped her hands primly in her lap, licked at her parched and blood-flecked lips.

"I'd like to see my mother now," Carol said eagerly, and Gaffney drove her the short distance to her home.